D0309363

MURDER BY THE SEA

MURDER BY THE SEA

LESLEY COOKMAN

ISIS

LARGE PRINT

Oxford

Copyright © Lesley Cookman, 2008

First published in Great Britain 2008
by
Accent Press Ltd.

Published in Large Print 2009 by ISIS Publishing Ltd.,
7 Centremead, Osney Mead, Oxford OX2 0ES
by arrangement with
Accent Press Ltd.

The moral right of the author has been asserted

British Library Cataloguing in Publication Data
Cookman, Lesley.
    Murder by the sea - - (Libby Sarjeant mysteries)
    1. Sarjeant, Libby (Fictitious character) - -
    Fiction.
    2. Women private investigators - - England - -
    Kent - - Fiction.
    3. Actresses - - Fiction.
    4. Detective and mystery stories.
    5. Large type books.
    I. Title II. Series
    823.9'2–dc22

ISBN 978–0–7531–8458–5 (hb)
ISBN 978–0–7531–8459–2 (pb)

Printed and bound in Great Britain by
T. J. International Ltd., Padstow, Cornwall

For Louise, Miles, Phillipa and Leo

Acknowledgements

Many thanks to Terry Miller, the people
of Cavus, Turkey, and all my Friends
and Writers, who Understand!

CHAPTER
ONE

They did boat trips around the bay. George took the *Dolphin* chugging round the uninhabited island in the centre every other day and Bert took the *Sparkler* to the little cove round the point. The next day they changed over. Tourists asked them if they didn't get bored doing the same thing all summer from Easter to September, but they just shrugged and smiled. The sea was always different, they said, the people were always different and the weather — well, the weather could be even more different. Sometimes they couldn't go out for a week; one year they hadn't gone out for the whole of August. Then they would sit in The Blue Anchor by the jetty, drinking tea and smoking, until the government forced them outside, where Mavis supplied them with a cheap canvas gazebo and an environmentally unfriendly heater.

But this year the weather was good. This year the regulars came back with smiles on their faces and the odd present of a bottle of whisky, which George and Bert would share on board the *Dolphin* or the *Sparkler* when the tourists went back to their hotels and apartments.

This year, too, there were the other visitors. Dark, olive-skinned, wary-looking, who worked in the hotel kitchens, cleaned the lavatories and worked on the farms outside the town. The tourists, for the most part, ignored them; the hoteliers and café owners despised them and paid them as little as they could get away with. The rest of the town's residents were divided in opinion. Those, like Mrs Battersby and Miss Davis, who complained bitterly to anyone who would listen and to a lot more who would not, that these people should not be allowed and should be sent back to their own countries, and those whose determinedly liberal attitude drove them to be fiercely defensive on the immigrants' behalf.

There were those, of course, who viewed both sides with amusement and detachment. George and Bert, and their friend Jane Maurice, who worked for the local paper, were among them. Jane would go down to The Blue Anchor and chat to George and Bert, and occasionally go out on the *Dolphin* or the *Sparkler* and help them entertain their passengers.

Which was what she was doing one day in July at the beginning of the school holidays. It was George's turn to go round the island, and, due to the unusually calm sea, the *Dolphin* was packed with families, nice middle-class families who preferred a traditional British seaside holiday to the dubious delights of sun, sea and Malibu, with unbearable temperatures and incomprehensible currency. Those families who, had they chosen to fly to the sun, would not have dreamt of looking for English bars, breakfasts and nice cups of tea, but who were secretly pleased that these essential delights did not have to be forgone.

It was Jane who spotted it. Something had been washed up, or dumped, on the far side of the island, but what made her look harder was its position, well above even the waterline from the high equinoctial tides.

"George, what's that?"

George squinted through his cigarette smoke, keeping one hand on the wheel while pushing Jane out of the way with the other. Then he reached for the radio.

"What's going on down there?" Libby Sarjeant peered round her easel in the window of her friend Fran's cottage.

"Hmm?" Fran wandered in from the kitchen with an enamel jug full of flowers.

"Down at the end by The Sloop." Libby stood up and leaned out of the open window. "There's a police car and — what's a blue and yellow car?"

"Eh?" Fran came forward and leaned over Libby's shoulder. "Oh — Coastguard, I think."

"I didn't hear the lifeboat, did you?"

"No, but they don't always send up a flare, you know. Anyway, perhaps the lifeboat hasn't gone out." Fran turned away from the window and looked round for somewhere to put the jug. "Much as I love my fireplace," she said, "I wish it had a mantelpiece."

Libby turned round. "Instead of a bloody great wooden lintel? I know which I'd prefer."

"I just need somewhere to put my flowers." Fran sighed and put the jug on the hearth. "I also need some more furniture."

"Ooh, look!" said Libby suddenly. "The lifeboat *had* gone out. It's on its way back."

Abruptly the window went dark.

"Oh, dear," said Libby and Fran together as the ambulance passed the cottage.

"Shall we go and have a look?" said Libby, wiping a brush on a piece of rag.

"Libby!" Fran looked shocked. "Don't be such a ghoul. Anyway, we wouldn't be allowed to get near the place."

"We could go to The Sloop for lunch?" suggested Libby hopefully.

"The Sloop will be cordoned off."

"The Blue Anchor?"

"No, Libby! Really, you're incorrigible." Fran went back towards the kitchen. "If you're going to behave like this, I shan't let you paint from my window any more."

Libby grinned and turned back to the easel, knowing this was an empty threat. She'd been painting pictures of this view for years without having been inside. Both she and Fran had owned pictures of this view as children, and now Fran actually lived here.

"How's Guy?" she asked now, considering where to position the next blob of white cloud.

"OK, I think."

"You think? Don't you know?"

4

"I'm still trying to keep him at arm's length," said Fran, and held up the kettle. "Tea? Coffee?"

"Tea, please. But why?"

"Why am I keeping Guy at arm's length? I told you before I moved here. If I wasn't careful he'd have moved in within a week, and I want time on my own."

"You can't really feel much for him, then." Libby stabbed at her painting.

"Hello, pot? Who are you calling black?"

"Ben and I are — what's it called — Living Together Apart. Or something. We've got our own spaces"

"Well, so have Guy and I."

"But you never see him."

"I do, so." Fran put a pretty bone china mug on the windowsill in front of Libby. "Almost every day. And he's been very helpful with things like tap washers and radiators."

"Taking advantage," said Libby, with a sniff.

"Not at all. He notices things when he's round here and offers to put them right."

Libby swung round to face her friend. "And are you still keeping him at arm's length in the bedroom?"

"Libby!" Fran's colour rose and she turned away.

"Look, we've had conversations like this in the past, and I know how difficult it all is, but for goodness sake! You've known him for a year, now, and I can't believe he's still hanging on in there. He's still an attractive man, and you're no spring chicken, pardon the cliché."

"Well, thanks." Fran sat down in the armchair beside the inglenook fireplace.

"Oh, you know me," shrugged Libby, with a sigh. "Speaks me mind."

"I had noticed." Fran stared down into her coffee mug. "As it happens, he *has* got past the bedroom door. No —" she held up a hand to stop Libby, "I'm not saying anything else. We respect each other's space. He'd still like to be round here every night, but I really do want to savour this experience on my own for a bit." She looked round the room with a smile. "It's just like a fairy tale. I still can't quite believe it."

Libby regarded her with an indulgent expression. "Well, I'm glad to hear it," she said. "You deserve your cottage, and you deserve Guy. Mind you, I don't know how you kept it from me."

"We don't live round the corner from each other any more, that's why, and Guy lives almost next door."

Guy Wolfe lived above his small art gallery and shop a few yards along Harbour Street from Fran's Coastguard Cottage.

"He might know what's going on by The Sloop," said Libby, turning to peer out of the window again. "The ambulance is still there."

Fran sighed. "Drink your tea, and we'll go and see if Guy knows anything," she said. "You'll never settle otherwise."

Libby smiled broadly. "How well you know me," she said.

In the event, it was Guy who came to them.

"I was going to take you both to The Sloop for lunch," he said, after kissing Fran lightly on the cheek, "but it looks as though it'll have to be The Swan."

"That'll be lovely, thank you," said Fran.

"Do you know what's happening?" asked Libby.

"Not sure, but an ambulance arrived as I was walking here, so whatever it is, it's serious."

"We saw it," said Libby. "I'll go and wash my hands."

"Look, the *Dolphin*'s come in," said Guy as they left the cottage. They walked over to the sea wall and leaned over. Sure enough, the *Dolphin* was gently rocking at its mooring outside The Sloop while the passengers trooped off, watched over by a couple of yellow-jacketed policemen.

"Perhaps that was it," said Libby, "an over-boarder."

"Perhaps." Guy frowned. "I hope not."

A passenger from the *Dolphin* broke away from the others and spoke to one of the policemen. Libby peered round Fran and tried to see what was happening.

"What's she doing?" she said.

"How do we know?" said Fran, exasperated. "Come on Lib. We're going to The Swan."

"I'm with the *Nethergate Mercury*," said Jane. "Can you tell me anything?"

The policeman looked her up and down. "If you've just got off the boat, miss, you know more about it than I do."

"Can I write it up for my paper?"

The policeman frowned. "Don't know about that," he said.

"Do you need me any more, then?" Jane had visions of bylines in the nationals and wanted to get to her phone.

"All passengers over there, miss. Names and addresses."

Jane sighed and went over to the group of passengers huddled round George, who was holding forth in aggrieved tones to another, harassed-looking policeman. Under cover of the argument, which seemed to centre on George's rights as a citizen being undermined, she dragged her daily paper out of her shoulder bag, looked up the number of the news desk and punched it in to her mobile phone. Several other people were on their phones, so her quiet conversation didn't appear out of the ordinary, neither did her second one to her own paper, which had been put to bed earlier in the day. Her excited news editor promised to try and halt production until they could get in a stop-press report and Jane, satisfied, put her phone away and moved up to hear what was being said by George and his policeman.

Fifteen minutes later, she and George were sitting outside The Blue Anchor with large mugs of coffee, supplemented, in George's case, with a generous tot of Mavis's whiskey.

"Treatin' me like a suspect," huffed George, lighting a cigarette with his ancient Zippo.

"No, they weren't, George," said Jane. "They had to get down exactly what happened, didn't they? And they talked to me as well."

"Hmph," said George as Jane's phone rang.

Her news editor said that he had wangled half an hour for her to put in a full report, so could she do so now? Jane filled in what she could, and being an honest girl, told him which national newspaper she had rung.

"No bloody scoop, then, is it?" grumbled the news editor.

"More local people will see the *Mercury* tomorrow, though," comforted Jane, "and I can also do an in-depth follow up, can't I? I know the area."

"If you can think of an angle, yes."

"Anyway, it'll have been on the local news before then, won't it? Radio Kent will have got it, and so will Kent and Coast."

"I know, I know," sighed the news editor. "Gets harder and harder for the poor newspaperman."

"Who do you think it was, George?" said Jane, returning to the table.

"How do I bloody know? Couldn't see its face, could I? Wouldn't be a local. More sense 'n to go gallivantin' on Dragon Island."

"Looked as though it'd been dumped, though."

"Hmph," said George again.

"I wish I could find out."

"Course you do, you're a bloody reporter ain't you? Police'll give a statement, won't they?"

"I suppose so." Jane sighed. "They won't give much away. I wonder who'll be in charge of the investigation."

"That there Connell, it'll be. If 'tis murder, anyhow."

"Inspector Connell? He's scary."

"Nah. That woman was scary."

"What woman?"

"The one what 'e got involved in that murder last winter. The body in the ole Alexandria."

Jane looked along the bay to where The Alexandria Theatre stood on the promenade, now surrounded by scaffolding.

"Weren't there two women? Oh —" Jane pointed a finger. "You mean that psychic, don't you?"

"Lives along 'ere, she does."

Jane looked surprised. "Does she?"

"Didn't you find that out when you was coverin' the story?" George looked sly.

"I didn't cover it," said Jane. "Bob did."

"Ah, the boss. Stands to reason. Anyway, she moved in round about that time, far as I remember. Coastguard Cottage, 'er lives."

"Does she now," said Jane, looking thoughtful.

"Look, now." George pointed. "Ain't got it all to yerself, now, 'ave you?"

A TV van was moving slowly along Harbour Street. Jane sighed.

"It must be serious," said Fran, as they watched the Kent and Coast Television van stop by The Blue Anchor.

"Not necessarily," said Libby, evincing a cynical view of local reportage.

"They were quick, weren't they," said Guy, wiping his soup plate with the last of his bread.

"Media wire," said Libby knowledgeably. "A reporter must have got onto it straight away."

"It'll be on the local news tonight, then," said Fran.

"Probably on the local radio news now," said Guy. "Shall we go back to mine and see if we can find out?"

"No, thanks," said Fran quickly, as Libby opened her mouth eagerly. "Libby will have to finish her painting, or clear things away, anyway."

"OK." Guy shrugged. "Will you be around this evening, Libby?"

"No." Libby sighed. "Peter wants a production meeting." Libby and her friend Peter Parker helped run The Oast House Theatre, owned by Peter's family, in their home village of Steeple Martin.

"For what?"

"The next panto, would you believe?" Libby sighed again. "I've written it this year, but I want to be in it, not direct."

"Is it mutually exclusive?" Guy regarded her with bright brown eyes full of amusement. "Would you be struck off if you did both?"

"It's too difficult to do both, to be honest. Anyway, I don't want to strain my poor brain any more than I have to, and directing's such a responsibility."

"Are you going to do it again, Fran?" Guy looked over at Fran, whose serene gaze was fixed on the horizon, her dark hair framing her face like a latter-day — and slightly mature — Madonna.

"No." Fran looked back at him. "I don't learn lines as well as I used to, and it's one thing turning out every night if you live round the corner, and quite another if you have a twenty-minute drive each way."

"Shame," said Libby. "I'll miss you."

"I said I'd help, Lib. Props, or something. As long as I don't have to be there all the time."

Guy was looking pleased. "So you'll be here more often," he said.

"More often than what?" asked Fran, looking surprised. "I'm here all the time at the moment."

"I meant more often than if you had been doing the panto," said Guy, with a cornered expression.

"Ah," said Libby and Fran together.

"Come on, then," said Fran. "Let's go back and see how that picture's coming along."

CHAPTER
TWO

Libby watched the Kent and Coast local news programme with her cat on her lap. Sidney the silver tabby rarely condescended to quite this much intimacy, and Libby concluded that he was intent on obliterating all scent of Fran's cat Balzac, an altogether more accommodating animal.

According to the reporter, standing on the hard outside The Sloop, where The Blue Anchor could just be seen on the left and the mast of the *Dolphin* bobbing in and out of the picture on the right, an unidentified body had been spotted by holidaymakers on the far side of what was known locally as Dragon Island. The body had been brought in by the lifeboat, summoned by boat owner George Isles. The reporter turned to George.

"'Tweren't me, son, it were Jane over there. She spotted it." The camera swung quickly away from the reporter's discomfited expression to where a young woman sat at a table outside The Blue Anchor.

"That's the person we saw speak to the policeman this morning," Libby told Sidney.

"A holidaymaker on your boat?" asked the reporter.

"No, she'm a local. Works for the newspaper," said George, obviously pleased with the effect he was having. "Helps me on the boat sometimes."

"Thank you, Mr Isles," said the reporter, "and now back to the studio."

"I wonder why they didn't edit that bit," said Libby, realising that the interview had been recorded not long after they had seen the television van that afternoon. "Made the reporter look very silly."

"Who are you talking to?" Ben Wilde appeared from the kitchen.

"Oh! You made me jump." Libby put Sidney on the floor and stood up. "I wish you'd call out when you come in the back way. I was talking to Sidney."

Ben came over and gave her a kiss. "I did."

"Not until you got in here," said Libby.

"What were you talking to Sidney about?" asked Ben, going to a tray of drinks on the table in the window and pouring himself a scotch. "Want one?"

Libby shook her head. "A bit early." She turned off the television. "We saw a television van in Nethergate this afternoon, so I was watching to see what had happened."

"Oh, that body," said Ben. "It was on the national news this afternoon."

"Really? I wonder why?"

"It's summer — the silly season. And it sounds as though this is a holidaymaker tragedy. That always goes down well with the public."

"Ben! That's awful." Libby sat down again and lit a cigarette.

14

"I thought you were giving up?"

Libby scowled. "I object to being forced into it by the government," she said.

Ben raised an eyebrow. "I would never have known," he murmured. "What time is this production meeting?"

"Never mind," said Bert, as he, Jane and George sat over a drink outside The Sloop. "At least yours will be an authentic eyewitness report. Bet you your boss will put it on the front page."

"Ha! One in the eye for that bloody telly reporter," said George, stubbing out his cigarette.

"Can we go inside now?" asked Jane, shivering slightly.

"You can," said George. "I'm having another fag."

Jane sighed.

"So how did they get on to it so quick?" asked Bert, taking a blackened pipe out of his pocket. Jane sighed again.

"Media wire," she said. "I got on to one of the nationals."

Bert and George looked at her as though she was speaking a foreign language.

"Ah," said George.

"Well, you want to get an angle," said Bert sucking noisily on the pipe stem while applying George's Zippo to the bowl.

"That's what I told my boss," said Jane. "An in-depth follow up."

"'Ow can you do that without knowin' 'oo the stiff is?" George was an avid viewer of the older-style American cop movies.

Jane was silent for a moment.

"Come on, ducks," said Bert. "Whatcher got in mind?"

"I wondered about that lady."

"What lady?" Bert raised his eyebrows.

"The one George was talking about," said Jane.

"'Er in Coastguard Cottage," rumbled George.

"Mrs Castle." Bert sucked on his pipe. "What about her?"

"She was involved with that murder last Christmas, wasn't she?"

"Oh, ah." Bert nodded. "That Ian Connell got her involved. I reckon he fancied her."

"Oh." Jane looked disappointed. "Do you mean she couldn't really help?"

"Don't know as I know," said Bert. "Some talk of her being psychic, wasn't there, George?"

"'Elped 'im afore. Some other murder."

"So she's official, then?" said Jane, leaning forward.

"Wouldn't say official, like," said Bert, "but done it before, yes."

"That's all right then," said Jane and stood up. "Anyone for another pint?"

The production meeting was taking place in The Pink Geranium. Harry, Peter Parker's civil partner, was chef and co-owner with Peter, and occasional helper at The Oast House Theatre. Tonight, there were only a few diners, and Peter, Libby, Ben and stage manager Tom had their favourite table in the window.

"So that's it, then." Peter leant back in his chair and picked up his glass of red wine. Libby topped hers up.

"Yes," she said. "That's the script. And I want to be in it."

"So do I," said Tom, "and I don't see how I can *and* stage manage."

"He ought to be Dame again, Pete," said Libby. "He was fantastic last year."

"And Bob and Baz as the double act again," said Ben.

"So who'll be stage manager?" asked Peter, looking harassed.

"Trouble is," said Ben, "the only people who want to do it aren't experienced enough, and we who are all want to be in it."

"I suppose you want to be in it too," Peter said gloomily.

"If there's a part for me," said Ben cheerfully. "Is there, Lib?"

"There's a couple you could go for," said Libby, "depending on the ages of the others in the cast."

"How about Tom and I overseeing design and build, then we'll train one of the others up to SM for the run." Ben beamed round the table. "That would work, wouldn't it?"

There was a murmur of agreement, and Peter sighed. "OK. But what about director?"

"You," said Libby.

Peter groaned. "I thought you might say that."

"Oh, come on, Pete," said Ben, "You've thrown your weight about during the other productions. You could do it legitimately this time."

Peter scowled. "You can push family feeling just so far, you know," he said to his cousin. Ben grinned.

"OK. What do we do about casting?"

Further discussion about auditions and pre-casting took them to the end of the bottle and Harry's assistant Donna was summoned with another. Harry appeared out of the kitchen and removed his apron.

"Have I been co-opted for anything?" he asked, pulling another chair up to the table.

"You're too busy every night, love," said Peter.

"I can do the bar a couple of times, can't I?" said Harry. "I did it for *The Hop Pickers* and *Jack and the Beanstalk*."

"If you're free," said Peter. "Thanks."

"How's Fran?" asked Harry. "I thought of her today when I saw that item about the body at Nethergate."

"We were there," said Libby proudly. The other faces round the table looked at her in horror and spoke with one voice.

"Oh, no!"

"For goodness' sake," said Libby crossly. "Not involved. We couldn't help it. Fran lives on Harbour Street and all the police and everything were down by The Sloop only fifteen yards away. Guy was there, too."

"So what was it all about, then?" asked Tom. "I haven't listened to the radio and I didn't have time to watch the news before I came out."

"A body was found on that island in the middle of the bay," said Harry. "The police think it was dumped, apparently, and that it could be an illegal."

"I didn't hear that," said Libby. "Illegal immigrant, you mean?"

"It was on the news this evening. I have the radio on in the kitchen."

"One of those poor buggers that try to get in through the tunnel, I suppose," said Ben.

"A bit far round for him, then, isn't it?" said Tom. "The tide might carry him if he'd fallen off a boat, but how did he get all the way across Kent from Folkestone if he came by tunnel?"

"All I know is they think it was dumped," said Harry. "Don't blame me."

"And don't worry about me," said Libby, looking virtuous. "Fran and I won't be involved this time."

Fran was watering the pots in her tiny yard outside the back door the following morning when she heard a knock at the front. Leaving Balzac, her beautiful black and white long-haired cat, to investigate the watering can, she went inside, wiping her hands on a tea towel.

"Mrs Castle?" The young woman on the doorstep was small, slight and brown haired. Little brown mouse, thought Fran.

"Yes?"

"I'm Jane Maurice from the *Nethergate Mercury*."

"Oh?"

"Yes. I wondered if you'd been invited by the local police to investigate the — um — murder that was discovered yesterday?"

"Murder? Yesterday?"

"You'll have heard it or seen it on the news? And it was in the *Mercury* this morning."

"I don't take the *Mercury*," said Fran, "and if you mean the body discovered on the island yesterday, I didn't know it was murdered."

"The police think it might be," said Jane Maurice. "That's why I thought they might have consulted you." She was fidgeting now, obviously having expected to be invited inside. But Fran was having none of it.

"I can't think why anyone should have consulted me, especially about a body." She made as if to close the door. "Now, if you'll excuse me —"

"But Mrs Castle —" began Jane, trying to step forward.

"Thank you, Miss — er. Goodbye." Fran closed the door and leaned back on it, her heart thumping. How had that happened?

She went slowly back to the yard, where Balzac greeted her with a chirrup. It was that last case, she thought, bending to stroke his head. Her part in it had been discovered by the local paper and her name had appeared more than once as "Inspector Connell's special investigator". Neither of them had confirmed it, and eventually, the paper had stopped including her. But they remembered, obviously.

As a reluctant psychic, Fran had been useful to the local police force once or twice, with a certain amount of help from an over-excitable Libby, but she wasn't comfortable with any of it. Libby would have had them setting up a psychic detective agency if she'd had her way, but Fran just wanted to be an ordinary person in an ordinary house now that she had Coastguard Cottage. Besides, one of her children was due to visit this weekend, complete with censorious husband, and she didn't think they would approve of anything even slightly out of the ordinary.

"Did you see that item on the news last night?" said Libby later, on the phone. "Harry said that on the radio they said it was an illegal immigrant."

"Yes, and I had a reporter round here this morning."

"You what?"

"Some girl from the local paper came round to ask me if I'd been consulted by the police."

"Oooh!" said Libby. "You're famous!"

"Oh, stop it, Libby. You know I've never wanted any of this. You're the one who always wants to go charging in to investigate things."

"If I didn't, you wouldn't be living here, would you?"

"I'd still have Coastguard Cottage."

"But you wouldn't know the rest of us. Or Guy."

"Once I was living six doors down from him, I expect I might have met him," said Fran. "He said he'd have wangled an introduction somehow."

"Oh, so you've talked about it?"

"Of course. I admit that my — er — involvement with you and Ben has somewhat changed my life, but I think Guy and I would have met anyway."

"Oh, OK." Libby thought for a moment. "So what did you say to this reporter? Did you tell her we'd actually been on the spot?"

"No, of course not. And don't you go getting in touch with her, either."

"No, I won't. Anyway, what I really rang up about was the panto. Did you mean it when you said you'd do props?"

When Fran rang off, she went to the window to look down Harbour Street towards The Sloop. The sky was greyer today, and both the *Dolphin* and the *Sparkler* were still moored up. She could see the two old boat owners, George and Bert, sitting outside The Blue Anchor, but no one else was around, which was odd for high summer. She wondered vaguely if perhaps Harbour Street had been blue-taped by the police, and was just going to open her door to look and see when there was a knock.

A tall young man dressed rather like a central casting geography teacher stood outside holding a briefcase.

"Mrs Castle?" he said, stepping forward before she could block the way. "Good afternoon. I'm from Kent and Coast Television, and I wondered if you would consider undertaking a psychic investigation into the body on Dragon Island on our behalf?"

Fran felt sweat break out along her hairline.

"I don't do that sort of thing," she said.

The reporter looked down his nose at her. "According to the reports, you do."

"What reports?" Fran pulled herself together.

He smiled. "From the *Nethergate Mercury*, for one. It's quite well documented that you've helped the police on at least one occasion."

"And I don't intend to do it again." Fran closed her lips tightly together.

The reporter leaned nearer with a smile. "Come on, Mrs Castle. This would be great publicity for you. And of course, we wouldn't expect you to do it for nothing."

"Publicity?" Fran recoiled in horror. "What on earth would I want publicity for?"

The reporter frowned. "Your job?" he said.

"My *job*? I don't have a job."

He looked confused for a moment, but rallied. That was *his* job, of course.

"I was told that you did this for a living."

"I *what*? Where on earth did you get that from?"

"Like the police, I have to protect my sources." He smiled again, but less convincingly.

"Well, whoever they were," Fran paused, tellingly, "*Jane Maurice* was wrong. I live here, on my own —" damn, she shouldn't have said that "— and I don't have a job, unless you count helping in the art gallery along the road. I've given my opinion to the local police on occasion, but that's it. And now I'd like you to leave."

The reporter looked stunned. Fran stood up. "Please?" she said.

Slowly, he stood up.

"I'm sorry," he said. "We really seem to have messed up this time." He held out his hand. "No hard feelings? I assure you, we were acting from the best of intentions."

23

Feeling guilty, Fran took his hand briefly. He wasn't so unpleasant really.

"Which were?" she asked.

"The intentions? Well, we thought maybe you could identify the victim —"

"He's an illegal immigrant."

"Sorry, yes, but they don't know where he came from. Just that he appears to be."

"That police investigation is ongoing, I believe."

"Yes, of course, but —"

"You thought I might help you steal a march on them?"

"And prove that people like you are genuine."

Fran sniffed. "There are television programmes that try and do that," she said.

"And no one believes them," said the reporter, triumphantly. "This would have been a genuine, news programme investigation." His eyes registered shock as he uttered the final damning words.

Fran was amused. "Into me."

He lifted his shoulders in resignation and bent to pick up his briefcase. "You've got me there," he said, and shook her hand again. "You wouldn't like to come and work for us, would you? You'd make a great investigative reporter."

Fran laughed, relaxing at last. "Maybe that would be interesting," she said, "but, to be honest, I'm a bit shy. I don't really like meeting new people."

"Well, thank you, Mrs Castle, and I'm really sorry to have bothered you." He went past her towards the door.

24

"And don't listen to Jane Maurice in future," said Fran as she held the door open. "She seemed a nice little thing, but I refused to talk to her, so why she thought I'd talk to you I can't think."

"She probably thought you would be swayed by a vision of fame and riches," laughed the reporter.

"So did you," Fran reminded him, "so you were both wrong."

He handed her a card. "If there ever is anything you want to talk about, will you give me a ring?"

"Do you mean about this investigation?"

"Anything, Mrs Castle, anything at all. If you think the Isle of Wight has fallen into the sea, just call me. I'll take you seriously."

She watched him walk up Harbour Street towards The Swan, noting that the blue tape was in place, then closed the door and looked at the card.

"Campbell McLean," she read out loud. She went to the window and looked out, but he'd disappeared. "Well, Campbell McLean, we'll see about you. And now for young Maurice."

She found her mobile and looked up the number of the *Mercury*.

"News desk," said a tired voice.

"Jane?" Fran said gently.

"Mrs Castle?" Jane's voice perked up immediately. "I'm so glad you called —"

"You won't be," interrupted Fran.

"Oh?"

"Who told Kent and Coast Television about me?"

There was silence.

"Don't worry, I know it was you." Fran sighed. "And don't you ever do it again. For a start, you know nothing about me. I am most definitely not a psychic investigator, or whatever they're called. I work occasionally in the art gallery in Harbour Street."

"But —"

"No buts, Jane," said Fran. "That's all I do and all I want to do."

"What about Goodall and Smythe?"

It was Fran's turn to be silenced.

"Goodall and Smythe?" she repeated. "What about them?"

"You did psychic research for them." Jane's voice was accusing.

Fran sighed again. "Not really. I used to go into houses for them if there was a suggestion of any — um — unpleasantness. That's all."

"That *is* psychic research."

"Not in my book, and I doubt it is in theirs," said Fran. "It was over a long time ago, anyway, and I haven't lived in London for the last year."

"So you're not helping the police?"

"No, Jane. I've already told you. And why the bloody hell you sicked Kent and Coast on to me I *don't* know. Now, leave me alone, please, and if you print anything about me, I'll sue."

"All right, all right," said Jane, "I won't. But you can't blame me for trying."

"I suppose not. Thought you'd got an angle on the story, did you?"

"Yes." There was a rueful note in Jane's voice now.

"Sorry to disappoint you. And now I must go, someone's knocking on my door."

And I hope it's not Mr Campbell McLean back again, she thought as she switched off the phone.

But it wasn't. On her doorstep stood Detective Inspector Ian Connell.

CHAPTER
THREE

Fran just stood and looked at him, knowing exactly why he was there.

"Fran," he said, holding out his hand. "How are you?"

"Fine, thanks," she said taking his hand briefly.

"May I come in?"

Fran sighed. "I suppose so," she said.

He came in to the sitting room and looked round. "Nice," he said.

"It is, isn't it?" she said. "Tea? Coffee?"

"Tea would be lovely, if it's no problem."

Fran went in to the kitchen and filled the kettle. He was going to ask her about the body. So had those reporters known? Was it just a good guess? Had something been said at a press conference? Although she knew it wouldn't. That wasn't the way the police worked. In fact, *she* wasn't the way the police worked normally, but since she and DCI Murray had come up against each other over a previous murder, Ian Connell had shamelessly picked her brains.

"The body on the island," she said, bringing in two mugs of tea.

Ian Connell turned sharply from the window.

"That's why you're here, isn't it?"

He came forward to take the mug she held out, looking sheepish.

"Yes. How did you know? Oh —" he held up a hand "— silly question."

"No, nothing like that," said Fran, sitting down in one of the huge armchairs by the fireplace and indicating that Ian should take the other. "I had a local paper reporter and then Kent and Coast Television both on to me asking if I was helping the police with their investigations."

"What?" Ian's eyebrows rose almost to his hairline. "Why did they think that?"

"The local reporter, Jane Maurice, had done her homework and knew I'd helped you in the past. She also knew I'd worked for Goodall and Smythe. When I wouldn't talk to her, she told Kent and Coast."

"Enterprising, isn't she?" Ian Connell was obviously amused. "Have you seen the *Mercury*?"

"No."

"She managed to get the front page."

"Not with me?" Fran was horrified.

"No. She was actually the one who spotted the body. She was out on George Isles's boat. Gift for a young reporter. She also got it into one of the nationals who sent it out on a media wire, but of course the local radio and TV networks had already got it by then."

"How? Libby said something about a media wire," said Fran, "but how did they know before that?"

"Oh, Fran." He smiled and shook his head. "They're ambulance chasers."

"Oh, I see," said Fran, who didn't.

"Anyway, young Miss Maurice was responsible for getting it out on a media wire and did herself a bit of good. I expect she thought she was on to a winner with you."

"Unfortunately, it seems that she was right," said Fran shrewdly.

"Ah." Ian looked down into his mug.

"Are you going to ask me to help?"

"That was the general idea, yes."

"But I'm nothing to do with this one at all."

"You were nothing to do with the last one, either, until you and Libby got personally involved. You could hardly do that with this one."

"You don't know Libby," muttered Fran.

"Oh, yes I do." Ian laughed. "And that reminds me, are you doing her panto again this year?"

"So what do we have to do?" asked an eager Libby sometime later when Fran rang to tell her about the visitors.

"We don't do anything," said Fran. "He wants to take me to see the body."

"Oh, yuck!" said Libby. "You're not going, surely?"

"No, of course I'm not. I did say I'd look at any belongings that might have been found, but apparently there weren't any."

"Oh, poor man," said Libby. "No clothes?"

"Only a shirt and trousers, and they looked old."

"Second-hand?"

"How do I know, Libby? Honestly." Fran shook her head at the telephone.

"So when is he going to show you these things?"

"I've got to go to the police station tomorrow morning. But they already think he's an illegal immigrant."

"Yes, I told you, Harry said that last night."

"But they think he might have been working over here, not one of those poor people who smuggle themselves in lorries."

"Oh. Does that make a difference?"

"Apparently. If he's been working, he may have been brought over by an illegal scam. Remember the Chinese in the lorry at Dover?"

"Oh, God, yes," said Libby. "And the Morecambe Bay winkle-pickers."

"Well, there are a lot more than that. It's huge business, and these people organise false papers and passports and get them working for peanuts in all sorts of places. Restaurants —"

"Chinese restaurants?" Libby put in.

"Possibly. I don't know. Fruit farms —"

"Oh, I know," said Libby. "The pickers round here are nearly all Eastern European, aren't they? Do you mean to say they're all illegal?"

"I don't know." Fran was beginning to sound exasperated, which, Libby reflected, was something that frequently happened during their conversations.

"Oh, well. Perhaps you'll know after you've been to the police station. When did you say you're going?"

"Tomorrow morning. I'll let you know what happens. I've got Chrissie and Bruce coming tomorrow, too, which makes life a bit difficult. I think they want to ask me a favour."

"Money?" asked Libby.

"I shouldn't think so . . . although Brucie Baby is quite likely to decide he can manage my investments or something. No, it's more likely to be something I can do for them, usually with maximum inconvenience to me."

"Let me know if I can do anything," said Libby, reflecting on her own children, who never seemed to want anything from her other than the occasional bed. Fran had already had an extended visit from her daughter Lucy and grandchildren Rachel and Tom, which had kept Libby away from Nethergate until they reluctantly returned to London. Not that she had anything against children, after all, she'd had three of her own, but they exhausted her and she never quite knew what to say to them. And she'd found Lucy a needy sort of person who resented her mother's independence and the removal of an on-tap babysitter.

"I might try and wriggle out of it, actually," said Fran.

"What, the police station?"

"No, Chrissie and Bruce. I could phone up and say the police need me, couldn't I? Bruce would hate that."

"Try it," said Libby, amused. "And let me know what happens."

After ringing off from Libby, Fran returned to staring out of the window, something she found herself doing far too often. Then, taking a deep breath, she punched in her daughter's number.

"Mum?"

"Chrissie. I'm awfully sorry, but we might have to put off your visit."

"What? Oh, Mum, you are the end. All our arrangements are made. What can be more important?"

"I have to go to the police station —"

She was interrupted by a shriek. "The police station? What have you done?"

"I've been asked to advise on a police matter," she began, but once more, Chrissie cut her off.

"Advise? What for? What could you advise on?"

"It doesn't concern you — or it needn't anyway. But I have got to be away for the whole morning and possibly the afternoon," said Fran stretching the truth somewhat.

"Well, I suppose if you have to," said Chrissie grumpily, "but I must say it's most inconvenient."

"Sorry, darling," said Fran, magnanimous in triumph. "Anyway, why don't you tell me what it was you wanted to ask me?" By the silence which greeted this question, she guessed she'd been right. "Are you all right?"

"Well, yes and no." Her daughter's breathless voice sounded faintly excited.

"Oh?" No point in saying anything else. All would be revealed.

"You know we're moving on Friday?"

Oh, god, she'd forgotten. "Yes?"

"Well, it's all got a bit much, and I wondered — if you weren't doing anything —" there was a pause while Fran racked her brains for what possible favour Chrissie wanted. "Well, could you come and mind Cass?"

"Mind Cass?" she repeated stupidly. Had she a grandchild she'd forgotten?

"Cassandra. The cat."

"Oh. Mind her? Why? Where?"

"Well, here. And there. She's in kitten, you see."

"I'm sorry, Chrissie, I don't quite follow. Why does she need minding?"

"Because she might go into labour in transit — or while we're unloading, or even before we've left. Supposing we lost her just as we were about to leave. You know what cats are like. They go off and find bolt holes."

"I thought that was when they died."

"Well, yes —" Chrissie sounded vague. "But I'm worried. Could you come? We won't ask you to do anything else, I promise."

No, of course they wouldn't. Chrissie's formal and uptight husband viewed Fran with deep gloom every time she wandered across his path, which was not very often.

"When do you want me?" As if it mattered. She wasn't exactly snowed under with social engagements.

"Friday morning? We can't put you up here because we'll have taken down all the beds. Could you get here then?"

"By what time?"

"Well, the van's arriving at eight —"

"Eight?" Fran yelped. "I'm not driving anywhere that early in the morning."

"Oh." Chrissie sounded deflated. "Well, I suppose you could sleep on the floor here — we're going to."

"No, Chrissie," she said firmly. "My sleeping-on-floors days were over a long time ago. Either I sleep in a decent bed there or I don't come. One or the other."

There was a muffled colloquy at the other end of the line, then Chrissie came back with renewed vigour.

"Bruce says we'll book you into The King's Arms for the night. Will that be all right?"

Fran smiled at the phone. "Fine."

"Er — we're eating there, actually, Thursday night, so would you like to join us for dinner?"

Fran chose to ignore the lack of enthusiasm. "Lovely. What time?"

"Eightish. Will you be all right getting here?"

"Yes, thank you, dear." She wasn't completely incapable.

"I'll give you the money for the petrol."

"Don't be silly."

"All right, then, Mum. We'll see you Thursday at The King's Arms at eight. You're sure it's all right? You weren't doing anything else?"

"Nothing I can't put off."

"OK then. See you Thursday. And thanks, Mum."

Fran cut the call and redialled Libby's number.

"Done," she said. "They want me to babysit their precious pregnant Siamese cat while they move."

"You mean they aren't coming tomorrow?"

"No. I told you, all they wanted was a favour. This was it."

"What about Balzac?"

"I'll ask Guy," said Fran. "After all, poor old cat was left alone for long enough before he came to me, wasn't he?"

"Meanwhile," said Libby, "you're now free to go investigating after all."

"No, Lib," said Fran, firmly. "Just free to go to the police station."

"And see Guy. I bet you weren't going to introduce him to Chrissie and Bruce."

"No," said Fran, with a sigh. "They'd have frightened him off for good."

"Or he might have frightened them off. When do you have to go and look after the cat?"

"Next Thursday. I'll be back Friday evening, I expect. I've made them pay for a hotel overnight," Fran added gleefully. "They didn't like that."

"So will you let me know what happens tomorrow?"

"Yes, I'll call you when I get home."

Libby put the phone back on its rest and went out to the conservatory. The picture started on Thursday was on the easel looking flat and dull. Perhaps she ought to go over to Nethergate again and have another go at it? She smiled and gave it a pat. Of course she should.

CHAPTER
FOUR

Saturday saw the sun shining once more on Nethergate. The Swan sat at one end of Harbour Street in all its black and white glory and The Sloop sat at the other in its more modest flint. Between the two strolled holidaymakers, passing and re-passing Fran's Coastguard Cottage. Lizzie's tiny ice cream shop was doing a brisk trade, as was The Blue Anchor, and the seagulls were having a field day with discarded chips. As Libby prepared to set up her easel opposite Coastguard Cottage, she noticed Mavis from The Blue Anchor scowling at a family whose children were distributing most of their lunch across the hard in front of them. Libby shook her head in sympathy. Visitors didn't realise how much harm seagulls could do, and how dangerous they could become.

The *Dolphin* and the *Sparkler* were both out and all signs of a police presence had been removed. Nethergate was back to normal.

Or perhaps not, thought Libby, noticing the small brown-haired person making her way purposefully along the sea wall towards her.

"Mrs Sarjeant?" said this person, slightly breathlessly.

"Yes," said Libby, cautiously, her brush poised in mid-air.

"My name's Jane Maurice."

Of course. The person she and Fran had seen on Thursday morning, and who had accosted Fran in her home yesterday.

"What do you want?"

Jane Maurice looked taken aback at Libby's tone. "I — I just wanted —"

"Mrs Castle has already told you she doesn't want to be bothered by the press, hasn't she?" said Libby, trying to look fierce.

Jane nodded vigorously. "I know. It's nothing to do with that. I wanted to talk to you."

"To me?" Libby put the brushes down. "What on earth for? And how did you know who I was?"

"Mavis told me." Jane looked sheepish. "I was down here to see George and Bert, only they've both gone out —"

"The *Dolphin* and the *Sparkler*?"

"Yes. I go out with them sometimes. And Mavis just pointed you out."

"Just like that?"

"Well, she said: 'There's that Mrs Sarjeant who does them theatricals over to Steeple Martin' or something like that, and said you were somehow instrumental in the restoration of The Alexandria. So I thought I'd come and ask you about it."

"Did you?" Libby looked sceptical. Coming hard on the heels of Jane's attempt to get Fran to talk, this was

38

hard to accept. The Alexandria itself had been mixed up in a murder, too, and this looked suspicious.

Jane noticed, and sank down on to the sea wall. "Oh, well, it was worth a try," she sighed. "I can't seem to get anywhere in this town."

"What did you want to know about The Alexandria?" asked Libby.

"Whether it really is being restored," said Jane, "and whether it will be a performance space, and if so what kind. I know you had something to do with The Oast House Theatre in Steeple Martin. Will it be like that?"

"It is being restored, but I'm afraid it's nothing to do with me," said Libby. "I don't know what use it will be put to. Could be a restaurant, or something."

This wasn't true, but Libby's knowledge of The Alexandria was highly confidential.

"Oh." Jane searched Libby's face for a moment, then sighed again and slid off the wall. "Thanks, anyway."

"Are you new down here?" asked Libby, picking up her brushes again.

"Not that new," said Jane, squinting out to sea. "I've been here about a year."

"What brought you here? The job?"

"No." Jane perched on the sea wall again. "I inherited a house."

"Goodness! That was a bit of luck," said Libby, "although not if you were very fond of the person who died, of course."

"Well, I was, but I didn't know her very well. She ran a boarding house here until the 1970s, then it became too much for her, so she turned it into little flats. She'd been in a care home for some time before she died, but the house was still there."

"And you inherited it? Tenants and all?"

"Two tenants," said Jane, "yes. They aren't any trouble, and an agent looks after that side of it. I just live in the top flat. I like it better than Auntie's ground floor one."

"So you moved down and got the job when you got here?" Libby had given up all pretence of painting now.

"No, I applied before I moved down. I was lucky. I was already working on another paper in the group and a vacancy became available."

"And how do you find it?"

"All right."

"Not so good?"

"I'm an outsider." Jane smiled a little crookedly. "Last year I went out on George's boat because he'd had an operation and needed help, and this year they've both let me go out with them whenever I wanted. Apart from them and a couple of people in the office, that's it."

"And now you can't get a story." Libby shook her head. "That's a shame."

"Thank you. But you can't get blood out of a stone —" here, Jane paused looking horrified. "Sorry. I didn't mean that."

"Yes, you did," said Libby, cheerfully, "and quite right too. But really, I've nothing to tell you, and neither has Mrs Castle. Even when she did help the police, it was all very hush-hush and no one believed it anyway."

"It seems to be quite well known, though. I knew about it because I worked on the paper, but I didn't cover the story. Was it true?"

Libby looked at her consideringly. "If I tell you anything, it's likely to end up in print, isn't it?"

"Oh, God." Jane shook her head. "You see? People don't trust me. Even though I'm only a reporter on a tiny provincial weekly."

"Who managed to get a front page story this week and something in one of the nationals."

"Just because I was on the spot and had my wits about me. It wouldn't have taken them long to find out, anyway."

Libby nodded. "So you're feeling a bit hard done by this morning."

"I suppose so." Jane slid back off the wall and stood up. "I'm sorry to have disturbed you, Mrs Sarjeant. I'll let you get on."

Libby looked ruefully at the picture. "I don't think I'm going to get on at all," she said. "How about we go and have a coffee in The Blue Anchor?"

"Really?" Jane looked stunned. "Why?"

"Because I'm not going to paint this morning after all and I've got to wait for Mrs Castle to come home, so I might as well wait in The Blue Anchor. It would be nice to have company and I'll buy you a coffee."

"Oh." Jane looked down at Libby's paraphernalia. "Can I help you carry, then?"

"That would be kind." Libby put away the brushes and covered the painting. "I'm parked behind The Sloop."

Ten minutes later, when they were seated outside The Blue Anchor, Mavis delivered a large mug of coffee for Jane and one of tea for Libby, who lit a cigarette and leaned back comfortably.

"I always sit out here with George and Bert because they smoke," said Jane, pushing the foil ashtray across the table.

"That's good of you," said Libby. "Most of us feel like pariahs."

"It's not good of me." Jane shook her head. "I wouldn't have anyone to talk to otherwise."

Libby squinted through smoke. "You're painting a very sad picture of yourself, you know."

Jane shrugged. "Maybe, but I think people in your age group think anyone under thirty-five is having a whale of a time with loads of friends and places to go. It isn't true."

"No?"

"Well, look at me. In a town I don't know, with no friends or family, working in a very small office with no one of my own age. What do I do? Go clubbing on my own? Go to a pub on my own? The most I do is come down here for a drink or a coffee with George and Bert or take myself to The Raj for a treat, to make a change from a take-away."

"Golly," said Libby. "You're right. I hadn't thought about it. What about college friends? Old school friends?"

"Oh, I've kept up with some, but they're scattered all over the country. And my school friends are mostly married with young children now, so we've nothing in common."

Libby stared out to sea for a moment. "What about interests? Hobbies?" she asked finally.

Jane laughed. "That's always the advice on the problem pages, isn't it? My only hobby is reading — not exactly sociable."

"Didn't you belong to any societies at college?"

Jane shook her head. "I told you, there's nothing I'm really interested in. At uni we worked or went drinking, the same as everybody else."

Libby looked at her meditatively. "Amateur dramatics?" she said.

"I know you're involved with The Oast House Theatre," said Jane, "but I'm really not that sort."

"You mean you're snobbish about amateur theatre?"

Jane flushed. "That wasn't what I meant."

"Oh, yes it was. I've seen it too often not to recognise it," said Libby, stubbing out her cigarette. "But there are amateur companies and amateur companies, you know. You might get a shock. After all, you did come asking me about The Alexandria."

"Well . . . yes. I wondered if it was going to put on amateur performances for the town. We haven't got a theatre here."

"You've got the Carlton Pavilion."

"It's not a proper theatre, though, is it?" said Jane.

"True, but it does put on live events."

"Music, mainly," said Jane, her eyes going towards where the Carlton Pavilion sat almost on the sand just below The Swan.

Libby sat up straight and stretched. "Well, I was going to invite you over to have a look at us, but I can see you wouldn't be interested."

"Look at you?"

"Our little theatre," said Libby, deliberately injecting a disparaging note into her voice.

Jane looked sheepish. "Actually, I'd love to," she said.

Libby beamed. "I thought you might," she said.

CHAPTER
FIVE

"So what happened?" Libby had left Jane at The Blue Anchor when she saw Fran arrive at Coastguard Cottage.

Fran shrugged. "Nothing. Ian showed me some clothes and that was it. No stunning revelations. Just clothes." She poured boiling water into a mug. "Sure you don't want one?"

"No, I'm awash."

Fran looked up. "Yes. So tell me, what were you doing having tea with Jane Maurice?"

Libby told her. "She's OK, really, Fran," she concluded, "just lonely. So I thought if she came over to the theatre she might meet people of her own age."

"We haven't got any young people," said Fran.

"There's Harry — he's young."

"Not available, though."

"And James." Libby's eyes lit up. "Ah! Now, James will be just about ready —"

"Libby, stop it! Don't start matchmaking. Invite the poor girl by all means, but don't try and interfere with her life, or James's, come to that."

"OK." Libby went into Fran's sitting room and to the window.

Fran frowned, suspicious of the ready acquiescence. "Come on, Lib. What are you planning?"

"Nothing." Libby turned and beamed. "Honestly, nothing." She came towards Fran and sat down in one of the armchairs. "So tell me what Ian said. Has he asked you to investigate anything?"

"No, of course not." Fran was looking uncomfortable, Libby noticed.

"What did he say, Fran? There's something, isn't there?"

"If you must know, he said it was a pity I hadn't taken up Kent and Coast's invitation."

"Wha-a-a?" Libby's eyes widened in astonishment.

"I know." Fran shook her head. "He seemed to think they could investigate undercover much better than the police could, and if I was on the spot I could — er — report to him."

"Spy, you mean? Gosh, what a cheek!"

"Well, yes. But he also thought I might pick up something, you know, hidden, if I was on the spot rather than remotely." Fran sighed. "I suppose he's right in a way."

"Are you going to do it?"

"What, after I sent that poor young man packing?"

"I'm sure you could get round that. Didn't you say he told you to get in touch?"

"I'll think about it." Fran stood up and took her mug back into the kitchen. "Did you want some lunch, by the way?"

"No, thanks, I said I'd meet Ben at the pub." Libby stood up and stretched. "We're going to the caff tonight. Would you and Guy like to come too?"

"I'll ask him," said Fran, blushing faintly. "Funny, isn't it? I still don't like instigating anything in the relationship."

"This isn't you, it's me," said Libby bluntly. "I'll go and ask him, if you like."

"No, don't be daft. I'll do it. I'm relieving him in the shop later, anyway." Fran went to open the front door. "I expect we'll see you tonight."

Libby relayed her morning's doings to Ben back at the pub in Steeple Martin.

"Are you," said Ben, nonchalantly lifting his pint, "starting to interfere a bit?"

"Interfere? Me?" Libby was outraged.

"Yes. Interfere *you*. Ever since I've known you —"

"No, I am not," Libby cut in. "And you didn't know me well before — before — well, before."

"OK, OK, since I've known you — intimately —" Ben leered over the table, "you've interfered in everything."

"I'm surprised you're still involved, then," said Libby huffily.

"Ah, but it's interesting," he said, reaching over the table for her hand. "And think of the opportunities for gossip."

"You're not supposed to gossip about police matters," said Libby.

"And you never do?"

"Well, only within the intimate circle." Libby picked up her glass. "You and Pete and Harry."

"Oh, that's all right, then." Ben chuckled.

"Fran and Guy might join us at the caff tonight," said Libby.

"They haven't been over for some time, have they? I thought maybe we'd upset them."

"I think it's just that Fran wanted to settle into Nethergate and not keep running back to us. She's got her own life to lead."

"You were worried about her moving down there, I seem to remember."

"Yes, but I needn't have. I still see her."

"Because you force yourself on her," grinned Ben.

"No, I don't." Libby was indignant. "I like painting down there, that's all. I always have, haven't I? I've been doing pretty peeps for Guy's shop for years."

"Guy's gallery, you mean," said Ben. "When it's paintings, it's a gallery, when it's cards it's a shop."

"Whatever." Libby shrugged. "Anyway, it's really good that they're together, even if Fran won't let him get too close."

"Oh?" Ben raised an eyebrow. "Don't they . . . ?"

"Ben! None of our business." Libby smothered a smile. "Actually, yes, they do, but only when Fran allows it, I gather."

"Well, that's the same as most couples, isn't it? I mean, we only —"

"Ben!" said Libby again, looking round the bar.

"I just meant," whispered Ben, leaning forward, "I can only make love to you if you want it, too."

"That makes me sound mean."

"Well, not exactly. You always do want it, too."

Libby swallowed. "This is not an appropriate conversation for a pub," she said in a strangled voice.

"Then how about carrying it on back at your place?" Ben stroked his thumb across her wrist and she shivered. "Purely in the interests of research, of course."

"Of course," said Libby, and finished her drink.

Later, when Ben sat on the cane sofa wrapped in the towelling dressing gown he kept in Libby's bathroom, she poured boiling water into her teapot.

"What do you know about illegal immigrants?" she asked, putting out two mugs.

Ben groaned. "I knew you were interfering."

"I'm not." Libby fetched milk from the fridge. "I just wondered. Seems there are all sorts of scams for getting them into the country. Like those Chinese at Dover, and the winkle pickers in Morecambe."

"Of course there are. It's always in the news."

"But there are whole organisations getting them false papers —"

"And jobs. I know, Libby. It's a scandal, but it's been going on for years. The worst of them are the prostitution gangs."

"Oh, yes." Libby, coming in with two mugs of tea, made a face. "I've seen a couple of TV programmes about that."

"Well, don't worry about it. I know the police are trying to get on top of it. The trouble is, we're in the front line being near the Channel ports."

"And being a fruit and veg growing area so we need lots of casual pickers." Libby curled up in the armchair with a sigh. "I think that's what our body was."

"*Our* body?" asked Ben suspiciously.

"Well, it's in our area, isn't it?"

"But nothing to do with you," said Ben, frowning.

"No, I know, but Fran might have to work on it."
Libby turned to look out of the window, avoiding Ben's
eyes.

"Oh, I see. For Fran, read Libby."

"No, I wouldn't be in on it," said Libby, looking back
at him with suspiciously wide eyes. "I think Ian wants
Fran to investigate with the television people."

"But I thought she'd already said no."

"She had. But Ian can be persuasive. And Fran's got
a conscience."

Ben sighed. "And you haven't."

"I just like helping people," said Libby, "and by the
way, I've invited that reporter to come over and see
what she thinks of the theatre."

"Which reporter?"

"The one who tried to interview me this morning.
She's lonely."

"Does she act?"

"She doesn't seem to do anything," said Libby, and
told him Jane's story. "So I thought it might be a
kindness to see if she'd like to get involved."

"We haven't got many youngsters here, either," said
Ben.

"But there are always more around for panto. She
might want to do chorus, or something."

Ben looked doubtful. "We'll see. When's she coming
over?"

"I don't know. When we have the audition, I suppose. I thought I might pop in and see her house some time in the next couple of weeks, just to keep in touch."

"You're sure you haven't got an ulterior motive?"

"No, of course not. Why would I have?" Libby was looking indignant again. "She's just a nice kid, and rather lonely."

Libby repeated this to Fran and Guy over quesadillas de hongos in The Pink Geranium later that evening.

"That's kind of you," said Guy. Fran turned down the corners of her mouth. Like Ben, she was suspicious.

"Oh, for goodness sake," said Libby. "Can't I do anything from a purely normal standpoint? Does everyone always think I'm up to no good?"

"A newspaper reporter does have access to a lot of things you might find useful," said Ben.

"If you were investigating something you weren't supposed to," added Fran.

Libby made a sound suspiciously like a snort. "Honestly," she said.

"Speaking of which, Fran," said Ben, "have you decided to do what Ian asked?"

"Eh?" Guy looked startled. "Ian? Connell? What's he been asking?"

"Don't worry, Guy, it's nothing carnal," grinned Libby.

"Libby!" Fran frowned at her. "It's complicated," she said to Guy, and explained.

"Why don't you do it?" he asked. "You could ask the Kent and Coast people not to actually put you on the box, but just to use your information."

"Would you have to say it was the police's idea?" asked Ben.

"Oh, I don't think so, or they might get the idea they had a privileged position." Fran poked meditatively at a piece of mushroom. "I'll phone that Campbell McLean person and sound him out, then I'll talk to Ian about how he wants me to play it."

"So you're going to do it, then?" Libby looked excited.

Fran sighed.

"Told you she had a conscience," Libby said Ben, triumphantly.

CHAPTER
SIX

Libby had to wait until Monday to find out where Jane lived. She called her at the *Mercury* offices, ostensibly to invite her to the audition for the pantomime. Predictably, Jane protested.

"You don't have to audition, Jane," said Libby. "I just thought you could come along and meet people. If you're with me you won't be on your own."

"No . . ." Jane was hesitant.

"Tell you what," said Libby briskly, "I'll pop a copy of the script over to you and you can have a read and see what we do. Mind you, panto reads very badly, so don't give us up just on the strength of the script."

"OK. Would you like me to pick it up?"

"No, I said I'll pop it over to you. Give me a chance to see your auntie's house."

"Oh!" Jane sounded surprised. "All right. I'm off this afternoon, actually, so would you like to come then?"

"That fits in nicely," said Libby. "I have to see Fran — Mrs Castle — today —" whether she likes it or not, she added silently "— so that's perfect. See you about three? What's the address?"

Libby then rang Fran to tell her that she would be visited.

"I'll be in the shop until two," said Fran.

"That's OK," said Libby airily. "I shan't be long."

Before she left for Nethergate, Libby booted up her computer and ran a search on illegal immigrants. The first few thousand entries appeared to be American, so she began to be more specific, until she finally came across some relevant news items from the Kent area.

"Poor things," she murmured to herself, as she read. It seemed the immigrants themselves were the victims, yet were continually abused and reviled by the press and the public. Conversely, there were the stories of criminal activity by the immigrants themselves, but Libby wondered how much of that had been forced on them by circumstances. She shook her head. It was a nightmare.

The biggest question, she thought, as she pushed Sidney into the conservatory to keep him away from the prepared vegetables in the kitchen, was why the body had been dumped on the island. Not killed there, presumably, as there wasn't anywhere to land properly, and it was only the size of a supermarket. But why there? He must have been taken in a boat, and at night, or he would have been seen, he and his killer. And night trips round Dragon Island were a very dodgy business, as frequently reported in the local news. Many an unsuspecting tourist had come to grief on its hidden rocks and the inshore lifeboat had been called out many times to rescue indignant holidaymakers who were convinced that Someone Should Have Told Them.

The only reason could be to delay discovery of the body and its identity. In which case, thought Libby, as she unlocked Romeo the Renault's door, the killer, or whoever dumped the body, wasn't local, or they would have known about George's and Bert's round-the-island trips. Nothing else ever came into the bay except the few yachts that tacked over from nearby marinas. A few privately owned small boats bobbed around in the tiny harbour, but Nethergate wasn't known for its watersports or sailing. The beach was mainly sandy and curved prettily towards its twin headlands, one of which sported an old fashioned and unused red and white lighthouse on a rocky outcrop. The beach shelved slowly, so swimming was easy and safe, unless you were unwise enough to venture too far out.

Perhaps that was it, Libby thought, perhaps he was a swimmer? But how would he have got so far above the waterline? And in a shirt and trousers? Perhaps someone was landing illegals under cover of darkness and he fell overboard? No, that wouldn't wash — she made a face at herself — he couldn't have got above the waterline. *That* was what made it so peculiar. If discovery were to be delayed, it would have been simpler to dump him in the water and wait for him to be washed up. She must find out where that would have been likely to be. Ask Jane to ask George and Bert.

Libby parked opposite Coastguard Cottage on a yellow line, assuming she wouldn't be very long. She knew she could watch for traffic wardens from her favourite window.

Fran opened the door and Libby began to pour out her thoughts of the last hour.

"So what do you think?" she concluded, running out of breath and sitting down.

"The same as you, basically," said Fran looking amused, "and the same as the police."

"Oh." Libby craned her neck to see out of the window. "They think the same. Have they got any answers?"

"I don't know."

"How do they know he's an illegal? And why do they think he was working here?"

"There were various physical clues, as far as I know," said Fran, "like dental work. And his clothes were from one of the supermarkets."

"Hmm. So have you called Ian? And Campbell thing?"

"I spoke to Ian this morning — he wasn't on duty yesterday — and he's going to call Campbell McLean. I think he thought the official approach would be best to save my embarrassment."

"So you don't know what you're going to have to do?"

Fran shrugged. "No idea. But TV investigations over the years have been really useful, haven't they? They've uncovered scandals and scams and all manner of things. Ian says it's because even if the police are undercover, it's often hard to get the money or the manpower to mount an operation, and sometimes it would amount to entrapment, which would then weaken the prosecution's case, or not even get past the CPS."

"Golly!" said Libby, round-eyed. "Don't you know a lot?"

Fran's cheeks showed two spots of colour. "Only what Ian's told me."

Libby's eyes narrowed. "You're not —" she began.

"No, I'm not." Fran shifted in her chair. "I'm cured of Ian."

"Does he know that?"

"I think so. Guy does, anyway."

Libby laughed. "Cor! Fancy having two men fighting over you in your fifties."

"They weren't fighting." Fran was on the defensive. "They just — well — fancied me. Never been known before."

"It must have been once, Fran. You've got three children."

"You know what I mean. Since I turned forty I don't think a man's as much as looked at me."

"And now look at you." Libby sat back and admired. "There's a definite glow about you these days. And I'm sure you've lost weight."

"I haven't, you know," Fran laughed. "Now I've got the roller-skate and I don't have all those stairs to climb to the flat I'm not taking as much exercise, so I've actually put it on, if anything. I think it's the clothes. You've taught me to be much more relaxed."

"Well," said Libby dubiously, "that's as maybe, but you certainly don't look like me. You still look tidy."

"That's partly my hair," said Fran, running a hand through her thick, dark, straight bob. "It just naturally falls tidily. Yours doesn't."

"No," said Libby, with a sigh. "Mine just looks like a rusty brillo pad. Ah well." She stood up. "I'd better go before Romeo gets a ticket. Did you want to come with me?"

"To see Jane? I think it would be embarrassing under the circumstances, don't you?"

"Perhaps. Can I tell her you're going to help with the investigation after all?"

"No, you can't! As far as I know, this is going to be completely undercover, and Kent and Coast have got to promise to keep me anonymous."

"Even when it's all over?"

"Not sure. I mean, I haven't even heard from Ian as to whether he's spoken to McLean yet."

"Will you let me know when you do? Or is this another one where you're supposed to keep me out of the picture?"

"I expect that's what Ian will say," said Fran with a grin, "but I can see a case for having a bit of camouflage along if I have to go poking around."

"First time I've ever been called camouflage," said Libby, with an answering grin. "Right, I'm off. I'll let you know what Jane and her house are like."

Jane's house was at the other end of Nethergate bay, on the higher cliff, beyond The Alexandria, which stood at the cliff edge looking down at the town. A tall, thin, flint house in a terrace of four, it, like Coastguard Cottage, looked out over the bay, but, as Libby discovered, with a very much more eye-catching view.

"Wow!" she said, as Jane led her into her living room at the top of the house. The window was long and low and had chairs set either side.

"Do you ever do anything except look out of the window?" she asked.

Jane laughed. "I didn't at first," she said, "but you do get used to it a bit. In summer the visitors provide most of the entertainment, and you've got the fairy lights all along the promenade, but in the winter it's a bit bleak."

"Still you've got a nice fire," said Libby, turning into the room.

"It's a gas coal one," said Jane. "I couldn't haul logs all the way up here, so I had the old gas fire taken out and this one put in."

"Did you have to do much to the house when you inherited?"

"Quite a bit. It had been maintained to a basic level while Aunt was in the home, but when I took over I had to start doing all sorts of things before the authorities would let me carry on letting."

"But I thought you said the agency dealt with all that?"

"They do, but ultimately it's my responsibility. I've got two good tenants, though, and Terry does loads of little jobs around the place."

"Terry?"

"My first floor tenant. He's ex-Grenadier Guards, and so neat and tidy you wouldn't believe. And conservative! Queen and Country before all things, and doesn't swear in front of the ladies."

Libby laughed. "A lot of the older generation are like that, though, aren't they? I suppose it's being in the army makes him so self-sufficient."

"Terry isn't exactly older generation." Jane smiled as she looked out of the window. "There he is now."

Libby looked down and saw a tall, immaculately suited, dark-haired young man climbing the steps to the front door.

"Goodness," she said. "Why did he leave the army?"

"No idea." Jane shrugged.

"And why isn't he with someone? Why is he single?"

"*I* don't know," said Jane, beginning to show the same signs of impatience Libby had noticed in her conversations with Fran.

"Sorry, sorry. I'm just incurably nosy," said Libby, turning away from the window. "Anyway," she fished in her basket, "here's a copy of the panto script. Now you're not to think of auditioning. I just want you to come over and see if there's anything you feel like getting involved in, even if it's only serving behind the bar on performance nights."

"It's a proper theatre, then, with a bar and everything?" Jane took the proffered script.

"Oh, yes. I thought you knew. You mentioned The Oast House Theatre on Saturday."

"I'd heard of it, probably in connection with The Alexandria." Jane's forehead wrinkled. "It was in our paper, wasn't it?"

"I expect so, it was in ours. I don't see the *Mercury*. Anyway, we're holding the audition on Thursday, so come over then."

Jane nodded. "Unless I get a shout," she said.

"What's a shout?" asked Libby, interested. "A story?"

"Yes." Jane put the script on a coffee table. "Can I get you some tea?"

"That would be lovely," said Libby, and followed Jane out of the room.

"Nice kitchen," she said, looking round the large, light space. "It must be lovely living here."

"It is," said Jane. "It would be perfect if it wasn't so lonely."

"What about your tenants? Don't you see them?"

"Terry comes up sometimes if he's found some job to do, and sometimes I ask him to do something. Mrs Finch has been here since my aunt converted the house into flats, in fact, I think she was a regular holidaymaker when it was a boarding house. She looks on me as an upstart." Jane pulled a rueful face. "And then there's the empty ground floor flat which was my aunt's."

"Can't you let it?"

"Not many people want to live here in the winter, and I don't want to do holiday lets, they're too much trouble."

"Which agents are you with?"

Jane gave her the name of the same agents who had handled Coastguard Cottage before Fran bought it.

"Well, they're very competent. Have you advertised it in your paper?"

"No, the agents put it in one of their ads regularly," said Jane, handing Libby a mug. "Sugar?"

"No, thanks," said Libby. "But surely you'd get a special rate on an ad? And you could put a picture in and really sell it. You're a writer."

"I suppose I could." Jane looked thoughtful. "But I'd want anyone who answered it to go through the agents. You don't know who might turn up."

"Perfect! You advertise it and put the agent's number. Not the front, though."

"Not the front? What do you mean?" Jane led the way back to the sitting room.

"A picture of the front. Someone might recognise it."

"Someone might turn up on the doorstep, you mean?"

"Yes, and that obviates the reason for putting the agents' number on."

"Right." Jane looked down into her mug. "I suppose I could get one of the paper's photographers to take some pictures for me."

"You don't sound too sure," said Libby.

"I'd rather it was somebody I knew."

"You know the photographers, surely?"

"Not well. They're mostly freelancers."

"You could ask Terry."

Jane looked up, colouring faintly. "I couldn't."

"You said you asked him to do the odd job. That's all this is."

"Mmm." Jane looked doubtful.

Libby deemed it wise to change the subject and began to ask questions about Jane's job, which led, inevitably, to the body on Dragon Island.

"I'm still the reporter on the case," said Jane, "but I can't get a handle on it. I get the police updates, but only the official take."

"They still think it's an illegal immigrant, then?" asked Libby, innocently.

"I think so. But I can't make out why he was so high above the waterline."

"I wondered that," said Libby, nodding approvingly. "But —" Suddenly, she got up out of her chair and went too the window.

"What?" said Jane.

"Suppose," said Libby, turning round with an excited expression on her face, "just suppose — he was *dropped!*"

"Dropped?"

"By a helicopter! Like a rescue in reverse."

"Surely a helicopter would have been noticed much more than a boat?"

"At night?"

"Even more at night," said Jane firmly. "It's much quieter, and a helicopter hovering over the bay would have everybody out of their houses immediately."

"Oh, bugger," said Libby. "I thought I'd cracked it."

Jane smiled. "Yes, I could see you did."

"Oh, well, I'll keep working on it." Libby grinned. "I expect all the talk in the pubs is about the same thing."

"George and Bert talk about it, anyway," said Jane.

"I must meet those two," said Libby.

"Come and have a boat trip one day," offered Jane. "It's a very relaxing way to spend a few hours. I'll let you know when I'm going out with one of them."

"Great." Libby came back to her chair and picked up her basket. "And now I'd better get back. I've got a meal to cook."

Jane saw her to the front door of the flat. "Don't come down," said Libby. "It's far too far to climb back. See you on Thursday unless I hear from you before then."

Satisfied that Jane's door was closed, Libby went down two flights of stairs until she stood in front of the front door to the first floor flat. She knocked.

The young man she'd seen from Jane's window opened the door, now clad in a pale blue T-shirt.

"Are you Terry?" asked Libby.

"Er — yes," said Terry, looking startled.

"I think Jane wants your help with something," said Libby. "Some photographs, I think."

"Photographs?"

"Of the vacant flat." Libby smiled sweetly. "For the paper."

"Oh." Terry still looked bewildered.

"She'll explain," said Libby. "Thanks very much." And she set off down the last flight of stairs, beaming.

But on her way home, her thoughts turned from matchmaking back to the body on Dragon Island. And, quite suddenly, she thought she knew. Someone had *wanted* it to be found.

CHAPTER
SEVEN

"Yes," said Fran. "The police think that, too."

"They do?" Libby felt deflated. "I thought I'd made a breakthrough."

"I've said before, haven't I, they always get there before we do."

"Then why are you going to do this undercover stuff for them? And why did Ian ask you in over the Alexandria business?"

"Specialist consultant," grinned Fran. "That's what he calls me."

"Well tell me, then. Has he been in touch again?" Libby peered out of Fran's window to check on Romeo, parked once more on the yellow line.

"Yes. Campbell McLean will call me, apparently."

"And he told you they thought the body was meant to be found?"

"I told him. And he agreed." Fran looked out of the window.

Libby looked at her thoughtfully. "When did you decide that?"

Fran shrugged. "I don't know. It was just there. You know."

Libby nodded. "Oh, well," she said, standing up, "let me know what happens next."

"I will," said Fran. "And don't go interfering in young Jane's life any more."

Libby felt colour rising up her neck. "I won't," she said.

Later that evening, Ben said much the same thing over Libby's painstakingly prepared stir-fry.

"I'm not interfering. Just making suggestions," said Libby. "Anyway, Jane's coming to our audition on Thursday, by which time the ad should be in the paper if young Terry comes up to scratch."

"Poor bloke," said Ben, forking up noodles. "He won't know what's hit him."

"I won't have anything more to do with him, will I? He can't take exception to one conversation with me."

Ben raised an eyebrow. "You probably scared him to death," he said.

Campbell McLean called Fran the next morning.

"I expect you know why I'm calling," he began.

"Yes," said Fran.

"I had a rather peculiar request from Inspector Connell."

"Yes," said Fran again.

There was a pause. "I'm not quite sure how to proceed."

Fran sighed. "Look," she said. "What did you want to do before?"

"I wanted to have you doing some sort of remote viewing on camera and then follow it up to see if it was right."

"As I said, investigating me rather than the murder."

"Yes, I admitted that. But now I don't know quite what to do. The Inspector seems to think we could do an undercover operation better than he could."

"You've done them before, haven't you? Into horse trading, and health issues?"

"Yes, but that was when we'd had tip-offs from the public."

"Well, this time you'll have to take a tip-off from the police."

"But what? They haven't got anything."

Fran thought for a moment. "I suggest you look at everything you've ever done on illegal immigrants. Somewhere there'll be a starting point. Then you get me in to have a look at what you've got and we'll go from there. Think what a scoop you'll get out of it."

Campbell McLean sighed. "Right," he said. "I'll get someone to start going through the archives. We did something last year on workers on farms with false passports."

"That's exactly it," said Fran, certain that it was.

"Really?" The voice on the phone sounded more cheerful. "Do you — er, well — did you —"

"I think I'm sure," said Fran with a laugh. "Don't ask me how I know, because I don't."

"OK. I'll get started in the morning. Speak to you then."

Ten minutes later, as Fran was getting ready to go to Guy's flat for a meal, Ian Connell called. Fran told him what she'd suggested.

"We've been questioning as many field and farm workers as we can, particularly after that big case last year," he said.

"What about the kitchen workers and cleaners?" asked Fran. "There's just as much of a problem there, isn't there?"

"Is that where you think the problem lies?"

"Not necessarily, in fact I felt it was farm workers, but I could be wrong."

"You're not often wrong."

"I still don't know how you expect McLean to go about this, though. I can hardly go traipsing through fields of potato pickers, or whatever they are, asking questions, can I? And it isn't like some of their previous investigations, where I could pose as a patient, or a prospective purchaser."

Connell sighed. "Look, just do your best," he said. "I'm sure McLean will come up with something."

The following morning McLean did, indeed, come up with something.

"Did you read about the cleaner at the council offices who was arrested?" he asked without preamble.

"I think I saw something about it on the news."

"She was an illegal immigrant, smuggled in four years ago, and she borrowed someone else's passport to apply for the job. After she was arrested she applied for asylum."

"Good lord! Did she get it?"

"Not yet," said McLean. "She's serving six months at the moment, and the judge said the application would have to wait until she was discharged."

"Is she serving six months, or only half of it?" asked Fran.

"Probably half, I expect, or even less if she was in custody before the trial."

"So she could be out already?"

"She could, but I don't know how we could find her."

"Was this a British passport? No, it couldn't have been, could it?"

"No. She's from Transnistria, I think, and borrowed an Italian passport."

"Transnistria? Where's that? I've never heard of it."

"I haven't had time to look it up," said McLean, "but it's there in the report."

"Could it be in Romania? It sounds like Transylvania."

"I don't know."

"Did she give the passport back to the Italian woman?" asked Fran.

"I suppose so."

"So what happened to her, the Italian?"

She heard a sigh. "I'll look it up. Do you think this is relevant?"

"Not sure," said Fran, "but it feels right."

"This actual case?"

"Not necessarily. Find out a bit more, and we'll see what happens."

After McLean had rung off, Fran went up to her spare room where she had installed her new computer.

Balzac followed hopefully, sniffing the keyboard and trying desperately to climb on Fran's lap under the desk.

The search engine provided her with the details of the case of the Transnistrian woman, but no mention of the Italian from whom she'd borrowed the passport. She also searched for Transnistria and discovered it to be a breakaway independent state between Moldova and the Ukraine, unrecognised by any other country. There was a lot of information which indicated that Transnistria was a hotbed of crime and a centre for people trafficking for both sex and labour, but right now, Fran didn't feel up to investigating. Libby, she was sure, would.

She had told McLean the case felt right, but so did the farm workers. This, she felt, was the problem with believing in her own "moments". Nobody had ever told her how to deal with them, and although she was more adept at using what Libby called her "powers" after the last three murders in which she had been involved, she was privately convinced that her brain manufactured incidents to trap her. She'd have to wait until she was given more evidence, and if nothing startling happened admit defeat and quietly withdraw.

Libby, however, was having none of it.

"Listen," she said, when she called Fran that afternoon after waiting for news all day, "it needs proper detective work. We can do that."

"No, we can't, Libby, we've nothing to go on this time. We've always had an 'in', if you like. This time we haven't."

Libby was quiet for a minute. Then, "Do we know how long the body had been there?"

"Not long, I wouldn't have thought. Either Bert or George goes round that island every day, more or less. It must have been the night before it was found."

"Bearing out the theory that it was meant to be found."

"Yes, we've established that."

"Well, couldn't we find out who took a boat out the night before?"

Fran laughed. "It could have come from anywhere, Lib! France even."

"No, because of the clothes. They were from here, weren't they?"

"Yes, and I suppose the police have already ruled out a boat from France."

"Perhaps they haven't," said Libby, "and we don't know."

"Then why would Ian have asked me to help? I can't help in France."

Libby thought again. "I know," she said. "Why don't we go and pay a visit to one of those farms where they employ foreign pickers?"

"On what excuse?" asked Fran. "I've already said that to Ian."

"What we need is a connection."

"That's what I've been saying," said Fran with a sigh.

"Not a psychic connection, a physical one. Someone we can connect with."

"Short of pretending to be a foreign cleaner without a passport I can't see how we do that."

"I'll think of something," said Libby. "Just see if I don't."

"But," she said to Sidney after ringing off, "I actually can't see how. We had somewhere to start with each of the other cases. But how do you find out about this?"

Sidney wove ingratiatingly around her legs until she moved away into the garden. With a look of resignation, he followed her and jumped on her chair before she could.

"The boat," she mused, turfing Sidney out. "I suppose the police have been on to the Coastguard or whoever it is looks after the sea. Would they know about boats appearing in the dead of night? It's not like aeroplanes, is it? Or the Channel. Or the Solent."

"You're talking to yourself again." Ben appeared from his private entrance to the garden, where it backed onto his parents' land.

"No, I wasn't, I was talking to Sidney." Libby stood up. "Tea?"

"Yes, please." Ben followed as Libby went back into the house.

"So what was *this* conversation with Sidney about, as if I couldn't guess?"

"Finding a connection." Libby moved the kettle on to the Rayburn. "Fran's taking on the investigation and we haven't got anything to go on."

"What's with the 'we' business? I thought it was Fran's investigation."

"Oh, I'm helping. You know that," said Libby airily, getting mugs out of a cupboard.

Ben sighed. "Even after last time?"

72

"Even after all three times," said Libby firmly. "It's always about helping people, really, isn't it?"

"And 'satiable curtiosity, like the Elephant's Child," said Ben.

"Good job somebody has it or nothing would ever get solved, would it?" Libby poured water into a teapot. Ben sniffed appreciatively.

"Nothing like real tea made in a pot," he said.

"That's the only reason you come here, isn't it," said Libby, grinning at him over her shoulder.

"Not quite the only reason," said Ben, sliding his arms round her waist from behind.

Libby giggled. "Do you know," she said, "you still make me feel like a sixteen-year-old?"

"And me a randy eighteen-year-old," he replied, nuzzling her neck.

"We probably wouldn't have liked each other at all," said Libby. "You know what it's like when you meet someone after twenty-odd years — you just want to see what they look like, what they've been up to, and that's that. If you'd really been friends you wouldn't have lost touch. Let me get the milk."

Ben let her go, regarding her thoughtfully. "So, the reverse is true? Don't like someone at eighteen and you'll probably like them at fifty?"

"No." Libby wrinkled her forehead. "I don't think I've thought this through properly. But when you think of the number of young marriages that fail because people change so much in their teens and early twenties. If you marry an eighteen-year-old boy, you might not like the twenty-five-year-old man."

"But there are some people," said Ben, accepting his mug, "who come together years later and love blossoms afresh. It happened on that old friends website, didn't it?"

"Yes, and look at the trouble it caused!" Libby led the way back into the garden. "Marriages were broken up because people got seduced into thinking their old love was their only love. Just novelty, that's all it was."

"Hmm." Ben pulled over a deckchair and collapsed into it. "I'm not sure it's always like that."

"Prove it, then," said Libby, removing Sidney from her chair. "Go on, find me a case study and prove it."

Ben raised his eyebrows. "Pleasure," he said.

"Too much introspection," said Guy, "that's what it is."

He and Fran were sitting outside The Sloop looking out at a particularly pretty sunset. Fran twisted her tall glass between her fingers.

"I can't help being introspective, can I?" she said. "I'm expected to be able to look inside my mind and come up with something startling. Trouble is I'm imagining things now."

"Because you're trying too hard, I expect," said Guy. "I don't think you should have taken this on. It's all so muddled, and I think Connell's got a cheek, involving you."

Fran sighed. "You're right, he has. Especially as I'd already said no to Kent and Coast. They must think I'm a nut."

"And Libby's keen, of course." Guy shook his head. "If it wasn't for her —"

74

"We'd never have met," Fran finished for him, despite what she'd said to Libby.

Guy looked up, brown eyes twinkling above his goatee. "So of course, I'll love her for ever," he said.

"You need her pictures, anyway," said Fran, "so don't try and kid *me*."

"Wouldn't dream of it," he said, reaching across to take her hand. "Now — your place or mine?"

CHAPTER
EIGHT

"The Italian woman's disappeared," Fran told Libby in the morning on the telephone. "McLean just called. So we're no further forward."

"Rubbish," said Libby. "What have the police found out about her? There must be something. They wouldn't just leave it there."

"Who did McLean ask about it?"

"Don't know. It wasn't this division as far as I know."

"Phone Connell. Tell him it's a line on the Dragon Island body."

"He'll want to investigate himself, then."

"Well? So what? If he's telling the truth about having you do an undercover job, he can't refuse to let you have the details to see what you come up with."

Fran frowned out of the window. "I suppose so."

"Say you had a 'moment' about her," said Libby, sounding more excited by the minute.

"The Transnistrian or the Italian?"

"Oh, I don't care, either."

"I'll have to say how I heard about her. I wouldn't have had a flash about something I'd never heard of."

"I bet you do, but you don't connect them up. Anyway, it doesn't matter, you can say McLean told you about illegal immigrant cases and this one caught your attention. That's true, isn't it?"

"Yes. You're right, I'll call him."

"Do it now," said Libby, and put down the phone.

It was Wednesday, and Steeple Martin's shops still adhered to the age old tradition of early closing day, so collecting her basket from the kitchen and shutting Sidney out, Libby left the house.

Allhallow's Lane was in full sunshine at this time of day, the ruts in the grass verge left by parked cars turned to hard-baked clay. The lilac tree which hung over the wall at the end now brushed Libby's head with dark green leaves. The high street was quiet, and after a visit to Ali in the eight-til-late, she went into The Pink Geranium and surprised Harry laying up tables for lunch.

"On your own?" she said.

"Donna'll be in soon." Harry waved her to the ancient sofa in the window. "Did you want something? Or is this just social?"

"I thought I might tell you all about Fran's new investigation."

"Oh, yes?" Harry looked interested. "Drop of wine, then, to help it along?"

Once he was settled at the other end of the sofa and a bottle of wine had been provided, Libby told him everything that had happened since the discovery of the body, including the pending introduction of Jane Maurice to The Oast House Theatre.

"Has she got anything to do with all this?" asked Harry. "The body and everything?"

"Only that she was the first one to spot it, and she was, I suppose, instrumental in getting Fran on the case. She also ran a front page article last week, and I expect she'll have quite a large feature this week. Why?"

Harry shrugged. "I don't know. There's no reason why she should be involved, I just wondered."

"How could she be?" said Libby. "She didn't know anything about the body!"

"No, I know." Harry frowned. "I dunno. Having one of Fran's moments, I expect."

"Oh, I do hope not!" said Libby. "One's enough."

Harry laughed and stood up. "Come and sit in the yard and have a fag and I'll make you some lunch," he said.

Libby sat in the cool, shady yard at the back of the restaurant and looked up to the flat above, where Fran had, for a brief time, lived.

"She's happy, you know," she called to Harry in the kitchen.

"Who?" Harry came to the doorway with his hands full of onions.

"Fran. I miss her being here, though."

"Oh, come on, Lib, she was only here for a few months."

"I know, but it was so great having someone round the corner."

"Hey! I'm round the corner." Harry was indignant. "And what about your *cher ami*? So's he."

"I know, I meant a woman friend. I haven't had one since I moved here."

Harry looked mystified. "But you've got us," he said.

"You're not women," said Libby, and giggled.

"Good job too," said Harry, and returned to the kitchen.

When Libby returned to number 17 Allhallow's Lane after lunch with Harry, she found a message waiting on her answerphone, and one on her mobile, which she had left, not unusually, on the kitchen table. Both were from Fran, informing her that she would be arriving in Steeple Martin in half an hour.

"From when?" muttered Libby, and found out almost immediately when she heard Fran's roller-skate outside.

"Ian found out about the Italian," she said.

"Great. Shall we go into the garden? Tea?"

"Tea would be lovely," said Fran, pausing to say hello to Sidney.

"So what's happened?" Libby came into the garden while she waited for the kettle to boil.

"Apparently, the investigation turned up the original owner of the passport, because details were taken, photocopied, I think, by the council. So, obviously, the police went looking for her at her registered address and found that she was missing. There was no record of her returning to Italy, so they tried to trace her family, but not very hard, I gather. I mean, they obviously had to get onto the Italian authorities, but these things take an awful long time, apparently. You have to put in requests and it can take months."

"And does it relate in any way to our body?"

"No, not as far as I can see," said Fran.

"I'll go and make the tea," said Libby, and went back into the kitchen.

Fran sat in the garden and absent-mindedly stroked Sidney's head while staring up into the cherry tree. Why did she still get the image of a farm? Somehow illegal immigrants working on farms didn't seem to be the answer, yet farms were still in her head. She shook it.

"Here." Libby sat a tray on her rickety table. "Biscuits as well. Bel showed me how to make these. They're ginger."

Fran peered at the plate. "Are you sure? They look like real ones."

"I know! Great, aren't they? Fancy my daughter showing me how to make something as good as this. Mind you, I'm getting through loads of Golden Syrup."

"Mmm." Fran bit into a biscuit. "They are good. Not for the figure, though."

"Oh, I've given up on the figure," said Libby, sitting down and kicking off her sandals. "Now, what about the Transnistrian? Where did she live?"

"I don't know." Fran looked bewildered. "I didn't ask."

"And have you found out any more about the country?"

"I haven't gone into it. It just seems a really odd place. Someone calls it the Black Hole of Europe."

"Sounds like somebody made it up," said Libby.

"That's what I thought at first, but it's a real place."

"Right." Libby picked up her mug and sat up straight. "Ask Mr Mclean. Then we'll go investigating."

80

"I don't honestly see what this has to do with the body on the island," said Fran. "I think you're grasping at straws."

"Maybe, but at least it gets us working. We've done nothing but potter about over the last week, and tomorrow you're off to Chrissie's, aren't you? So Saturday we really ought to be doing something."

"Look, Lib, we're not real detectives. And you're not even supposed to be part of the investigation." Fran eyed her friend warily, waiting for the outburst. Surprisingly, it didn't come.

"I know that, but you've been invited into it legitimately, and you said yourself I'd be useful. And you know you want to find out really. So we act like real detectives and start with whatever we've got." Libby sat back in her chair and closed her eyes.

"Right." Fran thought for a moment. "I suppose it makes sense. I'll phone McLean tomorrow and ask about the Transnistrian before I go to Chrissie's."

"OK." Libby opened her eyes. "And it's the audition tomorrow night. You won't be there for it, but can I say you're doing Props?"

"You can, but you can also ask for a volunteer to do it with me. I'm not doing it all on my own."

"Right," said Libby thoughtfully. "That's given me an idea."

"Oh, no," said Fran with a familiar groan. "Don't tell me. Jane Maurice."

"Well, of course," said Libby. "It makes perfect sense. She lives in Nethergate and so do you, so you could share the driving, and she wouldn't be doing something on her own."

"Always supposing the poor girl actually wants to do something."

"Look, you're just prejudiced because she tried to turn you into a media star," said Libby. "She's only trying to do her job, and as I keep saying to everybody, she's lonely."

"OK," said Fran with a sigh, "you ask her. And I'll find out anything else I can about our Transnistrian."

"That's the spirit." Libby beamed at her friend. "I've missed having something to do. And now, why did you feel it was so urgent you had to come over rather than ringing me?"

Fran looked sheepish. "I feel a bit silly, really."

"Not like you."

"No, I know. But I had this sudden desire to see where Jane lived, so I drove past thinking I'd go on to the supermarket afterwards."

"And?"

"Well, it was really odd. You told me Jane's Aunt had left her the house, didn't you? And I suppose that made me think about the similarity of our circumstances, especially as Jane's house is also converted into flats like Mountville Road was."

"Go on," said Libby, as Fran paused.

"I said it was silly," said Fran, peering down into her mug. "I suddenly thought, as I drove past, I knew which one it was and something nasty had happened there."

Libby stared. "You think it was just because of your own experience of Mountville Road?"

"I don't know what to think."

"Funny." Libby frowned. "When I had lunch with Harry he asked if Jane was anything to do with the body. I said only because she saw it first. But I wonder."

Fran looked startled. "Oh, come on," she said, "that's quite ridiculous. We're talking real life here, not coincidental detective stories. Besides, since when did Harry become psychic?"

"That's what I said to him, but I think he was just putting two and two together like we have in the past."

"And made five, also as we have," said Fran.

"Yeah, yeah, I know. But look, she spotted the body, didn't she? Suppose she was a plant?"

"You've met her. I don't think she'd be capable. And you're not suggesting she murdered someone and planted the body all by herself just to get a story, are you?"

"Of course not."

"Anyway," said Fran, "I didn't get a bad feeling about Jane but about the house."

"Oh, well, it was a thought," said Libby.

"You're the one who wants to befriend her. You can't have her as a suspect as well."

Libby grinned. "I know. Mass of contradictions, me."

"Well," said Fran, "I suppose I'd better go and do that shopping."

"And make that phone call." Libby stood up. "I shall phone young Jane and tell her what we've got in mind."

"I wouldn't," said Fran, following her out of the garden. "She might not come!"

"I shall merely invite her here first, then," said Libby loftily. "I know how to be tactful."

Fran raised her eyebrows and shook her head at Sidney.

"The trouble is, she believes it," she told him.

CHAPTER
NINE

"The Transnistrian girl is now in a detention centre waiting to be sent home," Fran reported the following morning. "Poor thing, straight from prison to a detention centre and now she's got to go back. Still McLean's going to see if the police will either let me talk to her or talk to her themselves. He seems to think it's a long shot and is fairly dubious."

"But he's got to give you the benefit of the doubt, hasn't he? Now the police have asked for the investigation," said Libby.

"Yes, but he's not nearly as keen, now. When it was all his idea it was a real project, but now he's got to play it by the police rules and not even feature me, he doesn't like it."

"Will he feature you at the end, do you think?"

"I hope not," said Fran with fervour. "He's supposed to keep me out of it."

"But that's cheating. How could Ian have harnessed his co-operation without you as a carrot?"

"I don't know. I have the feeling I might have to appear at the end, not necessarily in person, but as a hook to hang the story on." Fran sighed. "I hate this."

"Well, you go off to Chrissie's and have a lovely time babysitting Cassandra, and call me when you get back," said Libby. "Meanwhile, I shall take Jane to the audition and pump her for information about her house."

"Oh, Libby, don't do that," said Fran. "I'm not sure at all about what I felt yesterday. Just leave it."

But when Libby phoned Jane at her office to invite her to come to Allhallow's Lane before the audition, her house was obviously the first thing on her mind.

"I've had three answers to the ad," she told Libby gleefully. "That was so clever of you to suggest it. I don't know why I didn't think of it before."

"Oh, excellent," said Libby. "When are you seeing them?"

"Actually, Terry's going to show them round this afternoon," said Jane. "It was his idea. He said women on their own shouldn't do it, and it was as well to show them there was a man around."

"Well!" said Libby, grinning into the phone. Her instincts had been correct, then. "That's good. So are you still going to come to the audition tonight? I thought you might want to come to my house first, then we can go together. I've got a proposition for you."

"Oh?" Jane sounded wary.

"If you still want to come, of course."

"Oh, yes. I think you must be bringing me luck." Jane gave a little laugh. "Or just giving me a boot up the backside."

86

Libby privately agreed. "You were trying to be pro-active with the job," she said. "It just wasn't extending to your private life."

"No," said Jane. "Anyway, I'll come to your house this evening, if I may. What time and where?"

After Libby had given directions to Allhallow's Lane and arranged for Jane to arrive at a quarter past seven, she called Peter to discuss the audition.

"Is it going to be a problem if I go for the Fairy?" she asked. "Will people be annoyed and mutter about pre-casting?"

"Probably," said Peter, "but I couldn't care less. I'm going to announce Bob and Baz and Tom as pre-cast anyway, so I might as well add you. This lot aren't all as experienced as we are, so they should be pleased we've got good people in the lead parts."

"If you say so," said Libby. "Did Harry tell you I'm bringing along a new member?"

"Yes. He seemed a bit worried about her, though."

"Why? He's never met her."

"It seems you met her through this new murder," said Peter, and Libby could imagine the expression on his patrician features.

"I wouldn't put it quite like that," said Libby, bridling, "but yes, she was the first one to spot the body, which is hardly an involvement, is it?"

"If you say so. Anyway, if you think she's OK, that's fine by me."

"I thought she could assist Fran with props. Fran's happy with that, and as they both live in Nethergate they can share lifts and so on."

"Sounds all right to me," said Peter. "See you there then. Oh — and don't interfere."

"As if I would," said Libby to Sidney as she put down the phone.

Jane arrived at twenty past seven that evening full of apologies for being late.

"I completely missed the turning," she said. "I went sailing on towards Canterbury and realised I'd run out of village."

"Never mind," said Libby. "You're here now. Drink before we go?"

"I'd better not," said Jane, "I've got to drive home."

"Tea, then? Coffee?"

"No, I'm fine, thank you." Jane looked round the sitting room. "Oh, what a gorgeous cat."

"That's Sidney. My friends call him my familiar, but I think that's a bit mean. He's not the friendliest cat in the world, but quite a good guard cat."

Jane squatted down and held her hand out to be sniffed. Sidney obliged, then tucked his head back under his paw and pretended to go back to sleep. His ears gave him away.

"So tell me," said Libby, waving a hand at the armchair while she sat on the creaky sofa. "What happened with the prospective tenants?"

"There was quite a fight, apparently," said Jane, her little face lighting up. "The first person really wanted it, then the second offered to pay more, which is unheard of, according to the agents. The third liked it but said it was a bit too expensive, so the agents have said whichever of the first two supplies references which can be checked immediately, gets it. Oh, and if their cheque clears, of course."

"Won't they use a credit card? That clears straight away," said Libby.

"Oh, I don't know, but anyway, it looks as though I shall have a tenant at last." Jane smiled and sat back in the chair. "And all thanks to you."

"Nonsense," said Libby. "The agents hadn't marketed it properly or it would have gone long before this. Did Terry take the photos for you?"

"Yes, I meant to thank you for that, too," said Jane innocently. "He came up after you'd gone and said he'd seen you and you said I'd got a favour to ask. I never would have managed that on my own, you know."

"I know," said Libby, "that's why I asked him. Would have been a bit of a setback if he'd said no, but thankfully he didn't. So what happened?"

"He came up with his digital camera and took some shots of the rooms, then downloaded them onto my laptop, and after we'd chosen the best, I composed an ad and sent the whole package to the advertising department. It was a bit late, but they put me in on a news page, which probably made all the difference."

"I'm sure it did," said Libby. "What happened then?"

"Then?" Jane shook her head. "Nothing, why?"

"Didn't you even give the poor lad a cup of tea?"

"Oh." Jane blushed. "Yes, of course. Actually, we had a glass of wine."

Good start, thought Libby.

"And I'm taking him out for a curry tomorrow to say thank you." Jane's colour was by now so high she matched Libby's rug.

"Excellent," said Libby, beaming. "See? That wasn't so hard, was it? A friend. And now let's go and make some more."

On the way to the theatre, in between Jane's exclamations of pleasure at the quaintness of the village, Libby explained about her plan to give the props job to Fran and for Jane to assist.

"There won't be that much to do," she said, "especially not at first."

"It's very early, isn't it?" said Jane, as they turned into the Manor drive, which also led to The Oast House Theatre. "I thought panto was at Christmas."

Libby looked at her. "Of course it is."

"Then why are you having auditions at the beginning of August?"

"Because we have to start rehearsing in October and people need to know what they're doing. If they don't get a part in this they might want to go for something else with another company. We've got several people who belong to more than one group."

"Oh, I see." Jane nodded. "But you have one of the best reputations, don't you? I looked you up on the group files."

"The group files?"

"Yes, the group which owns the *Mercury*. I looked you up."

"Well, I don't know about that," said Libby, preening nevertheless. "My old group had one of the best

90

reputations, and we had several pros and ex-pros on both the technical and acting sides. I borrowed quite a lot of them when we did our first production here."

"Oh, that was the play when the murder happened, wasn't it?"

"Yes." Libby pushed open the glass doors of The Oast House Theatre. "Here we are."

Impressed, Jane looked around. "I didn't expect anything like this," she said.

"It helps when the son of the family who own the building is an architect," said Libby proudly, looking round with satisfaction.

"And who is also the best beloved of the company's best director," said Ben, coming up behind them and putting an arm round Libby's shoulders. "You must be Jane." He held out his hand. "I'm Ben."

"It also helps, of course, when the nephew of the family happens to be the best playwright and second best director," said Peter, descending the spiral staircase from his favourite place, the lighting and sound box.

"Oh." Jane looked slightly overwhelmed as she shook hands with them both.

"And you're going to be our new props assistant," said Peter.

"Well, I —" began Jane, but Peter clapped her on the back.

"Excellent," he said. "Ben, can I have a word?"

Later, when the auditions were well under way and Libby could slip away, she took Jane on a tour of the theatre.

"This is the play that will be on stage next," she said, waving a hand at the jigsaw of pieces which would eventually make up the set. "Wycherley's *Country Wife*."

"Oh?" Jane looked blank.

"Restoration piece," said Libby. "Some of the group members wanted to try something serious, although *The Country Wife* is hardly serious. Very bawdy, in fact. But classic English drama."

"Ah," said Jane.

"Anyway, look, here's what I wanted to show you. Their props table."

Set in the wings, but well back from the stage was a long trestle table, laden with odd items, tankards, handkerchiefs and parchment letters.

"There's another the other side of the stage," said Libby, "and a props cupboard in the corridor by the dressing room."

"It's all a bit complicated," said Jane, looking scared.

"Nothing to it," said Libby. "We have two tables, and it's the responsibility of each actor to pick up his or her personal props before going on stage. Large props are sorted out by the props team, and in the panto, that'll be you and Fran."

"Right," said Jane looking round at the stage and up into the flies. "Will they have finished the audition yet?"

Peter had the harassed look of someone who had heard the same thing too many times over. Libby waggled her fingers at him and he sat up straight.

"Right, thank you," he said to the actors before him, who stopped mid-sentence. "Now we'll try something with our pre-cast members and see how you all get on with them."

This part of the audition turned into an entertainment in itself, and Libby was gratified to see Jane laughing heartily. When invited for the customary drink afterwards, in the theatre bar rather than the pub, she accepted happily and was made a fuss of by several of the middle-aged men, who should, she said to Ben, have known better.

"But at least she'll feel accepted," said Ben, "and that's what you wanted."

"Yes, but I don't want her to lose out on Terry," grumbled Libby, seeing her matchmaking plans melt away.

"Who's Terry?" Ben looked bewildered.

"Oh, never mind," said Libby. "Come on, let's rescue her."

"I don't think she wants rescuing," said Ben with a grin. "But as you know, I always do as I'm told."

Libby quelled him with a look.

CHAPTER
TEN

The King's Arms was near the market cross in the very middle of town. A black and white building notable for its carved wooden beams, much like The Swan in Nethergate, it was a favourite venue for Bruce and his ilk. Fran peered in to the restaurant bar as she passed, in case Chrissie and Bruce had stolen a march on her and were enjoying pre-prandial cocktails, but they were nowhere to be seen, so she struggled up the wide, shallow staircase with her case, looking forward to a refreshing shower and change of clothes before she presented herself for inspection.

As it happened, Chrissie pre-empted her by knocking on her door at five to eight, while she was peering short-sightedly into the mirror to re-apply her lipstick.

"Hallo, darling." Fran leaned forward to kiss her daughter's round face. "How's everything going?"

"All right." A discontented frown settled on Chrissie's unlined brow. "It's hard work. I don't know why Bruce wouldn't pay for the removal men to do the packing as well."

"It costs quite a lot." Fran gave up waiting for an enquiry as to how she was, or how the journey had gone and went back to the dressing table. "I'll be with you in a minute."

Chrissie sat on the bed and picked at the knife crease in her tailored navy trousers. "If I had any money of my own —" she began.

Fran closed her eyes and counted to ten.

"If you'd only kept in touch with Dad," went on Chrissie.

"Your father had no more money than I had, and well you know it." Fran put her lipstick and hair brush into her handbag and turned to face the bed.

"Well, what about the house, then? Mountwhatsit Road? How much did you sell that for?" Chrissie's petulant face glared up at her mother.

"Oh, for goodness' sake, Chrissie," snapped Fran. "However did you become so mercenary?"

Chrissie stood up. "That's not fair." she said. "I just need a bit of money of my own, that's all."

"Then go out and earn it," growled Fran, pushing her out of the door and slamming it shut behind them.

"Lucy doesn't." Chrissie whined her way down the stairs.

"Lucy has two small children to look after. Anyway, she's looking for something to do now. Felix will forget to pay her maintenance if I know anything about him. So shut up and think yourself lucky." Fran opened the door to the restaurant and shoved Chrissie in ahead of her to where Bruce stood waiting for them, a fixed, welcoming smile on his bland features. "Or perhaps not," she mentally amended her last statement.

"Fran." He leaned forward and pursed his lips in the general direction of her left cheek. "Lovely to see you. Pleasant journey?"

"Very, Bruce. Thank you for asking." Fran shot an equivocal look at her daughter.

"Well, come and sit down. I decided not to bother with a drink before the meal, but I've ordered a nice bottle of the house white to go with it."

Fran hoped Bruce hadn't gone the whole hog and ordered the meal for her as well.

"And how's Cassandra?" Fran asked brightly, as they took their seats at a small round table overlooking the flower-filled courtyard. Ten minutes later, she was sorry she had asked. Her smoked salmon — not pre-ordered by Bruce — had arrived, along with Chrissie's predictable prawn cocktail and Bruce's pâté, and she had almost finished her first prettily chilled glass of very drinkable white wine.

"And, of course, when the kittens are born," Chrissie was saying, "they'll be worth a fortune."

"Lucy's got a new flat, by the way." Fran decided she'd heard enough about Cassandra.

"What new flat?" Chrissie sounded indignant.

"If you thought about anyone other than yourself you could have asked how your sister was when you mentioned her before, and then you would have known." Fran sipped her wine, which Bruce, unusually for him, had thoughtfully topped up. He fidgeted and looked away.

"I bet she didn't ask about me." Chrissie was sulky.

"Actually, she did," said Fran, keeping her fingers crossed and ignoring the fact that she had prompted Lucy's enquiry, "and Bruce."

"Nice of her." Bruce cleared his throat. "Moving, is she?"

"Well, she could hardly stay in that great big house on her own, could she? And Felix won't pay the rent on it. So she has to move somewhere smaller."

"So where's she going?" Chrissie demanded.

"Oh, a rented flat in the suburbs." Fran said vaguely.

"Why does she want to stay in London?" asked Bruce. "It'd be cheaper out here, for instance."

Fran forbore to tell him that Lucy wouldn't live within a twenty-mile radius of Chrissie and Bruce if she could help it and gave what she hoped was a tolerant, motherly smile.

"She'd have no friends, would she?"

"She'd have us." Bruce ignored his wife's sharp protest, which sounded, to her mother's fond ears, like a cat with its tail trodden on.

"Well, it doesn't arise, so let's forget it. It's your move we should be talking about." Fran smiled brightly. "Everything's organised, is it?"

The rest of the meal, which was delicious, Fran was relieved to observe, was accompanied by an exposition of Bruce's superior organisation. Everything, it appeared, had been taken care of, down to the last detail, which, Fran realised, was herself. When Bruce and Chrissie took themselves off to get an early night on the floor of their empty house, Fran heaved a sigh of relief and treated herself to a large gin and tonic in the bar before going back to her room to ring Guy and relieve her feelings.

Friar's Ashworth, the "new village" where Chrissie and Bruce were setting up home, wasn't quite as bad as Fran had feared. Most of the executive estates had been designed tastefully, with venerable trees allowed to live and green spaces preserved between the clusters of houses. Children could play safely, and there were walkways to the small parade of shops in the centre, but there was a curious sense of impermanence, as if the whole thing was a stage set that was due to come down at the end of the run.

Fran sat in the little room designated "the study" by the developers and tried to console Cassandra, who made her displeasure at her confinement known in no uncertain terms. Siamese were the most unprepossessing of cats, Fran thought, gazing into Cassandra's slightly crossed blue eyes, and they had the most cacophonous voices. But there, thought Fran, with a sigh, she was an expectant mother and as such must be pandered to.

By the evening, both Cassandra and Fran were suffering from almost terminal boredom and claustrophobia, and it was a relief when the door was finally closed behind the removal men and Chrissie gave orders for their release.

"Thank God for that." Fran stretched and yawned. "Can I go home now?"

"Home?" Chrissie looked bewildered. "I thought you were staying to help?"

Fran lowered her arms and looked at her daughter suspiciously. "And who told you that?"

"You did."

"I don't think so. As I remember, you asked me to come down and look after a pregnant cat during the move. I agreed, because you promised you wouldn't ask me to do anything else. I was surprised, because Bruce has never embraced me with all the pent-up love in a son-in-law's soul, but anybody can be of use, I suppose."

Chrissie picked a piece of fluff from her sleeve. "I don't think that's fair," she muttered.

"On whom?" asked Fran. "Me, you or Bruce?"

"Oh, Mum." Chrissie turned away and aimed for the kitchen. Fran followed, peering around interestedly.

"Wow, Chris. This is some kitchen."

"If it looked out at the front it would be better." Chrissie made her way between packing cases and picked up the kettle.

"Not if you've got children."

"Well, I haven't," snapped Chrissie.

"No, but these houses are designed for families, aren't they? You need the kitchen looking out on the garden so that you can keep an eye on the kids." Fran idly unwrapped a plate and looked round for somewhere to put it.

"Oh, put that down, Mum. If you're going, you'd better go, so that we can get on with the unpacking."

"I thought you were making me a cup of tea? And anyway, how am I supposed to get back to pick up my car from here? Is there a station?"

Chrissie looked at her mother with her mouth open.

"Station," repeated Fran. "Railway station. With trains. Where is it?"

"I don't know." Chrissie looked worried. "I hadn't thought —"

"Has Bruce? Where is he, by the way?"

"Putting the beds up. Hang on, I'll call him."

It transpired, as Fran had guessed, that neither Bruce nor Chrissie had given a thought to how she was to get back to their old house and pick up her car. Bruce was obviously torn between getting rid of her as soon as possible — before the new neighbours saw her — and keeping her on to help until it was convenient for him to drive her back. Fran herself solved the problem by suggesting that she called a taxi.

"But it's miles." Bruce was horrified.

"Well, how else am I to get there?" asked Fran, reasonably. "Unless you drive me."

"I know," said Chrissie, with an air of enlightenment. "You drive Mum back and pick up a take-away on your way, then we won't have to worry about food."

Fran suppressed her indignation at being left out of the catering arrangements in the interests of getting back to Nethergate and bade a fairly fond farewell to Chrissie and Cassandra, who by now was expressing her opinion of her new home in very unflattering terms.

"So, you're enjoying your new cottage?" Bruce asked after a fairly long silence while he reversed his car out of the new drive and made his way cautiously out on to the main road.

"Yes, thank you," said Fran. "I hope you enjoy yours."

"Oh, yes." Bruce smiled, a trifle smugly. "Chrissie's looking forward to putting it all to rights. Then she'll get herself a little job."

"Oh?" Fran raised her eyebrows. Did Chrissie know this, she wondered, so set was she in her anachronistic ways.

"And what was it you were doing with the police last weekend?" Bruce's tone had altered.

"Helping them with their enquiries," said Fran.

"What?" Bruce allowed his eyes to leave the road and gaze with horror on his mother-in-law.

"I occasionally assist the police," said Fran calmly.

"Assist them? How?" Bruce returned grimly to the road ahead.

"With aspects of their investigations. I give specialised advice." Fran looked at him sideways.

"Not —" he swallowed "— *psychic* advice?"

"Of course." Now Fran was openly smiling. "I'm sure you heard about it when I inherited Mountville Road. Chrissie was most interested in that."

"Yes, well." Bruce cleared his throat. "So what is it this time?"

"Murder."

"Murder?" If Bruce wasn't quite such a deliberately manly man, Fran would have said he squeaked.

"It usually is," said Fran. "It was when Aunt Eleanor died."

"Er, yes." Bruce obviously didn't want to think about murder in connection with his family-by-marriage. "Who is it this time?"

"Don't worry, Bruce. It's no one any of us knows." Fran patted his arm.

"Why are you helping, then?"

"I don't only help when it's something to do with me." Fran couldn't help laughing at his astounded expression.

"You mean — you're *called in*?"

"I've told you. That's what happens." Fran looked round. "Look, we're here. And the new people are already in your house."

Bruce pulled up and glowered at the front garden, now strewn with toys.

"They'll ruin my lawn," he muttered.

"Don't worry, it's not yours any more," said Fran opening the door.

"But I planted it," said Bruce. "Oh, sorry." He clambered out of the car and belatedly shut the passenger door after Fran. "Well, thanks for your help."

"Don't mention it," said Fran.

"And I'll have to call you in if ever I want someone found, won't I?"

Fran, assuming this was an attempt at humour, nodded smilingly.

"We had this bloke at work, you see. Damn nuisance." Bruce leant back against the car and folded his arms. Fran frowned.

"Really? Disappeared, you mean?"

"Well, not exactly," said Bruce. "This bloke coming in from Italy . . ."

"Italy?" Fran's voice sharpened.

Bruce looked surprised. "Yes, why?"

"I'll come with you while you get your take-away and you can tell me all about it," said Fran, pushing him back towards the car. "I knew today wouldn't be a waste of time."

CHAPTER
ELEVEN

"And so," concluded Fran, "this chap from Italy promised them this huge order, apparently, and then simply disappeared."

Libby shifted the receiver to her other ear and fumbled for a cigarette. "And this is something to do with our body?"

"He's *Italian*, Libby. There's a connection with the Italian girl."

"Oh, Fran, that really is stretching coincidence a bit far."

"I'm positive."

Libby could almost see Fran's lips closing in a familiar stubborn line.

"If you say so. What was his name?"

"Roberto something. Bruce couldn't remember. In fact, he got progressively more annoyed at my questions, so I didn't dare push any harder. Still," she said with satisfaction, "I did get a take-away out of it."

"And why is there a connection with the disappearing Italian girl?"

"It was in the same area that she lived in in London. That's where Bruce's firm is."

"That's simply coincidence," reiterated Libby.

"And he placed a huge order and disappeared himself. Cover, wouldn't you say?"

"Do you think he's our body?"

"No. Not sure what connection there is, but it's six degrees of separation, isn't it?"

"Eh?" Libby choked on a mouthful of smoke.

"The body on the island is the same nationality as the Transnistrian girl —"

"We don't know that," interrupted Libby.

"I do," said Fran. "Anyway, the Transnistrian girl borrowed the Italian girl's passport, the Italian girl disappears, an Italian man appears and subsequently disappears. Link it all back."

"Yes, I can see there's a nice neat chain, but absolutely no evidence that they're connected. And how do you know about the body's Transnistrian connection? Who told you?"

"No one told me," said Fran.

"Are you saying this is a psychic sureness? It doesn't sound like it to me." Libby threw her cigarette into the fireplace. "I think you're forcing yourself to interpret things the way you think they should be."

Fran was silent for so long Libby thought she'd cut the line.

"Fran?" she said eventually. "Are you there? I'm sorry, I didn't mean it."

"I'm here." Fran sounded weary. "And it's all right, Lib. To tell you the truth, I've been thinking the same thing myself. I was only saying so to Guy the other day."

"Too much pressure." Libby, relieved, sat back on to the sofa and drew her feet up. "Ian's put you under pressure."

"Yes, that's exactly what Guy said, and I agreed. But now and then I get a genuine flash."

"And have you had any about this whole case?"

"Jane's house and something to do with farms. That's about it." Fran laughed. "Pathetic, isn't it?"

"Well, forget it for a moment," said Libby. "Are you seeing Guy tonight?"

"It's a bit late, now, isn't it? I even wondered if it was too late to phone you."

"It's only just after ten, don't be daft. Give him a ring and suggest a drink or something. Take your mind off things."

"All right, I will. But before I go, what happened last night?"

Libby gave her a rundown on the audition and finished up by telling her about Jane's flat.

"So now she's got a new tenant, a tentative relationship with her Terry and a new hobby with us. Not bad, eh?"

"And all thanks to you," said Fran. "You and your interfering."

"Well, you see how good interfering can be if done with the best of intentions," said Libby. "Now I'm going back to Ben in the garden. You go and ring Guy."

Ben handed her a topped-up glass of chilled Cava as she came back into the garden.

"What was that all about?"

Libby told him.

"She wants to be careful," said Ben. "These TV people will be on her like a ton of bricks if she cocks up, and Ian won't be too pleased, either."

"She's not beholden to any of them," said Libby. "She's not getting paid for any of this, and she's only got to tell Ian it's no good and she'll be off the hook."

"With Ian, maybe, but can you imagine what capital Kent and Coast would make out of it? Fake Psychic Ruins Murder Investigation would be the least of it. And Fran could hardly muzzle them."

"But Ian could, if he thought it would harm the investigation."

"They'd only use it later, even if it was years later, as soon as the trial was over," said Ben.

"Always assuming there was a trial," said Libby. "I can't see them getting any further at the moment, can you?"

On Saturday morning, another bright beautiful summer day, Jane knocked on the door of Coastguard Cottage and invited Fran out on the *Dolphin*.

"Would Libby like to come, do you think?" she asked.

"It depends when you're going out," said Fran. "She'd have to get over here from Steeple Martin."

"Oh, not until eleven thirty," said Jane. "Just once round the island. People want to see it, so both boats are doing trips round it, one after the other. Ridiculous, really."

"Well, I'll come, thank you," said Fran. "I'll ring Libby and ask. What's happened about your tenant?"

"Oh, she told you, did she?" Jane looked excited. "Well one chap produced references immediately, apparently, and paid by credit card, so that's it, he's coming on Monday."

"References can be forged, you know," said Fran.

"Oh, no, I asked about that, as it seemed suspicious if he had them with him. Apparently he told them to look up some firm or other and ask for someone. Wouldn't even give them the number in case it was a false one with someone primed at the other end. And they did, and that was that. I call that honest."

And I call that over-prepared, thought Fran.

"Well," she said out loud, "I'm very glad for you. What did your friend Terry think of him?"

"I don't really know," said Jane; her colour was beginning to rise, Fran noted interestedly.

"How did you like the audition the other evening?" she asked, deeming it wise to change the subject.

"Oh, it was great! Libby showed me round the theatre and everyone was so nice to me. Some of them are really good, aren't they?"

"Certainly are," said Fran with a grin, wondering who the "some" were, and whether the rest would agree.

"Well, I must get off," said Jane. "I promised I'd get some stuff for George. Bert's already gone out on the first trip round the island, so I haven't got to get anything for him."

"I hope you're not letting them take advantage of you?" said Fran as she held the door open for the girl.

"Oh, no. They were both so kind to me when I was first here, I couldn't do enough for them." Jane smiled and almost skipped off towards the town. What a transformation, thought Fran. And all because Libby interfered. But, nevertheless, a girl who was far too trusting to be a reporter.

Libby was delighted to be asked to go on the *Dolphin* and promised to be with Fran by eleven fifteen at the latest. In fact she arrived at five past, so they strolled down to have a coffee at The Blue Anchor.

Mavis came out to present Libby with one of her battered tin ashtrays. Libby beamed at her.

"So," she said, when they'd given their order. "Are we looking for anything special?"

"What?" Fran looked startled. "How do you mean?"

"Well, clues." Libby lit a cigarette. "On the island."

"Of course not," said Fran. "This is just a pleasure trip." She looked out to sea. "I decided to give it all a rest. I'm not even going to think about it this weekend. And if nothing comes up then I shall tell Ian on Monday and he can call Kent and Coast off."

"Won't you tell McLean yourself?"

Fran shook her head. "He'd only badger me into it. I want it official, from the police. Even if it isn't strictly official, if you know what I mean."

Libby nodded. "Thanks," she said, as Mavis set down two large steaming mugs. "That's lovely." She turned back to Fran. "Well, I can't say I'm sorry."

Fran laughed. "That's not like you! You're the one raring to get your nose stuck into someone else's business usually."

"I know, but this one's nothing to do with us, we've got no personal interest and it looks pretty unsavoury.

Murder of an illegal immigrant." She shuddered. "Sounds so serious."

"Murder's always serious," said Fran, amused. "It's also always unsavoury."

Libby sighed. "I know. But somehow this one's different. Right outside the comfort zone."

"Which one of the others has been *inside*, then?" said Fran.

Libby pulled a face. "Oh, you know what I mean. Anyway, there doesn't seem to be any way of identifying our body, unless the police have had a bit of luck, and until that's done there's nothing anyone can do, so we might as well give it up and enjoy the weather."

Fran smiled and raised her mug in a toast. "Cheers," she said. "And speaking of enjoying the weather, here comes young Jane with a basket of goodies."

"Just like Red Riding Hood," said Libby, watching the small, brown-haired figure coming towards them at a trot.

"Hi," said Jane, slightly out of breath. "Glad you could come, Libby."

"Do you want a hand onto the boat with that?" asked Libby, surveying with interest the basket full of fresh French sticks and greaseproof wrapping which betokened an exciting selection of items from the local deli.

"No, it's fine," said Jane, shaking back her brown bob. "I'll take it over to George. We always give passengers a little something to eat."

110

"That's more than a little something," said Fran. "I hope he's not running at a loss."

"Oh, I shouldn't think so," said Jane. "He's quite a canny old bird."

"What a quaint expression for a modern young woman," said Libby, watching Jane climb down the steps on to the *Dolphin*.

"She's a very quaint modern young woman," said Fran. "I thought that when she turned up on my doorstep that day. And you can't tell me it's normal that she hasn't made any friends except those two old men since she's been here."

"I can understand it," said Libby. "It made perfect sense when she explained it to me."

Fran sighed. "I still think she's a bit of an oddity."

Libby laughed. "And you're not, I suppose?"

Fran looked affronted. "Only in one respect," she said. "Otherwise I'm quite normal."

"OK." Libby stood up. "Come on. It looks as though we ought to be getting on."

"Embarking," said Fran, standing up. "I'll go and pay Mavis."

George welcomed them aboard with an indifferent nod, and Jane smiled nervously.

"Sorry," she whispered. "He's not usually grumpy."

"You haven't made him take us for nothing, have you?" said Libby.

Jane's variable colour went up a notch. "Um," she said.

"Either that or you're paying for the trip." Libby frowned at her.

"Stop it, Lib." Fran tapped Libby on the arm. "It doesn't matter."

"Why didn't it matter?" Libby asked when they were settled on bench seats on the starboard side.

"You were embarrassing her. I think she arranged for us to come to say a sort of combined thank you and apology. And you were practically throwing it back in her face. Tact isn't always your strong point."

Libby was horrified. "Oh, bugger," she said. "I didn't mean it."

"I know you didn't, but she might not."

Libby looked down at her lap. "Should I apologise?"

"No, leave it. Just be nice to her."

Libby looked up again. "I *have* been! That's why she's making a thank you gesture."

Fran sighed. "Oh, Lib," she said.

The *Dolphin* swung out into the bay and began a wide sweep towards the island. Libby leaned over the side to catch the spray on her face. Fran sat and stared across the water towards the island, and Jane came towards them with a tray loaded with food.

"Wow!" Libby took a chunk of bread and some olives. "This is great."

Fran was still looking at the island. Her heart thumped inside her and she felt a familiar wave of blackness descend. From a distance she heard Libby asking if she was all right and then, nothing.

CHAPTER
TWELVE

"What was so annoying," said Fran, sipping at a glass of water, "was that it didn't mean anything. We already knew someone had been left dead on the island — it was hardly news."

"It was a bit frightening," said Jane, who still looked pale. "I've never seen anyone keel over like that."

"It could mean something," said Libby, looking thoughtful. "And at least it's settled one thing."

"What's that?" asked Fran.

"You're still functioning."

"Oh." Fran looked uncomfortably towards Jane.

Libby gave her a disarming smile. "Fran wasn't going to have anything to do with any more so-called psychic investigations, you see," she said. "Pity she can't switch off."

"Exactly," said Fran with relief. "But perhaps it wasn't that. Perhaps it was just a sort of strange seasickness."

"Do you feel sick?" asked Jane, moving backwards.

"Not in the least," said Fran cheerfully.

"Well, if you're OK now, I'd better go and hand round some more bread."

"Yes, I'm fine, Jane. Thank you for the water," said Fran, looking round briefly at the curious faces of the other passengers and giving them a small smile.

"You nearly dropped me in it," she said, turning back to Libby. "She's not to know I'm doing anything."

"All right, all right, I covered it up, didn't I?" Libby wiped her olivey hands on a tissue.

"I suppose so," said Fran. "And you said it could still mean something. What?"

"As far as I remember, from what you've told me, you only get those feelings at the actual site something's happened."

"Mostly, but not always."

"Yes, but you also felt it in Aunt Eleanor's room, didn't you? And at The Alexandria."

"Yes." Fran looked doubtful. "So what you're saying is that the murder could have taken place *on* the island? But that's impossible."

"Three impossible things before breakfast," grinned Libby. "Anyway, bet you that's what it means."

"Hmm." Fran frowned down at her glass.

"So now you've got to decide whether you tell Ian or not."

"Or Kent and Coast."

"No, they're only supposed to be giving you cover for investigations. Not to be told the results."

"That's true," said Fran, looking much struck by this. "But do I tell Ian or not?"

"Is he going to take any notice? They thought the body had been dumped there, didn't they?"

"Yes, and that was forensic evidence, so I don't see how it could be wrong."

Libby thought for a moment. "No, I don't either," she said finally. "But I still think you ought to tell Ian. Then you can decide whether you want to stop altogether after that."

"I'll do that." Fran looked over at the island, which now reared up looking quite forbidding as they passed across the back where the body had been found. "Just there, I think," she said, pointing.

"Yes," said Jane from behind. "That's exactly where it was."

"Right." Fran took a shaky breath. "Not that I really wanted to know."

"Can you really not switch off?" asked Jane curiously.

Fran looked across at Libby and made a face.

"I think things just pop into her head whether she wants them to or not," said Libby, coming to the rescue. "Annoying, I should think."

"Mmm." Jane studied the back of Fran's head.

"It's a lovely trip." Libby smiled brightly. "I love being out on boats."

"This one's not very interesting really, just an opportunity to see the back of the island." Jane sat down on Libby's bench. "The other one which goes out of the bay is better."

"Where exactly does it go?" asked Libby.

"Round the point and along a little way to where there's a cove. You can't get to it from the landward side, so it's always deserted. They stop there and people picnic on the sand."

"A real smugglers' cove?" said Libby.

Jane looked doubtful. "I don't know how any smuggled stuff would get off the beach again, though," she said.

"Oh, there's bound to be a secret passage through the cliffs!" Libby's eyes shone. "Shall we go on one of those boat trips, Fran?"

Fran at last turned back to them and laughed. "Is this Rupert Bear or the Famous Five, Lib?"

"Bit of both. I used to love those illustrations of cliffs and boulders in the Rupert stories, and I always believed you could actually have the sort of adventures the Famous Five had if only you lived in the right place."

"Did you go exploring when you were here on holiday?" asked Fran.

"I tried," Libby laughed. "Round the other headland, but all that was there was another beach with a lot of people on it. You couldn't get any further, so I used to fantasise that there were all sorts of caves and tunnels just out of sight that ran up to the top of the cliffs."

"But the top of the cliffs are built over," said Jane.

"Not then, they weren't," said Libby. "There were fields all the way along the coast."

"We used to walk along The Tops," said Fran. "That's what they were called, weren't they?"

"That's the name of an estate up there now," said Jane. "If you go right to the end of my road you come to the back of it."

"Doesn't the town look different from out here?" said Libby, leaning over the rail. "Much more picturesque. I can see your cottage."

116

"I should think so, seeing as it's on the harbour wall." Fran leaned over too. "And there's your house, Jane. It's closer than I thought to The Alexandria."

"And that's where The Tops were." Libby pointed. "Close to The Alexandria, too."

"Who's working on The Alexandria, Lib?" Fran turned suddenly to her friend.

"Eh?"

"The builders. Who are they?"

"How should I know?"

"I thought Ben was involved?"

Libby frowned. "I believe he was consulted."

Jane looked from one to another. "Is that the Ben I met the other night? He's involved with The Alexandria? What's happening to it?"

"I told you last week, I have no idea," said Libby. "If Ben was consulted, it was in his capacity as an architect. I wouldn't know about any of that."

Fran, looking chastened, had sat down again.

"So, Jane, when can we go out on the other trip?" said Libby.

"Most days, really. It's just that the body seemed to make everybody want to go round the island," said Jane.

"Ghouls," said Fran.

"Well, yes, but good for business. It's a shorter trip, so they can do more. Normally George would go round the island a couple of times, while Bert would go to the cove once, then the next day they'd change over."

"So somebody goes every day?"

"Unless the weather's bad. Sometimes if there aren't many people about they'll have a day off, or one of them will."

"Look we're nearly there, now," said Libby. "Any more of those olives left, Jane?"

"So what was all that about The Alexandria?" said Libby, as they walked back along Harbour Street after thanking Jane and George. "You know it's supposed to be under wraps."

"Sorry," said Fran. "I just had an idea."

"One of those special ideas? Or just an idea?"

"Just an idea." Fran looked up at The Alexandria. "I just wondered if any of the Polish community were working there."

"Oh." Libby looked up too. "Actually, that *is* a good idea. I suppose Ian's made enquiries among all the immigrant workers in the hotels? Wouldn't he have done the same with any builders? They're supposed to be very good, aren't they?"

"As builders? I think so."

"Well, wouldn't he have asked them?"

"I suppose so." Fran took out her key. "Are you coming in?"

"No, I'll get back home," said Libby. "But I really want to go to that cove. When do you want to go?"

"I'm not sure I do," said Fran, unlocking her door. "Won't Ben go with you?"

"Spoilsport. Oh, I'll get someone. And will you ask Ian about the builders? And your sea moment?"

"Yes, yes and yes," said Fran with a sigh. "Just give us a chance."

118

Libby drove home to Steeple Martin in a thoughtful frame of mind. She had thoroughly enjoyed the boat trip and wished it could have been longer, but what was worrying her more was Fran's state of mind. From warning Libby that she had nearly put her foot in it at the beginning of the trip to doing it herself at the end, she had been most unlike herself. Her "moment" had been the most dramatic Libby had witnessed, and was worrying in itself, but it was Fran's apparent searching for other ideas that had her friend puzzled.

Libby fully believed in Fran's intermittent psychic predictions as they had been proved right every time, but she was convinced that being put under pressure by the police in the shape of Ian Connell was forcing Fran to come up with ideas for which there was no evidence, psychic or otherwise.

"So what exactly is going on at The Alexandria?" she asked Ben a little later. "It all seems to be so hush-hush."

Ben shrugged. "It's because it's still legally owned by Bella," he said, "although that lawyer Robert Grimshaw's formed a trust to administer it, according to Bella's wishes. He thinks it will be adverse publicity if any of the details come out. And he's got a soft spot for Bella."

"Right. And the builders? Are they Polish?"

"Some of them, why?" Ben eyed her for a moment. "Oh, I see. The body on the island again. Well, nobody's been reported missing, so I doubt it's one of them. Anyway, there are loads of immigrant workers in Nethergate this year. Could be any one of them."

"Fran's got farms in her head."

"Well, yes, fruit pickers. Although the numbers are down this year because of the new government legislation."

"Oh, dear," Libby sighed. "More restrictive laws."

Ben grinned at her. "Absolutely. When are you going to cut and run, Lib?"

Libby sighed again. "If it wasn't for you and the children, I'd go now."

"Where to, though? Everywhere in Europe is subject to the same laws."

"And not the same interpretation," said Libby. "You know that full well. And I'm not going to get into an argument with you, so that's that."

"So, then. Fruit pickers. Legal numbers are down, so presumably illegal immigrants are taking up the slack," said Ben.

"And this bloke must be one of them." Libby gazed down at the soup she was stirring. "I wonder why the police haven't traced him yet?"

"He probably hasn't been reported missing if he's not supposed to be here."

"But they must have some idea of which farms are using these people?" Libby looked up. "They're being exploited, aren't they?"

"I'm sure the police are onto them, but it's probably quite a big operation. Connell will have already done something about that."

Libby ladled soup into two bowls. "I hope so," she said, "but I still don't really see what the Transnistrian woman and the Italian girl have to do with anything, do you?"

"No. I think it's Fran making assumptions."

"Exactly. She's under too much pressure." Libby put a bowl down in front of Ben and sat down herself. "And yet she did have this very convincing 'moment' on the boat."

"That's what's so interesting," said Ben. "She's had those before, hasn't she? When she went to The Laurels after her aunt had died? But this was even more dramatic, you said?"

"She all but passed out." Libby sighed. "The other times are when she sort of knows things without being told. And that's what she's trying to find now, I'm sure. Ian's investing in her to the extent of pushing her into the arms of Kent and Coast Television and she feels she's got to justify his faith, yet the only things that have really come out of it have been her sea moment and her feeling about Jane's house, which has nothing to do with anything at all."

Ben paused with his soup spoon halfway to his mouth. "Are you sure Jane's got nothing to do with all this?"

"Not you, too." Libby frowned at him. "That's what Harry said. How can she have anything to do with it? She's only been here a year, and she just happened to be on the boat when the body was spotted."

Ben sipped his soup. "But that's the point," he said. "She *was* on that boat."

Libby put her spoon down and stared at him in horror. "You're not suggesting she was actually *supposed* to be on that boat? To spot the body?"

Ben shrugged. "Well, it makes a sort of sense, doesn't it? No one else had spotted it."

Libby stared at him for a moment longer. "I just don't believe it," she said finally. "And why, for goodness' sake?"

Ben sighed. "I don't know, do I? You're the detective. I was just saying what seemed obvious."

Libby thought. "It doesn't seem obvious to me," she said eventually. "And it's no good asking Fran at the moment, is it? She'll go off on a wild goose chase."

"And that's usually you, isn't it?" Ben grinned slyly.

"They haven't turned out to be wild goose chases, have they?" said Libby. "I admit I'm not very scientific, but I've got there in the end."

"Well, let's forget about it, now," said Ben. "We've got the whole weekend to look forward to without thinking about bodies and Italians, so finish your soup and let's get on with it."

CHAPTER
THIRTEEN

Fran was somewhat puzzled to find herself outside Jane Maurice's house later that afternoon. Feeling confused and unsettled, she'd decided to go for a walk without thinking about where she was going. And now, here she was.

She gazed up at the house wondering why it seemed important. Turning to sit on a bench overlooking the sea, she tried to analyse the feeling. As usual, she was unable to do so. There was none of the suffocating blackness that she now associated with death, simply a feeling that the house was important. Not Jane herself, Fran acknowledged, just the house. But important to what? Surely not the body on the island? She searched her mind trying to find connections, aware as she was doing so that this was just what Libby said she'd been doing — trying too hard — when the front door opened and a man came down the whitewashed steps. Terry? she wondered. But this man looked older than Terry, whom Libby had described as around thirty.

Good-looking, she thought, very dark and going grey. This must be Jane's new tenant. Her eyes followed him down the hill and past The Alexandria.

"Fran?"

Fran jumped and turned round. "Oh, Jane! You startled me."

"I just wondered what you were doing sitting here outside my house." Jane stood with her arms folded, frowning suspiciously.

"Nothing." Fran laughed a little guiltily. "I just found myself here. I expect it was a result of our conversation on the boat." She nodded down the hill. "Is that your new tenant?"

Jane's expression cleared. "Mike, yes. He seems very pleasant."

"I thought he wasn't moving in until Monday?"

"Oh, the agents cleared his money and his references, so there didn't seem any point in waiting," said Jane. "Besides, the quicker he's in, the quicker I start getting rent."

"Is he English?"

"English? With a name like Mike Charteris? I should say so. Why do you ask?"

"He looks so dark." Fran smiled brightly. "Don't take any notice of me, I've got foreigners on the brain."

"Understandable, I suppose," said Jane. "Look, would you like to come up and have a cup of tea? Terry might come up as well in a minute. He's been doing something to the locks on the downstairs flat, so I owe him a cup."

"Love to." Fran stood up and smoothed down her skirt. "Won't Terry mind?"

"No, of course not. Why should he?" Jane led the way up the steps to the front door. Fran admired its stained glass panels and then, as she stepped inside, felt a shiver of recognition. She stopped.

"Anything the matter?" Jane turned back.

"No." Fran shook her head. "Just struck cool coming in from that sun."

"I know. Quite cold, these old Victorian houses, aren't they? Come on up."

So she'd been right, thought Fran. There was something about this house. But it was nothing to do with the body on the island.

While Fran was admiring the view over the bay, she heard the door open behind her.

"Oh, sorry."

Fran turned round to find herself face to face with a tall, good-looking young man in a T-shirt and jeans.

"You must be Terry?" she said. "I'm Fran."

"Oh, right." He wiped his hand on his jeans and held it out. "The lady who lives on Harbour Street?"

"That's right. Jane told you, did she?"

Faint spots of colour appeared on Terry's cheeks. "Yeah, well. We had a drink the other night."

"Right." Fran nodded. Libby was right, then. Romance was in the air.

Jane came in carrying two mugs, and went a similar shade of pink. "Oh, Terry," she said. "I'll get another mug."

"Doesn't matter," said Terry, backing towards the door. "You've got a guest."

"No, no," said Jane hastily, "I was telling Fran about you."

This time they both went even pinker, to Fran's amusement.

"I believe you met my friend Libby, too," she said, to defuse the situation.

"Yes." Terry nodded and looked towards the kitchen. "Shall I get myself a mug, Jane?"

Gosh, they've progressed quickly, thought Fran, remembering what Libby had told her about their relationship.

"No, I'll get it." Jane hurried back towards the kitchen and Fran sat down.

"Lovely view this flat's got," said Fran. "I suppose yours is similar?"

"Not as good, because it's lower down, but yeah. Good." Terry offered a small smile.

"And you were here when Jane's aunt still lived in the ground floor flat?"

"Only just. Before she went into a home." Terry shifted in his chair and looked towards the kitchen. His expression changed to one of relief as Jane came through the door.

"Aunt Jessica?" She put Terry's mug on a side table by his chair. "She went into a home a year before she died, didn't she, Terry?"

"Yes." Terry took an unwise sip of his hot tea and winced. "I wasn't here all the time, and Mrs Finch couldn't get up and down from the basement, so no one could look after her."

"Basement?"

"What they call a garden flat. The ground floor is actually above ground level."

126

"Of course, the steps up to the front door. So Mrs Finch has her own entrance?"

"Yes, which is at the back with no steps to go down. Ideal for her. She's quite old." Jane sipped her own tea and flashed a glance towards Terry. "You help her, though, don't you, Terry?"

Terry shrugged. "Now and then. Little jobs, you know. Like I do for you."

Fran looked from one to the other and hid a smile. It was rare, in her experience, to see a young couple in the throes of this sort of old-fashioned courtship. She hoped it would last.

"Mrs Finch was here when your aunt was here, too, was she?"

"Yes. She used to come here when Aunt Jess ran it as a B&B. I told Libby, I think she looks on me as an upstart."

"Your aunt must have inspired loyalty," said Fran.

"I think her guests liked it because it was informal and Nethergate is such a lovely, traditional seaside place."

Fran's gaze turned back to the window. "It certainly is. I've loved it since I used to come on holiday as a child."

"Libby said something about that," said Jane. "Where did you stay?"

"In the cottage I live in now," smiled Fran. "My uncle owned it."

"Oh, I see. Like me, then." Jane grinned happily.

"More or less," agreed Fran. "Did you stay with your aunt when you were a child?"

"Yes, often. I didn't see her so much after I grew up, and now of course, I feel guilty."

"Did she have no children of her own?" Fran tutted. "Sorry, that was insensitive. She can't have done if she left the house to you, can she?"

"No, she never married," said Jane. "There was some talk in the family about a man during the war, but I was too young to know anything about it."

"Was she a career woman?" asked Fran. "After all, this house must have cost quite a lot, whenever she bought it."

"I've never thought about that," said Jane. "I suppose she must have bought it, because otherwise it would have been left to her *and* my grandfather."

"He was her brother?"

"Yes. My father was her nephew and she treated him like a son." Jane gazed at the window.

"Sorry, I've been being awfully nosy," said Fran.

"No, you haven't. It's fascinating." Jane turned bright eyes on Fran. "I shall have to do some digging." She looked across at Terry who was trying to look as though he wasn't there. "Will you help me?"

He cleared his throat. "Yes. Of course. Whatever."

Fran finished her tea. "I must be going. I didn't intend to stay out this long. Will you let me know if you find anything out? Not if it's personal of course. It's just as you say, it's fascinating."

"It is, isn't it?" Jane got up to see her out. "I've just never thought about it before. It was always Aunt Jess's house — it never occurred to me to wonder how she came by it."

"And it shouldn't have occurred to you, either," said Libby later, answering her mobile. "You're seeing mysteries where there aren't any."

"Jane thought it was interesting, too," protested Fran.

"Jane was probably in a state of high excitement because Terry was there."

"Oh." Fran looked out of her window at her own view of the bay. "Oh, and I saw the new tenant too."

"Really? He's all above board, then?"

Fran sighed. "Yes. Very English and normal-looking."

"So nothing to investigate there?"

"No," said Fran, sitting down suddenly. "Nothing at all."

Libby sighed gustily. "So, what are you going to do? Speak to Ian about your sea moment and the Polish builders?"

"If there are any Polish builders. They might all be bona fide British builders."

"Or bona fide Polish builders."

"You know what I mean." It was Fran's turn to sigh. "But yes, I'll call him on Monday."

"And Kent and Coast?"

"I'm going to try and get out of it."

"No, don't do that," said Libby slowly. "I've got an idea."

Behind her, Ben groaned.

"What?" said Fran.

Libby turned and scowled at Ben. "I'll tell you tomorrow," she said. "When I'm alone."

★ ★ ★

"So did you call Ian?" Libby, on Monday morning, floundered through a muddy farm track in her borrowed Wellington boots, while a fine rain created a mini-stream down the back of her neck.

Fran, a few paces ahead following the disapproving back of Campbell McLean, nodded.

"What did he say?" Libby gasped, sliding dangerously close to the splits.

"Not a lot." Fran's voice wafted back covered in icicles. That makes me today's most unpopular person, thought Libby, wondering why, if they all felt this way, they'd actually agreed to make this investigative trip. Campbell McLean wasn't even filming.

"Bet his editor's not too keen," muttered Libby to herself, as the recalcitrant boots took her face to face with an enquiring cow over a wire-link fence. "All this time wasted on nothing, when he could be doing lovely little fillers all over the region."

"What did you say?" Fran stopped and looked back.

"Nothing." Libby concentrated on getting the boots back on track.

"If you're complaining, you've only got yourself to blame." Fran turned and began to pick her way along the track. "This was your idea."

"I'm perfectly well aware of that," said Libby, drawing herself up to her full height and looking haughtily up at Fran. "And if it was such a mad one, why have both you and McLean over there gone along with it?"

Fran was silent.

130

"There see, you've got nothing to say, have you?" Libby looked smug.

Arriving in a somewhat dilapidated and run-down looking farm yard, Fran stopped and watched as Campbell McLean, braving the unfriendly overtures of a sheepdog, disappeared round the side of a barn.

"After our conversation yesterday, I called Ian, told him about the sea moment and the Polish builders," she shot Libby a further frosty look, "and then mentioned your idea. He said as there'd been nothing from the television end so far, we might as well follow it up. So he set it up with McLean. And you saw how pleased *he* was about it when we got here."

"Why didn't you tell me this before?"

"When? I didn't have it confirmed until this morning, and I didn't think I had to report to you after every telephone conversation."

Libby looked up from under her brows. "Hmm," she said.

"And what does that mean?" Fran let out her breath in an angry gust.

"Nothing," said Libby again. Fran stared at her for a long moment.

"Almost monochromatic in the rain, isn't it?" said Libby after a few minutes silence. "I wonder where that man's got to?"

She was answered shortly by the man's reappearance, trailing a stocky individual wearing a body warmer and a cap.

"Farmer," muttered Libby. "Central casting."

Fran compressed her lips.

"Fran, Libby, this is Mr Budgen," said Campbell McLean, as he came level with them.

Fran smiled and held out her hand. Mr Budgen, with a surly nod, shook it. Libby kept her hands in her pockets. The sheepdog was circling them making unpleasant noises and Campbell McLean watched it nervously.

"So what was it you wanted, then?" Budgen looked from one to the other of the women.

"Just a short piece on the overseas farm workers for the evening news," said Fran, and hesitated.

"Because of the new legislation," put in Libby, earning herself surprised looks from all her listeners. "There are fewer workers, aren't there? This year? And if you can't get your crop picked in time, you'll lose money?"

Budgen's sandy brows drew down until they formed a straight line above his eyes.

"So?"

"Strawberry crop was affected, wasn't it?" Libby noticed with satisfaction that her words were striking a chord. "Because only Romanians and Bulgarians can come over now, and the other EU workers don't want to do fruit picking any more."

"How do you know this?" Fran asked in astonishment.

Libby smiled in triumph. "Ben. He knows all about it. Well, he would, wouldn't he? Now he's in charge of the Manor Estate."

Campbell McLean screwed up his eyes and glared at Libby. "And he is?"

Libby glared back. "My partner. None of your business."

McLean looked taken aback.

"So," she continued, returning to Budgen, "you've still got workers, but not through SAWS?"

"Eh? Saws?" said Fran in a faint voice.

"Seasonal Agricultural Workers Scheme," said Libby offhandedly. "Open to abuse of course."

Fran shook her head. "I'm lost," she said.

"No, I remember," said McLean. "We've done pieces on it before, several times, and there was that big case a couple of years ago, wasn't there?"

Libby nodded, a teacher bestowing approval on a bright pupil.

"So, Mr Budgen, is that what's happening?" Libby turned back to the farmer, who was looking distinctly uncomfortable.

"I've got workers," he muttered.

"Bulgarians and Romanians?" asked Libby.

Budgen nodded. "Far as I know."

"Could we talk to some of them?" said McLean.

"Don't know much English, most of 'em," said Budgen.

"Well, can we bring the cameras back and interview you and film some of them working?"

"Behind enough as it is," said Budgen. "Don't want no more interruptions."

"Are there any other farms who might be willing to talk to us?" asked Fran.

Budgen shrugged. "'Ave to ask 'em, won't you? Who gave you my name, anyways?"

"Picked you out with a pin," said McLean with what he obviously hoped was a winning smile. It didn't win Mr Budgen.

"Got to get on," he said. "See yourselves off the land." He clicked his fingers. "Gal," he said, and the sheepdog followed him reluctantly from the yard.

The three of them watched him go, then Libby turned round with a sigh.

"Anything?" Campbell asked Fran.

Fran shook her head.

"Do you think he's really only got Bulgarians and Romanians?" asked Libby. "Because I don't."

"Undercover operation, do you think?" McLean stepped up to walk alongside her down the muddy track. The rain had stopped.

"Yours, you mean?" Libby turned to look at him. "How would you do that? And I thought Inspector Connell only wanted you to provide a cover for Fran?"

"He did, but the understanding was we could do our own investigation. That was the whole idea in the first place."

"But not an investigation into Fran," said Libby.

"No." McLean sounded regretful.

"I don't see how you could go back there now. He'd be on the lookout for everything."

"We could find someone else to go in."

"And say what? No, if you want to do secret filming you've got to have someone who isn't suspicious of you to start with. A different farmer." She looked up at him. "How *did* you find him, by the way?"

"I was obfuscating a bit back there." Campbell grinned. "I knew perfectly well about SAWS and the court case in 2003. He was one of the farms that came under scrutiny. He wasn't charged with anything, but I took a punt on him anyway."

"Any other farms on that list?" asked Libby.

"I'll see what I can come up with." He looked at her with renewed interest. "You're the detective-minded one here, aren't you? Not Fran."

Libby laughed. "So I'm always told. My nearest and dearest get very exasperated with me."

"How did it start?"

Libby looked up, frowning. "You're not going to do a number on me, now, are you?"

"Not unless you're psychic as well," he said.

Libby told him about the murder in Steeple Martin that had introduced her to Fran, and the subsequent cases in which they had been involved.

"But you must know that," she concluded, "or you wouldn't have come after her in the first place."

"I do now, but only because Jane — Maurice, was it? — on the *Mercury* told me." He looked back at Fran, who was trailing some paces behind them. "I don't think her heart's in this."

"No." Libby looked back, too. "She would far rather forget all about it and live a normal life."

"That's what she said to me when we first met," said Campbell. "I was gobsmacked when that Inspector called and said she'd agreed to do the investigation."

Libby sighed. "Yes. And I haven't helped, really. Still, at least you've got a vague lead for a story, haven't you, even if it isn't anything to do with the body on the island."

"The illegal workers, you mean? Yes, if I can work out how to get into it. I'll talk to my editor."

"Who won't be pleased that you've wasted this morning?" grinned Libby.

"Ah, but I can justify it, now, can't I?" He grinned back. "Reconnaissance."

CHAPTER
FOURTEEN

"Come on, then," said Fran, when she and Libby were seated in the pub in Steeple Martin. "What's all this SAWS stuff? I felt such an idiot back there."

Libby looked a little shamefaced. "I only found out about most of it yesterday," she said. "You know I said I'd looked it all up on the internet last week? Well, I wasn't really looking in the right places, and Ben knows all about the current legislation from farmers, so we went through it yesterday afternoon. It's what we thought was going on, about the illegal workers, but the gangmasters have moved on to other countries, now, which is why we had the Transnistrian connection."

"So what happens? How do they operate?"

"Well," said Libby, taking a sip of her lager, "they recruit people overseas who want to come and work over here, and provide them with false documents. Then they have farmers who will turn a blind eye over here. In fact, SAWS isn't in force any longer, because of this new legislation, and as I said earlier, apparently the other migrant workers don't want to do seasonal fruit picking."

"But it was in force when this Transnistrian woman first came over?"

"Must have been. She must have come over on false papers, then as she wanted to stay here, borrowed the Italian girl's passport and got the council job."

"Mmm." Fran gazed down into her tonic water. "But as you said, it's got nothing to do with the body on the island."

"No." Libby glanced quickly at her. "Sorry about this morning. I genuinely thought if you had your mind set on farms it might trigger something and you would have a breakthrough."

"And I didn't." Fran sighed. "In fact the only things I can be sure of are nothing to do with the body."

"The sea moment was."

"Yes, but I already knew about that death." Fran shook her head. "No, I'd better give it up. I'll tell Ian." She grinned at Libby. "And you can go on and be Campbell's right-hand woman instead."

"No, neither of us could stand it." Libby grinned back. "What did Ian say about your sea moment, by the way? Or the case in general?"

"I told you — not a lot. 'Our investigations are continuing', was more or less it."

"But what about the boat?"

"He didn't seem to attach any importance to it. After all, as we said, we were near the site of the body, and I don't have to be at exactly the same spot as someone died, do I? I knew about it, that was enough."

They sat in silence for a moment, while the rain, which had started again, dripped down inside the huge fireplace.

138

"So do you think that farmer is employing illegal workers?" asked Fran eventually.

"From the way he reacted, yes," said Libby.

"And he wouldn't know if one of them was missing?"

Libby looked at her. "He wouldn't want to know, would he? Why?"

"So there'd be no way of tracking them back to their employer?"

"If they're dead with no clothes on, no."

"Don't be sarcastic. You know what I mean."

"I do, and it's fairly obvious, isn't it? No one's going to own up to losing an illegal worker."

"No." Fran sighed, and they relapsed into silence.

"What are you going to do now?" Libby finished her lager and twirled the glass.

"Go home, I suppose. Unless you want another drink?"

"No, I didn't mean that. I meant in general. With your life."

Fran raised her eyebrows. "Good heavens! That's a big question."

"Well, if you're giving up on this investigation, you must want something to do. You don't have to work any more. Will you take up a hobby?"

Fran laughed. "I've got one already, haven't I? Props lady for the panto."

"That doesn't start for months yet."

"Macramé? Crochet? The WI?"

Libby frowned. "Don't be silly. You know what I mean."

"Yes, Lib, I know what you mean. But for the last few months I've been quite happy pottering around in the cottage, haven't I? Helping Guy occasionally in the shop."

"But it was a novelty, then. Now it's real life. And especially when the tourists go, it'll be bleak and cold, and Guy won't need you in the shop."

"I moved in at Christmas, Lib. I've done bleak and cold in Nethergate."

Libby sighed. "You're determined to misunderstand me, aren't you?"

"I do understand you. And yes, I shall probably want to do something with my time. I've always had something to do, even if it was waiting for non-existent calls from my agent. Or investigating houses for Goodall and Smythe."

"So what will it be?"

Fran put her head on one side and looked at Libby. "What do you think about writing?"

"Writing?" Libby looked bewildered. "I do that. Pantos."

"Fiction. A novel, perhaps."

"Blimey!" Libby was awed. "Do you think you could?"

"I don't know, but I'd like to try."

"How will you start?"

"I thought I might try a creative writing course. There's a couple of evening classes."

"Where? Could I come?"

Fran hesitated.

"Oh, well, if you'd prefer that I didn't." Libby sat back in her chair looking huffy.

"I just wanted to do something on my own." Fran looked down at the table. "You're such a strong character, Lib, that no one notices me, and soon it would be your writing class, not mine."

An appalled silence fell. When Fran finally looked up, she was horrified to see tears streaming down Libby's cheeks, while she fumbled in her basket for a tissue.

"I'm sorry, Fran." Libby hiccupped and blotted her eyes. "I'm such an insensitive cow."

"Oh, God, Lib, don't." Fran reached across and took her friend's hand. "I shouldn't have said anything."

"Yes, you should." Libby took a deep breath and sat up straight. "I try and run people's lives, that's my trouble. Everyone accuses me of interfering, don't they? You, Ben, Pete, Harry — and you're all right. What I forget is that sometimes it actually hurts people."

Fran laughed. "Don't be humble, Lib, it doesn't suit you. And none of us would want you any different, you know that. As long as you know when to pull back."

"I might need you to tell me," admitted Libby, "like you just did." She gave her face another swipe with the tissue. "God, look at that. Mascara all over the place. What does my face look like?"

"Shiny," laughed Fran, "but not blotchy. Come on, have another drink and I'll tell you all about my writing project."

Later in the afternoon, when Fran had driven back to Nethergate, Libby mooched up the Manor drive in search of Ben. The theatre was, of course, locked, but the front door of The Manor itself was open.

"Hello?" Libby pushed the door and stepped into the hall.

"That you, Libby?" A voice called from somewhere to her left.

"Hetty? Yes, it's me. Are you in the kitchen?"

"Yeah — come on in. Kettle's on."

The Manor kitchen was warm, the Aga on permanently, summer and winter alike. Ben's mother, Hetty, stood by the deep butler sink looking out at the drowned fields and copses that constituted her domain.

"Sit down, gal." Hetty waved Libby to the Windsor chair by the Aga. "Our Ben's somewhere outside. Got 'is mobile number?"

"Yes, but it doesn't matter," said Libby, sinking into the chair. "I just needed company."

"Yeah?" Hetty cocked her head as she lifted up the singing kettle. "Don't normally come lookin' for company."

"No." Libby stared at the Aga miserably.

"Well, I ain't goin' to be much company if you don't want to talk. I'll just pop into the scullery to get the milk and see how you feel when I get back."

Libby stood up and went to look out of the window. She had to admit to feeling a bit silly now. A childish desire to unload her woes had driven her up here, and yet she could hardly tell Hetty, who one day might be her mother-in-law, all about her character flaws. The thought made Libby go hot all over, and she hurriedly turned on the cold tap and held her wrists underneath the water.

"Hot flush, gal?" Hetty came in with a bottle of milk.

Libby made an ambivalent noise in her throat and turned off the tap.

"So what you investigatin' now?" asked Hetty, pouring strong tea into large mugs.

"Nothing," said Libby. "Not any more."

"Ben said something about that body on the island."

"Not now. Fran was asked to help, but she can't, so that's that."

Hetty sat down at the long table. "She got something else to do?"

"No, she just can't — um — see anything, if you know what I mean."

"Oh, ah. Can't psychic it up?"

Libby giggled. "That's right."

"Just as well. Shouldn't go gettin' involved in all them murders."

"It wasn't our fault, Hetty," Libby protested.

"Still, don't want to go lookin' for 'em."

"No," sighed Libby.

"So is that what's gettin' you down?"

"Not really." Libby looked down into her mug. "Fran told me off for being overbearing."

"Told you off?"

"Put me right. Very gently."

"Hmm." Hetty made a face.

"I know, I know. They all tell me I'm nosy and interfering, but I didn't realise I was that bad."

"Don't suppose you are, gal. You have a think about what she said, and I reckon you'll find out that it wasn't that bad after all."

Libby looked up. "You could be right, Hetty."

"Course I'm right. Had to be, haven't I? All these years." She reached across and patted Libby's hand. "And you're part of the family, gal, and I know my family."

For the second time that day, Libby found tears filling her eyes, and she swallowed hard. "Thank you," she whispered.

Hetty administered a final pat and stood up. "You call our Ben, now," she said. "He'll be lookin' for an excuse to come in out of the rain."

Libby fished another tissue and her mobile out of her basket, and after wiping her eyes and blowing her nose, punched in Ben's number.

"He's coming in," she said, finishing the call and returning the mobile to the basket.

"Thought so." Hetty turned away from the sink and flapped a hand at a trug full of potatoes. "Want to give me a hand peelin' those? Stayin' for dinner, are you?"

"I ought to go back and get out of these clothes," said Libby, "and feed Sidney."

"After you've seen Ben you can pop back and change, then come up her for your dinner. Go on, I don't see enough of you these days." Hetty gave her a brief smile, and Libby hugged her.

"Thanks, Het," she said. "I'd love to."

144

When Ben arrived in the kitchen, Hetty shooed them off to her sitting room and Libby told him everything that had happened that day.

"Oh, Lib," he said when she'd finished.

"Was she right, Ben?"

He smiled and put an arm round her shoulders. "Of course she was right, but you've taken it the wrong way."

"Hetty said something like that. Your mum's lovely, you know."

"I know she is, and very wise indeed."

"So how should I have taken it?"

"The only thing you're guilty of is sometimes not seeing the effect you have on other people," said Ben carefully.

"I realise that," said Libby.

"Fran was right — you do have a strong personality. You're warm, funny and impulsive, and nobody can ignore you. Yes, you're nosy and you do interfere, but only from the best motives. The trouble is, as Fran said, if you went to classes with her you would become so enthusiastic that they would be *your* writing classes, not hers. It shouldn't matter, but it does. She wants to do something of her own."

Libby nodded. "Of course I see that, I just feel so guilty that I hadn't noticed. How many times have I done that to other people, do you think?"

Ben laughed. "Dozens, I expect. Oh, don't look at me like that, I didn't mean it."

"But, Ben, Fran has got something of her own. She's got her talent. No one else has that."

"I know, but she doesn't like it, does she?" He gave her shoulders a squeeze and kissed her cheek. "Now go on, you go home and feed the walking stomach, then come back here all polished and perfumed and have dinner with us. You can fascinate my dad. He needs cheering up."

"Oh, dear." Libby stood up. "Isn't he too good?"

Ben shrugged. "Oh, you know. Much the same, but it's obvious that he's getting weaker."

"Poor Greg," said Libby.

The rain had stopped again as Libby splashed through muddy puddles all the way to Allhallow's Lane. Sidney greeted her with the anguished howls of the starving, and after replenishing his food bowl, she went to run herself a bath.

Well, she thought, that was an interesting day. From the meeting at Budgen's farm, where she was sure they had stumbled on a nest of illegal workers, to Fran giving up the investigation and unwittingly bringing Libby face to face with herself.

Ben and Hetty had both gone a long way to making her see that it wasn't quite as bad as she'd first thought, but it still made her feel churned up inside. Thoughtfully, she slid down into the warm water.

Her thoughts turned back to Budgen and his workers. He hadn't confirmed whether they were Romanian and Bulgarian, and Libby was positive they weren't. Why she should be so certain, she couldn't say, unless it was simply his unco-operative attitude and the generally forbidding aspect of his farm, but she really hoped Campbell McLean would carry on that part of the investigation and expose him. Because, of course, that was the only investigation that was going to be done, now. And she and Fran were no longer part of it.

CHAPTER
FIFTEEN

Ben brought a cup of tea and the telephone to Libby's bedside at half past seven the next morning.

"That Jane from the *Mercury*," he said, bending over to kiss her. "See you later."

Libby struggled on to one elbow and took the phone.

"Jane?" she said. "You're very early. What's happened?"

"Sorry, Libby, I just thought you ought to know. I tried to ring Fran but she wasn't answering."

"Ought to know what?" Libby managed a sip of rather too hot tea and winced.

"Terry. He was attacked last night." Jane sounded as though she was near to tears.

"How awful," said Libby, wondering why Jane thought she ought to know. "Is he very bad?"

"He's in hospital. There's —" Libby heard a gulp "— a policeman by his bed."

"Oh, lord. That does sound serious."

"Yes. I stayed at the hospital as long as I could, but he's under sedation now, so they said I should come home."

She wants company, thought Libby. That's why she's ringing.

"Where is he? Kent and Canterbury?"

"Yes. I'm outside there now."

"Come here, Jane. It's on your way. You won't go in to work, will you?"

"No — I can't. Can I really come?"

"Of course, silly. Are you all right to drive?"

"Yes — yes. I think so."

"Do you want me to come and get you?"

"No, I'll be fine. I'll take it slowly, and I'll be going against the traffic, won't I?"

"All right, then," said Libby, swinging her legs out of bed. "I'll have the kettle on. See you in a bit."

By the time Jane arrived, Libby was dressed and tea was made in the big enamel teapot.

"Or would you prefer coffee?" Libby asked, as she shepherded Jane into the garden.

"No, tea would be lovely, thanks." Jane subsided into one of the chairs under the cherry tree. The rain had disappeared overnight and the sun was doing its best to dry up the remaining puddles.

Libby brought out a tray with mugs and biscuits and Sidney butted Jane's legs. She smiled.

"Tell me all about it, then," said Libby, handing over a mug.

Jane drew a breath. "He was mugged," she said.

"Did you find him? Is that why you were at the hospital?"

"No, it was the new tenant on his way home." Jane sipped her tea and Libby sighed.

"Yes? Where?"

"Oh — on the steps."

"The steps of the house? Was the front door open?"

Jane looked puzzled. "I don't know."

"Just that if it was, he must have come out of the house. If it wasn't, he was just going in."

"Oh, I see." Jane frowned. "The police didn't say anything about that."

"They've questioned you?"

"Yes."

Drawing teeth wasn't in it, thought Libby. "At home?"

"No." Jane shook her head. "Sorry, Libby, I'm being a bit dim, aren't I?"

"Doesn't matter," said Libby, "you've obviously had a shock. Just tell me from the beginning — if you want to, that is."

"Right." Jane took another sip and put her mug on the table. "Last night I was in the office until late and didn't get home until nearly eleven. There was a policeman on the doorstep and Mrs Finch and Mike were in the hall talking to two more. Apparently, Mike came home at about twenty past ten and found Terry on the steps. I don't know about the door. He called the police and an ambulance."

"So what happened next?"

"Well, the policemen asked who I was and where I'd been, then they asked me to let them into Terry's flat, where they had a look round. There were no lights on, or anything, so I suppose he'd been on his way in when it happened. Then I asked if I could collect a couple of things and take them to Terry in hospital, although they both looked a bit gloomy and said they didn't think he'd need them, which really worried me."

"But you took them anyway? You knew where to find things?"

Jane coloured. "No, I just went into the bathroom — oh, it's so clean and neat, Libby, you wouldn't believe — and took his toothbrush and toothpaste." The colour deepened. "And a deodorant. I just took what he might think of as essential."

"So you went to hospital."

Jane nodded. "They sealed his room after me, and I left them my key. Then I went to the hospital."

"Did you see him?"

"Oh, yes. And he was sort of conscious. He recognised me, anyway." The colour, which had faded, returned. "I held his hand, while I was allowed to, but not when the doctors were there, of course."

"So did they operate? What exactly is wrong?"

"They didn't tell me a lot because I'm not his next of kin, but he had head injuries and broken ribs as though he'd been kicked. They did something to him and he's in a side room now."

"Not intensive care?"

"No." Jane brightened. "I never thought of that. That's good isn't it?"

"I would have thought so. Did he say anything to you? You said he recognised you."

"He tried to smile and say 'Jane' when I first got there, but I think he was under a bit of sedation then, too. After that, he didn't say anything. I had to sit in the waiting area most of the time, but they let me in to his room again about five this morning. Then they told me I should go home."

"What about his next of kin?"

"I don't know. They asked me when I first got there, but nobody said anything after that."

Libby looked thoughtful. "I expect they had a good look around his flat and found an address book or something." She sipped her own tea. "So it was just a straightforward mugging?"

Jane looked surprised. "Well, yes. What else could it have been?"

"Oh, I don't know. Just seems odd. You know, with Terry being ex-army. I would have thought he'd have given as good as he got."

"Not if they came up behind him and hit him on the head. That's what seems to have happened."

"Did they get anything? Wallet? Money?"

"Do you know, I didn't ask." Jane frowned and picked up her mug. "I suppose they did."

"Well, perhaps you'll find out more later. Will they tell you anything over the phone — with you not being next of kin?"

"I shall go back later," said Jane, "and they know who I am, now."

"It might be different staff, though."

"Oh, well." Jane shrugged. "I'll sort it out somehow." She stood up. "Thank you for the tea. I suppose I'd better ring the office, then I'll go back and try to get some sleep."

"You've only been here five minutes," said Libby. "You still look a bit shaky. Why don't you try and have a nap in my spare room?"

Jane hesitated. "I don't know," she said. "I feel I ought to be at home in case anyone tries to get in touch."

"But you've got your mobile, haven't you? If the police want you?"

"Yes." Jane sat down again. "Perhaps I will, if you really don't mind. I do feel a bit wobbly."

"Lack of sleep," said Libby. "Have another cup of tea and I'll go and check on the sheets."

When Libby came back into the garden ten minutes later, Jane was asleep with Sidney on her lap. Libby smiled, picked up the tray, took it inside and found her mobile.

"Fran?"

"Hi."

"I've got Jane Maurice here, and guess what?"

"What?"

Libby told her everything Jane had told her and waited for a response.

"She tried to call me," said Fran eventually.

"I know, she told me, but you didn't answer."

"I was in the shower." Fran sounded defensive and Libby grinned.

"Anyway, what do you think?"

Fran sighed. "You want me to say it's something to do with what I felt about her house, don't you?"

"Well, I did wonder."

"I've no idea, Lib." Fran sighed again. "I think my brain's completely switched off, now. Do you think it's connected?"

"I just thought it was a coincidence, that's all. Especially as the new tenant's moved in."

"Are you suspicious of him?"

"Well, he was the one who found Terry."

"Not surprising if Terry was on the steps of the house where he lived, I would have thought."

"All right, all right. Don't be sarky."

"Sorry, Libby. I'm not being obstructive, I'm brain dead. Perhaps this is the end of my moments altogether."

"OK." It was Libby's turn to sigh. "I'll go off and do the Florence Nightingale bit. Speak to you soon."

Jane was still asleep and Libby, mindful of the sun working its way out of the branches of the cherry tree, shook her gently awake.

"You'll get sunstroke if you stay here," she said. "Come on upstairs."

Blearily, Jane followed her through the cottage and upstairs to where there were fresh navy sheets on the spare bed.

"Bathroom just there," said Libby. "I won't disturb you."

She went downstairs and cleared the tea and breakfast things, before going into the conservatory and staring at the painting begun on the day the body was found on Dragon Island.

She knew she ought to do more work on it; she also knew she should think about doing more paintings. Guy could always sell her work, which was reasonably priced, and he'd even used some in reproduction on birthday and Christmas cards. While it didn't exactly make her rich, it was an income she would hate to be without, even though Ben had assured her he was well able to "take care of her", as he put it. But their Living Apart Together relationship, a LAT as it was now officially known, didn't seem to Libby to fit into the traditional — or even out-dated — mould where man the hunter looked after woman the gatherer, and she preferred to remain independent.

But somehow, painting wasn't holding her attention right now. It never did, she realised, when there was something else going on in her life. It was partly because it had now become a job rather than a hobby, which it had been before her marriage broke up and she moved to Steeple Martin. But now, despite the (almost) mutual decision to give up on the investigation, Libby found she couldn't let it go. And it was disturbing her concentration.

But which investigation? Libby gave up on the painting and went back into the garden, where Sidney joined her as she lit a cigarette. The body on Dragon Island or Jane Maurice's house? Or were they, as Fran had postulated, connected somehow? Libby shook her head at Sidney, who flattened his ears. And what, she wondered, had Fran said to Ian Connell about giving up the investigation? And come to that, what had Kent and Coast Television, in the shape of Campbell McLean, had to say about it? They wouldn't be best pleased to have wasted their time.

But then again, Libby reflected, as she had thought yesterday, at least McLean now had a handle on the boorish Budgen and could possibly follow up the lead of illegal farm workers. There had been raids on restaurants employing illegal migrant workers recently, she knew, but had there been any on farms? If there had, they hadn't featured on any news programmes as far as she knew, so perhaps McLean was in for a scoop after all. Especially if it turned out that the body was one of his workers, although, Libby conceded to herself, that would be a coincidence too far, as, indeed, the relationship between the body and the Transnistrian woman suggested by Fran was.

And then there was Jane Maurice's house. Why did Fran feel there was something there? She hadn't even said what, exactly. Something that had happened there? Something was hidden there? Or just someone who lived there? If so, and it had been the hapless Terry, Libby was certain Fran would have picked up on it, and the same applied to the new tenant, Mike Charteris, so that was that. Unless Fran was right, and her brain had shut down as far as picking up any extra sensory messages was concerned. "And that," Libby told Sidney firmly, "would be a tragedy."

With that, she stood up and went inside to phone Harry.

CHAPTER
SIXTEEN

Harry, when appealed to, chose to come to Allhallow's Lane rather than wait for Libby to join him at lunchtime. He appeared, in shorts and sandals, bearing a bunch of old roses that Libby correctly assumed were from the cottage garden behind the house he shared with Peter.

"So, what's it all about?" he asked, settling into the chair recently vacated by Jane, and adjusting a battered straw hat on his head.

"Where on earth did you get that?" asked Libby, distracted.

"I found it in an old trunk of Pete's. He thinks it was his dad's."

"Doesn't he mind you wearing it?"

"Course not. And James thinks it's hilarious."

"Dear Jamie. How is he?" Peter's young brother was a favourite of Libby's.

"Fine. Good to his mother." Harry cackled.

"Oh, yes, how is Millie?"

"Still mad as a box of frogs. But seems to accept Pete and me, now."

"Well, yes. She came to your wedding, didn't she?"

"Try and remember it was a Civil Partnership, dearie. I didn't actually go down the aisle in ivory tulle and a tiara."

"No, all right, but if I want to think of it as a wedding, I can, can't I?"

"Stupid old trout. Yes, you can. I give you permission." Harry took off the hat and waved it in front of his face before returning it to his head. "Now, come on. Tell all."

Libby glanced up at the open spare room window. "Quietly," she said. "I don't want her to hear."

"I'll whisper, then," said Harry.

Libby told him everything that had happened yesterday, including Fran's decision to "retire" and finishing up with Jane's story.

Harry frowned. "And you want me to say what?" he asked in a stage whisper.

"It all seems too much of a coincidence to me," said Libby. "All of it. You agreed with me the other day. About Jane being involved."

"Ah, but *you* didn't agree with *me* at the time," said Harry, fanning himself with his hat again.

"No, I know, because other stuff hadn't happened. Anyway, what do you think?"

Harry looked up into the cherry tree. "Not sure why you're asking," he said.

"Because I want to know if I'm barking up the wrong tree," said Libby.

"Was that a pun?" laughed Harry, tapping the trunk behind him.

"No." Libby scowled at him. "Be serious."

"I am. And again, I'm asking why you want to know? Fran has decided not to be involved any more, therefore you aren't either. Not that you ever had any official standing, anyway. So — why do you want to know what I think?"

Libby stared at him.

"Don't look so taken aback, Lib." Harry leant forward and patted her arm. "It's true, isn't it?"

"Yes," said Libby, glumly.

"You just can't break the habit, that's the problem," continued Harry. "The Miss Marple persona's gotcha!"

"I told you, I'm not a Miss Marple."

"You said that to Ben when we had those accidents at the theatre," said Harry, "but look what's happened since."

"Not my fault," said Libby, looking like a sulky child.

"You needn't have got involved with Fran's auntie last summer, or all the stuff last December."

"But Fran was *asked*," insisted Libby. "And I'm better at ferreting things out than she is. I *had* to be in on it all."

"All right, I'll give you that," said Harry, "but now Fran's given up, no one's going to ask you, so you can stop ferreting."

Libby glowered at him. He laughed.

"So now what do you want to know?" he said.

"Am I seeing connections where there aren't any? Jane's Terry's been attacked, Fran thinks there's something about her house and was she actually *supposed* to see the body? That's all," Libby finished plaintively.

"I think you *are* seeing connections where there aren't any, old love," said Harry. "I know I wondered about Jane when you first told me about it all, but I can't really see it. Just let it alone. You're providing a shoulder for missus upstairs, if anything else happens she's bound to tell you, but until then just get on with being our nice old trout. Why don't you and Ben go away for a few days?"

Libby sighed. "I can't leave Sidney."

"Do that walking stomach good to starve for a few days," said Harry.

"And Ben doesn't feel he can leave the estate. Hetty couldn't manage and Greg's too poorly."

"I didn't think there was that much of the estate left."

"There isn't, but what there is has to be managed. We might be able to get away in the autumn, perhaps, before panto rehearsals start."

"Nah, that's daft. You want to go away now, while the weather's good." Harry looked at his watch. "Well, if you're not going to offer me any refreshment, I'd better get back to the caff. Have to prep up for lunch. Can't do anything in advance in this heat."

"I thought yesterday's rain would have cooled things down." Libby stood up. "Do you want tea? Is it too early for a beer?"

"Regretfully, I must decline, fair lady. But if you're at a loose end when your guest goes you can pop down for a livener with me." Harry stood up and jammed his hat back on his head. "Put those roses in water or they won't last."

"Thanks for the advice," said Libby, as she opened the front door for him.

"Don't be sarcastic," he said, dropping a kiss on her cheek. "See you later."

Well, that's that, thought Libby, after putting the roses into a pretty china jug. An unbiased opinion. Leave it. With a sigh, she went back into the conservatory and prepared to paint.

Jane woke an hour later full of apologies and thanks.

"I'll go home and change now," she said. "You were right — I couldn't have made it earlier. Then I'll go back to the hospital."

"Don't forget to let me know what's happening," said Libby, standing in the doorway once more.

"I won't." Jane got into her car and waving, began reversing slowly down Allhallow's Lane.

Libby went back to her painting for another hour, then reproving herself for alcoholic tendencies, washed her brushes and set off to The Pink Geranium for a drink with Harry.

"Ben and Pete are coming in," he told her, polishing glasses on his apron. "Lunch trade was pretty non-existent, so I sent Donna off. She's off tonight anyway, so she might as well have a nice long afternoon."

Libby sat down at the table in the window and reached behind her to pull down the blind.

"Is this a council of war, or just a warn Libby to stop ferreting party?" she asked.

"Just a get-together." Harry brought a bottle of wine and the glasses over to the table. "The old gang. Also, I think there's something Pete wants to talk to us about."

"That sounds alarming," said Libby, accepting her wine.

When Peter arrived, Libby was surprised to see him followed closely by Lenny, Hetty's brother, and his partner Flo Carpenter, with Ben bringing up the rear.

"Me, it was actually," said Lenny, when they were all settled round the table, and Peter had supplemented the wine with some from his own stock. "My idea." He looked proudly round the table.

"What was?" asked Libby, when nothing else seemed forthcoming.

"The party." He raised a triumphant glass. "For Het."

Ben smiled. "Birthday party."

"Blimey," said Harry.

"Golly," said Libby.

"She'll kick up," said Peter.

Ben nodded. "That's why Lenny's going to do it," he said.

"I don't understand," said Libby. "Won't she like it?"

"You know my mum," said Ben. "Don't hold with no fuss."

"But she always does the tenants' party," said Libby, "and she loves having loads of us to entertain."

"That's different, gal," said Flo. "It's not for her, is it. She feeds us all, looks after old Greg, loves it. Not when it's her, though."

"So how did this come about?" asked Harry, tipping back on his chair until Peter told him off.

"I arst Len what we was doin', and he arst Ben," said Flo.

"And he says she don't want no party. So I says, that's what she thinks." He beamed round the table. "And I says to young Pete, what about the theatre? Then we could do it for a surprise, like."

"And I says yes," said Peter, "but I still say she'll kick up."

"No, she won't," said Ben. "She'll be thrilled to bits. Nobody ever does anything for my mum, and she's had a lot to put up with over the last eighteen months."

Everyone looked solemn and sipped their drinks in silence.

"So when is it?" asked Libby, after a decent interval.

"Saturday week," said Ben. "Not much notice, I know, but Lenny's only just thought of it. I asked mum ages ago, and she said I could take her and Greg to the pub for a meal."

"Not The Pink Geranium?" said Libby, laughing. "How dare she!"

"Doesn't like veggie food," said Harry.

"Bet you're doing the food, though," grinned Libby.

"If I'm arst," he said, looking down his nose.

"I thought," said Peter, "we could do up the stage like a marquee."

"What, with chairs and tables?" Libby was alarmed. "There won't be much room."

"A couple of tables with a few chairs and a long table at the back with the food and booze. People can go and sit in the auditorium."

"We'll get food all over the seats." Libby wrinkled her nose.

"Don't be a killjoy," said Peter. "If we don't mind, why should you?"

"Oh, OK." Libby finished her wine. "What do you want me to do?"

"Think of some entertainment," said Flo. "You know, songs, an' that."

"Ooo!" A smile spread across Libby's face. "Yes!"

"Oh, dear," said Harry.

"Shut up." Libby gave him a poke. "A piano. That's what we need. Well, we've got a piano, haven't we? What we need is a pianist."

"Piano?" Puzzled looks were exchanged, but Flo and Lenny looked delighted.

"That's it, gel," said Lenny. "You 'it the nail on the 'ead!"

"A joanna! A pianna player," said Libby. "Real pub piano, with all the old songs."

"War-time songs," said Flo, "like we used to sing down hoppin'."

"We could do a proper set, too," said Libby, warming to her theme. "An old pub."

"Brilliant." Ben slapped her on the back and made her splutter. "Fantastic idea. I could get on to the brewers —"

"I'll download lyrics," said Peter. "We can have song sheets for those who are too young to remember."

"'Ave you got that old hoppers' hut you had for that play?" asked Lenny.

"No, that's all broken up, now," said Ben, "and anyway, I don't think Mum would be too pleased with that, one way and another."

Lenny looked crestfallen. "No," he said. "Spose yer right."

"We'll stick with the pub," said Peter. "Now, Lib, all you've got to do is find your proper pianna player."

"Oh," said Libby.

CHAPTER
SEVENTEEN

Life for both Libby and Fran slipped slowly back into routine. Libby called everybody in her phone book trying to locate a suitable pianist and came up with no one. By the end of the week, she was panicking.

They had both visited Jane a couple of times to keep her spirits up, as Terry was still in hospital. Libby was smug about her role in bringing them together, but Fran pointed out that living in the same house they probably would have done anyway.

"What, like you and Guy?" scoffed Libby. "I know you said you would have got the cottage regardless of me and therefore met Guy, but you didn't even know it was there, did you?"

"I'd have worked it out," said Fran, looking grumpy. "And you don't *know* that Terry and Jane have got it together, do you?"

"Well, look at how this has affected her. I'd say it was a safe bet." Libby grinned and jabbed Fran in the shoulder. "I'm going to set up as a dating agency. Just call me Dolly."

Saturday morning saw a meeting at the theatre to discuss progress on the party so far. The "pub" set was coming on nicely under the aegis of Ben, with considerable input from Lenny and Flo, Harry had decided on bangers and mash as being appropriate food, with a quantity of vegetarian sausages for those who wanted them.

"Then it isn't too complicated," he told Libby. "We can't have authentic desserts as what there were during the war and just after were horrible, so it's jelly and ice cream as a suitably nostalgic substitute, and a big birthday cake."

"So what about the pianist?" asked Peter, as they all admired the piano decked in red, white and blue bunting.

"I can't find one," muttered Libby.

"Oh, hell," said Ben.

"If anyone takes up the piano these days it's classical or Elton John," Libby said. "No one knows the old stuff. Why would they?"

"But they could read the music, surely?" said Peter.

"I'm not sure I could afford to download about a hundred songs," said Libby, "and there would be bound to be at least a dozen you'd forget."

"I thought you could download songs free from the internet?" said Harry.

"Lyrics, yes, but not music." Ben sat down on one of the benches. "I don't know why, but I thought it would be easy."

"I wonder if any of the other drama societies could come up with a pianist? They'd be the best bet," said Libby. "I don't know why I didn't think of that."

"Have you got any contacts with other societies?" asked Peter.

"I can try," said Libby, "but it will have to wait until I get home and get my phone book."

But the next call on her mobile put pianists right out of Libby's head.

"It's Jane," said a breathless voice as Libby was walking back down the Manor drive.

"Hello, Jane," said Libby. "How's Terry?"

"Well, that's the thing, Libby. He's coming home."

"Blimey, that was quick," said Libby. "I thought head injuries were kept in for much longer than that."

"I don't know about that, I wasn't told everything. His parents came down and the doctors talked to them."

"Were they nice?"

"The parents?" Jane hesitated. "Oh, yes. Very grateful, you know."

"So did you want to ask me something?"

"Well, yes. This is a bit awkward."

Libby stopped walking and waited. "Well, go on, then," she said. "What's awkward and what do you want me to do?"

"I wondered if you were doing anything later on this afternoon?"

"Nothing I can't put off," said Libby.

"Only, you see, Terry's coming home in an ambulance, and I said I'd be there to, er, look after him."

"Yes?" prompted Libby. "Why do you need me?"

"Because of Mike."

"Mike?"

"Charteris. My new tenant."

"Oh?" Libby's ears pricked up.

"You see, he's been coming up to see me all week and he said he'd help me with Terry today."

"Ah." Libby smiled to herself. "I see. So you want me to come along so you can say, no thanks I've already got help?"

"Exactly." Libby heard Jane's sigh of relief. "You seemed the right person to ask."

"OK." Libby made a fast decision. "What time do you want me?"

"Whenever you can come. I don't know what time Terry will get here."

Interpreting this to mean "come as soon as you can", Libby said, "When I've had some lunch I'll be on my way."

She called Ben as she continued her walk home, telling him she would be back that evening as soon as she could. As they had no plans to do anything other than watch television and perhaps pop out to the pub for last orders, this wasn't a problem.

Ali at the eight-til-late had started making fresh sandwiches, and Libby called in on her way past to pick up a ham and mustard on brown. When she'd eaten this, washed down with a glass of water, she cleaned her teeth, dragged a brush through her hair and left the cottage.

On the way to Nethergate, she pondered the situation. Fran, who had seen Mike Charteris, reported that he was slightly older than Terry, but good-looking nonetheless. A good-looking, single (presumably) man exhibiting concern for his young attractive landlady was

169

not notably peculiar, but if the landlady had already fallen for one of her other tenants who was temporarily incapacitated, it would undoubtedly be unwelcome, unless, of course, the landlady had femme-fatale leanings. Which, obviously, Jane didn't.

It being Saturday in high season, Libby eventually had to park in the car park at the end of The Tops rather than in the street outside Jane's house. By the time she rang the door bell, she was hot and sticky.

"Lead me to a glass of water," she said as Jane opened the door.

"Sorry, Libby." Jane shut the door. "Did you have to park miles away?"

"Far enough," said Libby. "Now I just want to get to the top of these stairs and sit down."

"It's really kind of you," said Jane, after she'd supplied the required glass of water. "Only Mike kept coming up to see if I was all right, or if I'd heard any more from the hospital, and — oh, I don't know — it made me a bit uncomfortable."

"And he wanted to be here to help today."

"Yes." Jane nodded. "I know he's only trying to be helpful, but I don't know him, and —" she broke off.

"And?" prompted Libby, after a moment.

"I can't explain it." Jane looked down at her hands. "He seemed to keep trying to get into the flat. It frightened me a bit."

Libby suppressed a smile. "You are an attractive young woman, Jane."

Colour crept up Jane's neck. "Well, I don't know about that," she said, clearing her throat, "but it didn't quite seem like that, if you know what I mean."

"Do you mean he was threatening?"

"No." Jane shook her head. "I can't put my finger on it. Perhaps I'm just not very good with men."

"Except Terry," said Libby naughtily.

"Well, I've known him a lot longer," said Jane, her colour now rising to her hairline.

"But only just got to know him properly," said Libby.

"Yes." Jane looked up. "Thanks to you, actually, Libby."

One in the eye for Fran, thought Libby triumphantly.

"Oh, I'm sure you would have — um — got together eventually," she said aloud.

"Well, I'm really glad you asked him to come up and help. Not," she added hastily, "that things have gone very far, but we've had a couple of meals and been out for a drink." She smiled. "It's been lovely."

"And then this has to happen," said Libby.

Jane's face fell. "I know. And I still can't understand it."

"Did you ever find out whether they took his wallet?"

"Oh, yes, apparently, and his cash and keys. That's why I had to leave the police my pass key that first night."

"Right," said Libby. "And no witnesses?"

"No. Mike didn't see anybody as he came along the road, but it must have only just happened, because Mrs Finch had brought her bin round to the front door only minutes before."

"Oh, of course, Tuesday was collection day. So this bloke took a real chance, then?"

"No more than normal, I suppose." Jane shrugged. "The muggings I report on could have been seen by any number of people. They're just chancers."

"And Terry was just coming in, too, you thought, because all his lights were off."

"Yes."

"Then it's odd that Mrs Finch didn't see him, too."

"If she didn't see the mugger, why would she have seen Terry?"

"True. But the other funny thing is, if Mike was walking home, presumably from the direction of the town, why didn't he see them ahead of him?"

"The mugger must have gone, and he wouldn't have seen Terry until he got right up to the steps, would he?"

"No." Libby shook her head regretfully.

"What are you getting at, Libby?"

"Nothing." Libby stood up and went to look out of the window, just as Jane's front door bell rang.

"Is it the ambulance?" Jane sprang up from her chair.

"No, I can't see who it is," said Libby, craning her neck.

"Oh, God, it'll be Mike again." Jane's shoulders drooped.

"I'll go," said Libby briskly and started out of the door before Jane could stop her, hoping it was Mike, and not some perfectly innocent visitor.

Just outside the door of Jane's flat stood a good-looking man with greying dark hair.

"Oh!" he said, looking surprised.

172

"I'm sorry," said Libby with a quizzical look. "Can I help you?"

"I just came to ask if Jane was all right. I believe Terry's coming home today. I'm one of the tenants." His voice was deep, with a hint of a London accent.

"Yes, she's fine, thank you," said Libby. "I'm here to help with Terry. But thank you for offering."

"Are you Jane's mother?" He peered at her.

Libby suppressed indignation and simply smiled. "No, I'm a friend," she said. "Thank you so much for coming." And, still smiling, she gently closed the door.

"Thanks, Libby," said Jane, when Libby returned to the sitting room. "Did he seem angry?"

"Angry?" Libby raised her eyebrows. "No. Why on earth should he have been?"

"I don't know." Jane shook her head again. "That's part of the feeling I always get. That he's angry that I don't let him in."

"Just a determined suitor," said Libby, although she privately wondered if Jane would be safe alone after she'd gone. Silly, she apostrophized herself. Jane had been alone here all week, except for Mrs Finch in the basement. "What else do you know about him? The agents checked his references, didn't they?"

"Oh, yes. He's staying down here doing some sort of contract work. He has a flat in London, but didn't want to commute. He'll only be here for a few weeks, but I thought, you know —"

"A bird in the hand," Libby finished for her.

"Exactly. And the agents are trying to find me a permanent tenant. Unless —" she broke off again.

"Unless what?"

"I sell the house."

Libby was surprised. She hadn't expected that.

"Why would you want to sell it?"

"If things don't work out for me in Nethergate I'd be silly to stay here. I wouldn't get much for the house with sitting tenants, but it would be enough for a reasonable deposit for a flat back in London."

"When you say, work out for you in Nethergate, what do you mean?"

"Well," said Jane, "as I told you, I haven't exactly made many friends here, have I? And the job really hasn't got any prospects of promotion. So if things stay as they are, there isn't much to keep me."

"What about Terry?"

Jane's colour returned in a rush. "I don't know," she said.

As Libby heard a vehicle drawing up outside, Jane was saved the embarrassment of continuing the conversation. The door bell rang, and the next twenty minutes were taken up with getting Terry into his flat, after which Libby tactfully left while Jane fussed around him, and once more managed to divert Mike Charteris from his obvious intention to help.

CHAPTER
EIGHTEEN

Terry was persuaded to eat the fish and chips Libby fetched for them all, and perked up enough for her to feel comfortable about asking a few questions.

"I don't know much," he said, prodding a chip into a puddle of tomato sauce.

"You didn't see anyone, obviously?"

"I don't know." He frowned underneath the bandages. "I can't remember anything except walking up the road towards the house. The doc said that was normal."

"Handy for the attacker. Wonder if he knew that."

"Knew that Terry wouldn't remember?" Jane looked startled.

"Well, even I know about post-traumatic amnesia," said Libby.

"Really?"

"I think this kind is called retrograde," explained Libby. "And if Terry remembers walking up the road, it isn't too bad. It means he can remember events only a few minutes before the attack. Isn't that right, Terry?"

Terry started to nod, and winced. "Yeah. I saw the other kind in the army. Nasty."

"The other kind?" Jane turned towards him.

"Don't remember anything after the attack. You get guys doing all sorts of things they wouldn't do normally. We had one who took all his clothes off and kept calling for his mum. He didn't know anything about it afterwards. But he couldn't work, either."

Jane looked appalled. "I never knew."

"Most people don't know that bit," said Libby, "but a lot of people know about the ordinary sort, where you lose the memory of what actually happened."

"What's your point, exactly?"

"Well, whoever did it could rely on Terry not being able to give evidence about it."

"But I should remember eventually," said Terry. "The doc said."

"When it's too late, though," said Libby. "What have the police said?"

"That's a bit odd, actually." Terry tried to push himself up against the pillows and Jane rushed to help. "This flat was searched."

"I know," said Jane. "I gave them my key."

"Not by the police," said Terry.

"You mean —?" Jane was shocked.

"They'd already used your keys before Mike came along, then." Libby nodded to herself. "But what about Mrs Finch? She'd only just been out with her bin, Jane tells me, and you weren't on the steps then."

"I don't know." Terry's face was losing colour. "But someone searched my flat."

"Was anything taken?"

"Don't know." Terry closed his eyes and Jane frowned at Libby.

176

"OK." Libby stood up. "Can I do anything else for you, Jane? If not, I'll be off home before it gets dark."

Jane smiled in relief. "No, nothing, thanks, Libby. It was so good of you to come."

"Yeah, thanks," said Terry, briefly opening his eyes.

"There's something odd about this," said Libby quietly, as Jane saw her to the front door.

Jane nodded. "I know. I'll see if he knows anything else in the morning. He needs to rest now." She looked down at her hands. "Um — you're suspicious of Mike, aren't you?"

"Perhaps I shouldn't be, but it all strikes me as a bit odd and coincidental," said Libby. "Although I can't for the life of me think why Mike should steal from Terry, or what he might want to find in his flat."

"But you think he took the flat deliberately?"

"Well, maybe. But that would mean he knew Terry already, and that he lived here. If so, why hadn't he tried to burgle him before?"

Jane looked up quickly. "There was a burglary before," she said.

"Really? When?"

"Ages ago. Before I moved in here. I should have said attempted burglary, because no one actually got in. The front door had been jemmied, but that was it. The police thought whoever it was had been disturbed."

"So only Mrs Finch and Terry were here, then?"

"Yes."

"So it looks as though it's Terry they're after?"

"They?"

"Whoever it is, then," said Libby impatiently. "Have you told the police about this?"

Jane shrugged her shoulders and spread her hands. "Tell them what? This is pure speculation, Libby." She looked uncomfortable as she said this, and Libby realised belatedly that she was doing it again. Pushing her nose in where it wasn't wanted and putting two and two together and making a hundred and five.

"Yes, you're right." She sighed. "It's the amateur detective in me. I can't seem to stop."

"If I had my newspaper hat on, I'd be after that story like a jack-rabbit," said Jane, with a little laugh, "but in real life, I'd have to say it looks like complete fantasy."

"And it's how rumours start," agreed Libby, nodding. "Say that to anybody else, and it turns into Chinese whispers, and the next thing you know is poor Mike being hounded out of town."

"Exactly." Jane leaned forward and gave Libby an unexpected kiss on the cheek. "Thanks so much for coming. I promise I'll ask Terry if he knows anything else in the morning and let you know."

"If you're sure," said Libby. "And now I'd better go."

She walked back up to the car park, now almost empty in the gathering twilight, and looked out over Nethergate bay. From here, she could see The Alexandria just below and to her left, then further down The Swan on the town square, then Harbour Street, and The Sloop overlooking the harbour itself. To her right, where the open fields of The Tops used to be, the edge of the new estate and the beginning of Canongate Drive, where Ben's friend old Jim lived.

Libby peered down at the people strolling along the promenade and Harbour Street, lit by the fairy lights, and wondered if Guy and Fran were down there. She had a sudden desire for normality and safety, turned hurriedly and got into the car.

"What's the name of Jane's house?" Fran asked Libby over the phone on Sunday morning.

"The name? Has it got one?"

"It's only a short terrace, and each one has a name on the stone lintel above the door. Didn't you notice?"

"No, can't say I did. Why do you want to know?"

"If I said I wanted to send flowers you wouldn't believe me, would you?"

"No," said Libby baldly.

"I thought not," said Fran with a sigh. "I wanted to look it up on the internet, that's all."

"Why?"

"To find out why I've got this feeling about it."

"Perhaps you were doing what's-it-called, precognition? About Terry's accident?"

"No. I'd have seen it, wouldn't I? Or felt something about him, rather than the house."

"Right," said Libby, grudgingly. "So you're going to investigate this, rather than our body?"

Fran sighed again. "No, Libby. I just want to know if the house has a history, that's all. But if you don't know, I'll take a walk up there and see what the name is myself."

"Will you see Jane?"

"No, I don't think so. She'll have her hands full with Terry, won't she? How was he?"

Libby told her what had happened the previous day, reluctantly including her own suspicions, and eventual retractions. Fran laughed.

"You're learning," she said.

Switching off the phone, Libby looked thoughtfully at her own computer. If Fran was going to do it, so could she.

She was checking emails before searching for any reference to Cliff Terrace when her phone rang again.

"Libby, it's Jane."

"Hello," said Libby, surprised that after yesterday Jane would have called, despite her promise. "How's Terry?"

"Much better," said Jane, and Libby wondered if she was blushing. "Mind you, he was awake at six. Hospital conditioning." She gave a little laugh.

"Good job you stayed down there, then," said Libby.

"Er, yes." Jane cleared her throat and Libby grinned. "What I wanted to tell you, though, was that one of the policemen came round earlier. Terry asked if I could stay while they talked, and afterwards I told Terry I wanted to tell you. He didn't mind."

"Oh, right." Now Libby was even more surprised.

"Apparently, it turns out that they think Terry was mugged much earlier than when Mike found him."

"How could that be?" asked Libby. "Why didn't Mrs Finch see him?"

"They seem to think he was in the hall. They found traces of blood. Then he was dumped outside on the steps."

"And his flat was searched while he was unconscious in the hall?"

"Yes."

"So do they think he was dragged outside to make it look like a random mugging?" said Libby.

"Yes, that's it exactly, but listen, that's not all." Jane paused and Libby bit her lip in frustration.

"Well, what?" she said.

"It was searched again this week!"

"*What?*"

"I know. Unbelievable, or what? It must have happened when everyone except Mrs Finch was out. Well, obviously Terry was, but when Mike and I were at work, or maybe when I was at the hospital and Mike was out. I know he goes to The Swan to eat most evenings. That's where he'd been on Monday night."

"So how do they know?"

"They'd secured the door, they had to come and unlock it yesterday for Terry to come home and that's when they discovered it."

"But discovered what, exactly? Was the room trashed, or what?"

"No, this detective said that both times you would hardly know anything was wrong, except that the first time a couple of drawers and cupboards had been forced — and window frames, oddly. Then yesterday, obviously their own arrangements had been disturbed and there were other tell-tale signs in the flat." Jane sighed. "So it looks like you were right, after all."

"That someone's after Terry, you mean?"

"Yes. That seems to be the way the police are thinking, anyway. But they can't find out why, and Terry doesn't know. He hasn't got a record, he was in the army and had nothing to do with this area until he got his job."

"Did you find out why he came here?"

"I think," said Jane slowly, "that he came here with a girl."

"Ah."

"Yes. I don't want to question him about it, though. It's not my place."

"No, of course not," said Libby, grinning.

"Anyway, I thought you'd like to know," said Jane. "If Terry thinks of anything else, he says I can tell you."

"That's good of him, but why?"

"He knows all about your other cases. I told him. And he likes you."

"Does he?" Libby found herself smiling. "That's nice."

"He said —" Libby heard Jane take a deep breath "— you'd brought us together."

"Aaah!" Wisely, Libby refrained from making a triumphant comment, but saved it up to repeat to Fran. "Well, that's lovely, and now I mustn't keep you from him."

"Oh, it's OK, he's sleeping. He's going to get up when he wakes, and I'm going to do a proper Sunday roast." Jane sounded so cheerful, Libby could hardly

182

reconcile her with the rather mousey creature she'd met a couple of weeks earlier.

"What number Cliff Terrace are you, by the way? I think Fran was thinking of sending flowers? Or has the house got a name?" Libby privately congratulated herself on this strategy.

"There's really no need," said Jane, "but it's very nice of her. It's got both actually, number two and Peel House. Melbourne, Peel, Palmerston and Disraeli, all Victorian prime ministers. They were built while Disraeli was in office I think, or there might have been one more — Gladstone."

"Or Salisbury," said Libby, "and even Russell. He was before Peel, wasn't he?"

"Oh, goodness, I don't know," said Jane. "Anyway. That's it. I think there's even a piece about it in an online magazine about Nethergate."

After ringing off, Libby could hardly wait to track down the magazine article Jane mentioned. Peel House itself was slightly more difficult, as there seemed to be a plethora of Peel Houses all over the web, but eventually Libby found the Nethergate online magazine, and sure enough, a short article about Cliff Terrace, which had originally been called Victoria Place, apparently. When the town expanded, the promenade, being more important, was renamed Victoria Place, and Cliff Terrace given its new name.

The phone rang again.

"Found it," said Fran.

"So have I," said Libby.

"What?"

"I've found Peel House on the internet. Jane just called to tell me something about Terry and his accident and told me the name so I looked it up. I've got it in front of me."

"What, exactly?"

"Peel House, second in a terrace of four named Cliff Terrace."

"And?"

"Well, that's more or less all," said Libby. "Why? What have you found?"

"Peel House was owned by Jessica Maurice —"

"We know that," interrupted Libby, "she was Jane's aunt."

"Jessica Maurice," continued Fran, "the wartime mistress of Fascist sympathiser and Mosley follower Simon Madderling."

CHAPTER
NINETEEN

Libby gasped. "Golly," she said.

"Do you know anything about him?" asked Fran.

"No, but I know about Mosley, obviously. Must have been famous, this Simon — what did you say? — Madeleine?"

"Madderling. Yes, he was. At the time, anyway. I'd heard of him vaguely, but there's a whole potted history of him on the net. You can look him up yourself."

"Hold on," said Libby, and typed the name into the search engine with one hand. Sure enough, pages of results came up.

"If you go to the second site listed, you'll see," said Fran. "That's the one that mentions Jane's aunt, but it looks as though this wasn't made public until very recently."

Libby, scanning the article quickly, said, "How did you come up with the connection to the house? I mean, does it say anywhere 'Jessica Maurice, owner of Peel House, mistress of etc etc.'?"

"No. I put in Peel House followed by Jessica Maurice and came up with various hits, but none together. It's easy enough to follow, though, if you happen to want to know."

"And you did?"

"Well, of course." Fran sounded much happier than she had for some time, thought Libby. "I knew there was something about that house, and this is it. I would bet that Madderling bought that house for Jessica during the war. I was also sure, and this is actually what I found out about Jessica herself, that she was some sort of government agent. Madderling disappeared in '43, I think, and was never traced. The popular theories were that he'd been disposed of by the British government or the fascist fraternity."

"But I thought the fascists were all imprisoned during the war?" said Libby.

"Not all of them. The high flyers were, of course, like Oswald and Diana Mosley and the members of the Right Club."

"The Right Club? What was that?"

"Hang on — here we are — 'The main object of the Right Club was to oppose and expose the activities of Organized Jewry'."

"Good God!" gasped Libby.

"That's what Fascism was, basically. Extreme right. Anyway, you know enough about Fascism to know about Cable Street and William Joyce and stuff —"

"Lord Haw Haw?"

"Yes. Anyway, it turns out that Madderling was an MI5 agent who infiltrated the Right Club. There were others, Joan Miller for one."

"Who she?"

"A former deb. There were lots of them working for the government in one capacity or other. From what I can piece together, she and Jessica were friends."

"So that's why you think she was an agent, too?"

"It seems logical, doesn't it?"

"Yes, it does. Jane doesn't know any of this, does she?"

"No, I'm pretty sure she doesn't," said Fran. "I told you when I asked her what her aunt did and how did she afford the house, she said she'd never thought about it. She said there'd been some talk in the family about a man during the war, but that was it."

"And this man was what's-his-name?"

"Simon Madderling."

"Well." Libby sat back in her chair and drummed her fingers on the table. "That's all very interesting, but why do you think that's why you had one of your moments about the house?"

"I'm not quite sure yet, but it stands to reason, doesn't it, that a house with that sort of history will have some kind of event attached to it?"

"Ye-es," said Libby slowly.

"Well, it does," said Fran firmly.

"Have an event?"

"I'm certain of it," said Fran, once again sounding so much like her old self that Libby almost cheered.

"That's a definite, then," said Libby. "And does it link with the attack on Terry?"

"Ah, now that I'm not sure about. It certainly wasn't the event that drew me to the house, but it doesn't exactly feel out of kilter."

"I'm not sure I understood all that," said Libby. "Was it a yes or no?"

"A maybe," said Fran.

"Oh."

"Anyway," said Fran, "what about Terry? You said Jane called this morning?"

Libby recounted the conversation with Jane, adding her own questions to Terry from the previous evening. She also included the positive comments on her matchmaking.

"Told you so," she concluded. "Matchmaker extraordinaire, that's me!"

"You said there was an attempted burglary before?" asked Fran, ignoring this.

"Yes," Libby sighed. "That's why I thought — and so do the police, apparently — it must have something to do with Terry."

"Hmm," said Fran.

"Hmm what?"

"I don't know. Let me work on it."

"You've obviously been working on it for some time already."

"Since yesterday evening," said Fran.

"Wow. But you only asked me about Peel House this morning."

"I started researching Jessica last night."

"So you got all that stuff about the Right Club then?"

"Some of it," said Fran.

"Right. Oh, and by the way, in order to obtain the information you didn't want —"

"Eh?"

"The name of Peel House."

"Oh," said Fran.

"I told Jane I needed the number of the house because you were thinking of sending flowers."

"Oh, right. Well, I can't do that on a Sunday, can I?"

"No," said Libby, "but I can go and get some nice ones from the supermarket and take them round from both of us."

"Lib, be careful. Don't start interrogating Jane about this. Or Terry, come to that."

"What do you take me for?" said Libby indignantly. "Of course I won't."

"I know you, don't forget," said Fran. "Just wait until I've done some more research. Oh, and you don't happen to know if Jane's parents are still alive, do you?"

"No, but if her father had been, surely he would have got Peel House. Jessica treated him like a son, Jane said, didn't she?"

"Yes, that's right. Bother. He would have known more than Jane."

"Her mother might, if she's alive."

"Why shouldn't she be? She'd be our age, wouldn't she?"

"Probably. I'll let you ask Jane about that."

"Gee, thanks."

"Will you go today?"

"I can do. Before lunch, though. Het's doing us a roast and Lenny and Flo are coming."

"That's twice in a week she's fed you," said Fran. "Is she buttering you up?"

"No, she just likes cooking for people. And I think she gets a bit lonely. Ben's not there most of the time, and Greg's not much company these days."

"Poor old Greg," said Fran. "Is there a prognosis?"

"I don't know. Ben just says he's getting frailer."

"But still a charmer," said Fran.

Libby called Ben to ask what time she should be at The Manor, then got into Romeo the Renault to drive to the supermarket. She didn't like forsaking Ali at the eight-til-late, but the only flowers he ever had were of the garage forecourt variety. Having purchased a large and impressive bouquet and resisted the lure of the food aisles, she went on to Nethergate and parked on the yellow line outside Coastguard Cottage.

"I thought you could sign the card," she said to a surprised Fran. "Or would you like to come with me? I'm not going to be long. I've got to be at The Manor by one thirty."

Guy appeared at Fran's shoulder. She blushed.

"Been helping with the research, Guy?" asked Libby cheerfully.

"Yes, it's fascinating, isn't it? Just shows how little we know about the war years." He gave Fran's arm a squeeze. "Why don't you go with Libby? I'll book a table at The Swan for us for when you get back."

"OK." Fran was obviously still hesitant. "Let me do the card, anyway."

They went inside Fran's living room, where she found a pen and added something to Libby's message.

"Come on, then," said Libby. "Quicker we go, the quicker we'll get back. And you can keep me in check."

"In check?" queried Guy.

190

"Asking too many questions," grinned Libby. "You know what I'm like."

Outside Peel House, Fran stared up at the terrace.

"It's attractive, isn't it?" she said.

"It is. And a gorgeous position. They aren't terribly big, though. I wonder who lived in them when they were built?"

"Merchants, I think. And I expect they became houses families took for the season."

"Oh, like Bella's Shepherd family?" Libby referred to an investigation the pair of them had become involved with last winter.

"Exactly. Kitchen in the basement, nursery and servants in the attics."

"Well, it's the attics where Jane lives now, and Terry's got the first floor. That's where they'll be."

Libby pressed Terry's bell and Jane's breathy voice came through the grille.

"It's us, Jane," said Libby. "Bearing flowers."

Terry was sitting in a chair in his living room looking self-conscious.

"Thanks," he mumbled. "Nice of you."

Jane looked at him proudly, like a mother with a precocious toddler. "I'll put them in the kitchen sink until I find a vase," she said. "Would you two like tea or coffee?"

"No, thanks," said Fran before Libby could accept. "We won't hold you up."

"So, did you think of anything else, Terry?" asked Libby, while Jane took the flowers away.

"No. Nothing was stolen. Can't understand it."

"Libby said drawers and a cupboard were attacked, is that right?" asked Fran.

"Yeah. And a window frame." He shook his head and winced. "Mad."

Libby noticed Fran's face was alight with interest. "Do you think it's the house they were interested, not you?" she said.

"The house?" Jane had come back into the room. "Why on earth would it be the house?"

"I don't know. I know nothing about it, except that your aunt owned it."

"Would your parents know anything about it, Jane?" asked Fran. "You said your father was like a son to Jessica."

"My father died years ago," said Jane, "or he would have got the house. I don't think mother liked Aunt Jessica very much, although she did her duty by her. It was Mum who organised the home. And it was a very good one."

That confirms that, thought Libby.

"Anyway, what's the house got to do with it?" asked Jane. "It was Terry who was attacked."

"Just a thought, as nothing of his was stolen," said Fran carelessly. "Anyway, glad to see you're recovering, Terry." She stood up. "We'll leave you in peace."

Libby opened her mouth to protest, but stood up silently on meeting Fran's steely gaze.

"Bye, Jane," she said. "Call if you need anything."

"So?" she said to Fran as soon as they were back in Romeo. "What was that about?"

192

"I'm going to phone Connell," said Fran, getting out her mobile. "It's the house. There's something there."

"Connell's got nothing to do with this case," said Libby, starting the car. "He's doing the body on the island, if you've forgotten."

"I know, but he'll know who's handling this case."

"Which is probably only down as GBH and burglary, not murder."

"GBH is serious enough," said Fran, holding the phone to her ear. "Now shut up."

"Ian's not on duty at the moment," she said, switching off after a short conversation. "But they'll pass on a message."

"And what do you expect to happen then?" asked Libby, drawing up outside Coastguard Cottage. "I don't suppose you're Ian's favourite person after letting him down over the body on the island."

"I'm sure he understands what I do isn't an exact science," said Fran, unfastening her seat belt.

"At the beginning of the week you had convinced yourself it wasn't a science at all," said Libby. "In fact, it didn't even exist, if you mean your own particular brand of science."

"I know," sighed Fran, pausing with her hand on the door handle. "But as soon as I realised that this feeling about Peel House was getting stronger and stronger, I had to give in to it."

"And now you've justified it."

Fran nodded.

"So what about that connection you invented about the body being connected to our Transnistrian girl?"

"I was just looking for connections — anything. It was tenuous, to say the least, wasn't it?" She smiled faintly at Libby.

"I'll say! But interesting. Pity we couldn't follow that one up as well."

"Lib," warned Fran. "Don't go trying to investigate things on your own. It's nothing to do with us. You're welcome to help me with the research into Jessica Maurice and Simon Madderling if you really want to."

"Of course I want to, it's fascinating, as Guy said. But you must tell Jane. It wouldn't be fair to keep her in the dark."

"No." Fran looked thoughtful. "But I'd really like to speak to her mother first. I wonder how I could manage that?"

"I'll find out," said Libby. "I'm good at that sort of thing."

"Just don't get into trouble," said Fran opening the car door. "You're good at that, too."

CHAPTER
TWENTY

However, it wasn't as easy as Libby had hoped to trace Jane's mother. Short of asking outright, she couldn't decide which way to go. She didn't even know Jane's birth date, so the Family Records office route was closed to her. When she got back to Allhallow's Lane after lunch at The Manor, she spent the afternoon on the computer trying to work out how to do it, but decided eventually there was no way it was possible. She phoned Fran.

"Can't get Jane's mother's name without asking Jane," she said. "What do you want to do now?"

"Ask Jane, I suppose. Damn."

"You'll have to tell her why."

There was a short silence. "Is she going back to work tomorrow?" Fran asked eventually.

"I expect so. She was only off for one day last week. Terry seems well enough to cope on his own during the day."

"It'll have to be today, then. I'll ring her."

"Do you want me to do it?"

"No, I will." Fran sighed. "I'll ring you back and let you know how I get on."

"What's going on now?" asked Ben coming in through the kitchen. "Are you interfering again?"

"No, I'm not!" Libby scowled at him. "I tried to find something out for Fran and couldn't, so she's going to do it on her own."

Ben looked dubious. "Is this to do with the body?"

"No. Something entirely different and nothing to do with the police."

"What, then? I thought Fran had retired."

"So did she, but it appears that her psychic energy, or whatever it is, is still in full working order." Libby thought for a moment. "But not *to* order, if you see what I mean."

"I always thought that was the case," said Ben, sitting down on the cane sofa with a creak. "We really must get you a better sofa."

"When she did stuff for you and Goodall and Smythe it *was* to order," objected Libby.

"Just wandering round buildings to see if anything came to her. Bit different."

"I suppose so," said Libby.

"So what is it that's got her interested this time?"

"Jane Maurice's house," said Libby.

"Ah! See, that's obviously what she does best. Houses."

"But it's what she's discovered that's so interesting," Libby went on, coming to sit in the armchair. "It turns out Jane's aunt who left her the house was the mistress of some famous bloke in the war."

"Famous bloke?"

"Fascist sympathiser, but a double agent working for MI5. Simon something." Libby wrinkled her brow.

"Madderling?" said Ben. "Good God, that is high flying."

"You've heard of him?"

"Yes, although I don't know much. I read a lot about the politics of the Second World War when I was younger. But it's only recently it came out that he was a double agent."

"Yes, that's what Fran said. Anyway, she thinks there's something in the house, and that's why Terry was attacked."

"Lost me." Ben shook his head.

"Terry was attacked and his flat searched, although nothing was taken except his wallet and keys."

Ben frowned. "Why attack Terry? Jane would be the one to attack, surely?"

"Apparently there was an attempted burglary before Jane moved in. Perhaps whoever it is is trying the flats one by one."

"If they do, it's going to look very suspicious, isn't it?"

"Well, that's Fran's theory, anyway. She's phoning Jane to tell her all about her aunt right now."

"You mean Jane didn't know?" Ben lifted his eyebrows in surprise.

"Doesn't seem like it." Libby stood up. "Tea?"

It wasn't until the tea was poured that the phone rang.

"What happened?" asked Libby.

"She was — well, she was —"

"Gobsmacked?" suggested Libby.

"You could put it like that! Anyway, she confirmed that she hadn't known anything about it, and was going straight upstairs to check it all out on the computer."

"So what about her mother?"

"She wants to talk to her herself." Fran made an irritated sound. "Which I really didn't want. I don't suppose the mother will talk to me after that."

"Why not?"

"Oh, Lib, can you imagine? Jane saying, 'Well, now you've told me all about it there's this strange psychic woman who wants to talk to you'?"

"If she's a sceptic Jane will convince her."

"I haven't given Jane much reason to trust me, have I?"

"What about your blackout on the *Dolphin*?"

"Not much to go on, is it?"

"Buck up, Fran," said Libby. "At least Jane might find out a few more facts for you. And then you can tell Ian in the morning."

"That's if her mother tells her anything, and if she does it tonight."

"Well, there's nothing else you can do, now," said Libby, "so just get on with having a nice Sunday evening and forget all about it."

"That's rich, coming from you," said Ben, when she switched off the phone.

"I shall," said Libby. "I shall sit on the sofa with you and watch mindless television all evening."

"There's a charity quiz at the pub," said Ben.

"Even better," said Libby. "Let's go and win."

The red light on the answerphone was winking when they returned, having come a respectable third in the quiz. Libby pressed the button.

"Lib, Jane phoned back and says her mother will talk to us," came Fran's voice.

"Us!" said Libby to Ben.

"So I've to ring in the morning to arrange a convenient time. Can you ring first thing and tell me when you've got time to go up to London? Bye."

"She doesn't say what Jane told her," said Libby, following Ben into the kitchen, where he was collecting whisky and glasses for a nightcap.

"She'll tell you in the morning. Don't worry about it," said Ben. "You've got your wish, you're on the investigating trail again, so just relax and enjoy it."

"Is that your way of telling me I'm a pathetic, obsessive nerd?"

"Absolutely," said Ben.

"You haven't yet told me what Jane said about her mother," said Libby, as Fran turned what Guy called her roller-skate onto the Canterbury Road the following morning.

"I haven't had time, have I?" Fran changed into fifth gear and settled back. "It isn't much."

"Well, what did she say when you told her about Jessica?"

"She was angry at first. She started telling me off for prying into her business, until I said it was all available on the internet and I'd come across it accidentally because I was interested in the house."

"Which was true," said Libby.

"In a way, yes, it was. So then she calmed down and asked me about it. You remember she said her mother didn't like Jessica? Well, she said she first thought that when she was a child and heard this vague mention of a man. It would make sense, wouldn't it? It was dreadful in those days to live in sin, and especially if the man was known to be a spy."

"But he wasn't known as a spy, then," objected Libby. "He was only known as a Fascist sympathiser, and follower of Mosley."

"Well, even worse," said Fran. "I expect most ordinary people thought any Fascist sympathisers *were* spies."

"We can put her mind at rest about that, anyway," said Libby. "He was a spy, but on our side." She looked out of the side window. "I wonder what happened to him?"

It was lunchtime by the time they hit London and Fran made her way along the Embankment towards Battersea.

"Where is it?" asked Libby.

"Somewhere between Battersea Park and Wandsworth Road," said Fran. "Not my side of the river."

"It is mine, but I don't think I could find my way round there any more. Wandsworth and Wimbledon, possibly, but not this bit. And even if I could, they'll have turned all the roads one way and shut them off, won't they?"

"True. Anyway, you've got the road map I printed off, so once we get across the bridge you can direct me."

Libby glowered at her, but took the maps and tried to figure out where they were. Across the bridge, and Battersea Park looked familiar, but that was about all. However, they eventually found 31 Jubilee Road, one of the Edwardian terraced houses that proliferate all across London, where Jane's mother lived in the downstairs flat. After finding a parking space several streets away, by the time they rang the doorbell they were nearly fifteen minutes late.

"Mrs Maurice?" said Fran, as the door opened. "I'm so sorry we're late. We couldn't find a parking space."

The woman gave a very small smile. Libby could see traces of Jane in her face, but it was stronger and less good-humoured. Flawless make-up could not disguise the crêpey lines, and the rigidly set hair could not completely cover the glimpses of pink scalp beneath. Only a few years older than Libby and Fran, she seemed like a completely different generation.

"I understand you want to talk about my husband's Aunt Jessica," she said, after ushering them into a sitting room at the back of the house, whose tall French windows opened onto the garden, as rigidly arranged as Mrs Maurice herself.

"If you don't mind," said Fran. Libby was wondering why this woman had even allowed a phone call about Jessica, let alone a whole interview. The answer soon became clear.

"First you must tell me why, and how you much you already know," said Mrs Maurice.

Fran took a deep breath and glanced at Libby.

"I'm sure Jane has told you about the attack on one of her tenants?" she began.

"No," said Mrs Maurice, looking surprised. Libby wasn't.

"He was attacked last week, and it appears that the attacker wanted to search the house. There had been an attempt over a year ago, before Jane moved in, as well."

Mrs Maurice said nothing, but gave a slight nod.

"Mrs Sarjeant and I researched Peel House on the internet to see if there was any reason that the house could be important, or hold some sort of secret. That was when we came across the fact that it was owned by Jessica Maurice and had, in fact —" and here Libby saw a slight involuntary movement of Fran's hands "— been bought for her by her lover Simon Madderling."

Mrs Maurice's face had tightened into even more of a mask than it had been before. Scored a hit there, Fran, thought Libby.

"Then there is very little else I can tell you." The woman fixed her eyes on a point above Fran's head. "Jessica Maurice worked for some sort of civil service branch in London during the war as many women did. She met this man who apparently worked for the same service but who was a follower of Mosley." She spat the name out of her mouth like a bad taste. "I believe she lived with him in London until he bought the house in Nethergate."

Result! thought Libby.

"But did you know," Fran said, "that Simon was a British spy?"

"Even worse," said Mrs Maurice. "He betrayed his country doubly, then."

"No, not at all," said Fran hurriedly. "He was posing as a Fascist to infiltrate the organisations." She glanced briefly at Libby for support. "Did you ever know a friend of Jessica's called Joan Miller?"

"I wasn't even born then," said Mrs Maurice. "How would I have known any friends of Jessica's? And where did you get that nonsense about that man?"

"It was published a few years ago," said Fran. "You must remember when the 50-year rule came to an end? When all the wartime documents were released?"

Mrs Maurice shook her head. Fran sighed and glanced again at Libby.

"So you never knew or met Simon Madderling or Joan Miller?" said Libby.

"Of course not. I wasn't born until the end of the war."

"Oh?" said Libby.

Faint colour crept up Mrs Maurice's unlovely neck. "1942, actually, if you must know. But I was far too young to know anything of this. I didn't meet Jessica until after I met my husband."

"Of course," said Fran. "Did he tell you anything about his aunt?"

"I heard all about her from his mother," said Mrs Maurice. "He always supported her. Jessica Maurice, that is."

"Yes, we heard she treated him like a son," said Libby innocently. Mrs Maurice's lips clamped together and her colour flared.

"So there is, in fact, nothing you can tell us," Fran put in hastily. "Nothing we don't already know."

"You don't *think* you know. She was no better than she should be, that woman. A bad influence on my husband and my daughter. I warned Jane about going to live there. That house was bought from immoral earnings." Mrs Maurice's voice had risen considerably, and noticing a blob of spittle at the corner of her mouth, Libby was uncomfortably reminded of Peter's mad mother Millie.

"It was good of you to see us," said Fran, rising quickly.

"Yes, thank you, Mrs Maurice," said Libby, following her example. "We'll say hello to Jane for you."

They made their way silently through the hall, across the blue and green floral carpet, past the gold-painted ironwork mirror and hall table and through the reeded-glass inner door. Jane's mother closed it firmly behind them without another word.

"Whew!" said Libby as soon as they reached the pavement. "No wonder Jane wants to live in Nethergate."

"I wonder why she didn't warn us," said Fran, looking up at the house. "She must have known what would happen."

"Perhaps she thought she would open up to us," said Libby, gesturing with her head towards the flick of a net curtain in the bay window. Fran nodded and turned to walk away.

"No," she said, "I think it was to punish us for finding out facts she thought supported her mother's dislike of her aunt."

"Eh?" Libby turned a puzzled gaze on her friend.

"We found out about her having a wartime lover who was supposed to be an enemy of the state. Jane's mother had always disapproved of Aunt Jessica, and this may have seemed to Jane to explain it. Then she probably felt guilty for blaming her mother for her dislike of Aunt Jessica."

"Oh, I see! Thinking it must have been justified, you mean?"

"Exactly. And the thing is, until those documents were published, in her own lights she probably was justified."

Libby shook her head. "I can't believe her attitude, though, can you? I mean, she's only a few years older than we are —"

"Ten," said Fran.

"All right, ten years older than we are, but she's only in her sixties. She sounds as though she's still in the fifties."

"Nineteen fifties?"

"Of course nineteen fifties! Immoral earnings indeed!"

"Yes, but Libby, until comparatively recently, people thought Madderling *was* a fascist spy."

"It doesn't excuse her completely out-dated attitudes, I'm sorry." Libby trudged along with a mulish expression on her face.

"No." Fran glanced at her friend with amusement.

"So what did we learn? Precisely nothing. Waste of time and petrol." Libby exhaled gustily.

"We had our suspicions confirmed. Simon did buy the house for Jessica."

"That's about all, though." Libby frowned, deep in thought. "I reckon we ought to find out more about this Joan Miller."

"I think we're in danger of digging too deep," said Fran.

"What?" Libby stopped and turned to her friend. "You were the one who had a thing about the house. You were the one who thought Terry's attack was the result of something hidden there."

"I know, but I really don't think we're looking for something that's of national importance, and going into Joan Miller's life takes it into that sort of realm."

"Was she that important?"

"Even I'd heard of Joan Miller," said Fran. "She left MI5 to get married before the end of the war. She wrote a book about it all. I think the powers that be tried to get it suppressed. I don't know how true it was."

"Oh." Libby began walking again. "I suppose it does seem a bit far-fetched. But you were certain yesterday."

"I know," sighed Fran, "but now it looks a bit pathetic. Am I trying to justify myself?"

"Oh, don't start that again," said Libby, "if only for my sake. Let's go home, go and tell Jane what her ma said, and then go and have a nice soothing drink at The Sloop or The Swan. Ben can come down and pick me up."

"All right," said Fran. "And Peel House can keep its secrets."

"Whatever happens," said Libby darkly.

206

CHAPTER
TWENTY-ONE

Settled at a table in The Sloop overlooking the harbour, Libby ordered drinks while Fran talked to Jane on her mobile.

"She's coming down to join us." Fran sat down at the table and put the phone back in her bag.

"What did she say about her mum?"

"Nothing. I just said we were back, she asked where we were and she said she'd come down. I don't know whether she was at work or at home."

While they were waiting for Jane to arrive, Libby phoned Ben and asked him if he could come and fetch her from Nethergate.

"Not too popular," Libby said to Fran. "He was busy doing something mechanical on the estate. I shall just have to wait until he's ready."

"That's OK," said Fran. "You can come back and wait with me." She turned her head. "Here's Jane."

"Hi," said Libby. "You look bushed."

Jane coloured faintly, in a much more attractive way than her mother.

"I had to get up early to make sure Terry had everything before I went to work," she said.

"I hope he's fully appreciative," said Fran, as Libby got up to get a drink for Jane.

"Oh, he doesn't think I should be looking after him," said Jane with a little laugh. "I think he thinks it's unmanly."

"From what I've seen of Terry that sounds very likely," said Libby, coming back to the table. "But I bet he likes it really. Have his parents gone home?"

"Oh, yes. As soon as they saw he was all right, they went back. His mother's coming down on Wednesday, I think, just to see how he is."

"Good. Now," said Fran, pulling her chair forward, "tell us why you didn't warn us about your mother."

Jane looked down into her glass. "I don't know what you mean," she said.

"Your mother," said Libby, "is a living breathing miracle. Transported from the last century."

Jane looked up and opened her mouth. Fran stepped in.

"Century before last, Lib," she said, defusing the situation. "What Libby means is, your mother seems to have the same morality as *her* mother's generation. She hasn't moved with the times."

Jane subsided. "No," she said. "I always wonder if it's just me, but then I meet other people's parents." She looked up. "And you two. You're nearly the same age as my mother, aren't you?"

"About ten years' difference," said Libby, "but, yes, nearer her age than we are yours."

"She's always been like it. Drove my dad and me mad. And my grandmother was just the same. It was almost as though she was my mother's mother, not my father's."

"What was your grandfather like? Jessica's brother?" asked Libby, leaning her elbows on the table.

"Quite jolly. I don't remember him very well, but I would think Dad was more like him. Aunt Jess was the same. My mother was scandalised when she opened the house as a B&B, but that was Aunt Jess. Independent. Wouldn't be beholden to anybody."

"Well, your mum confirmed that Simon Madderling bought the house for Aunt Jessica during the war, obviously before he disappeared, and that she thought he was a fascist spy."

"And you say he wasn't," said Jane slowly.

"That's what the official documents said when they were released," said Fran.

"Yes, I know."

"You know?" Libby raided an eyebrow.

"I looked him up, of course. I can't believe I didn't know any of this." Jane shook her head.

"I don't suppose your father would have told you, and your mother certainly wouldn't. The only person who might have done would have been Jessica herself, and I expect she thought it was best to let the past stay buried," said Fran.

"I talked it over with Terry last night," said Jane, "and we wondered why, as Jess left the house to me, she didn't tell me if there was something hidden there. That's your thinking, isn't it? That's why Terry was attacked?"

"It's one theory," said Libby. "Only because we were working on Fran's — er — insights."

"And have you told the police?" asked Jane.

"I've left a message for my friend Inspector Connell," said Fran.

"He's not the one in charge of Terry's investigation, though, is he?"

"No, but none of the other officers are likely to take anything I say seriously," said Fran.

"What, not even after those other cases you've helped with?" Jane looked surprised.

"My involvement was blown a bit out of proportion," said Fran. "Your chap at the *Mercury* was somewhat intrusive."

"That's Bob, the news editor," said Jane. "But you did help, didn't you?"

"A bit," said Fran. "So did Libby."

"Yes." Jane looked at Libby for a moment. "So what do you think now?"

"Not much." Fran sighed and shifted in her chair. "I think maybe I was getting something from a long way back and just assumed it had something to do with Terry's attack."

"You don't think there's any danger of anything else happening?"

"I've no idea," said Fran. "I was interfering. Sorry."

Libby looked at her in astonishment. "*You* were interfering?"

Fran laughed. "Yes. Now you can tell *me* off."

Jane frowned. "What are you talking about?"

210

"I'm the nosy interfering one," said Libby. "Everybody tells me so. Especially Fran."

"Oh." Jane twirled her glass. "Well, I think you're very good at interfering, and I wish you'd go on doing it."

Libby and Fran both looked at her and then at each other.

"What, exactly, do you mean?" asked Libby.

"Not so that I can do a piece on you," said Jane, looking at Fran, "even though I wanted to at first. No, because everything you've been doing interests me, and I want to find out more about Aunt Jessica and Peel House. And Simon Madderling, of course. As I said, I googled him this morning and found out quite a bit about him and it even mentions Aunt Jessica on one of the sites."

"It was the house that led me to the information," said Fran, quoting what she had told Libby the previous day.

"Yes. Well, there must be more to find out, surely?" said Jane, looking from one to the other. "Couldn't you look into it?"

Fran looked uncomfortable.

"She doesn't really do stuff to order," said Libby. "That's why she doesn't like helping the police. She's only happy if something comes to her sort of — oh, I don't know — spontaneously."

"But the house did, didn't it?" persisted Jane. "And there must be more to find out."

"I'm sure there is," said Fran, "but do you really want me to? I mean, our visit to your mother wasn't very successful, was it? I could just be wasting time."

"My mother confirmed what you thought, that Simon bought the house. See," said Jane, "you knew about it all along, really, didn't you? You remember that first time you came to the flat you asked about my aunt's job and how she'd afforded the house?"

"I hope I didn't sound as rude as that!" said Fran, frowning.

"No, it wasn't rude. It was — um — enlightening." Jane looked down at the table. "I really think I ought to know if there's anything there. To be found, I mean. I think I *need* to know."

Fran sighed. "Well, I'll have another go. Can I have a wander round the house sometime?"

"Any time!" said Jane. "We can go now if you like."

"Haven't you got to get back to work?" said Libby.

"Oh — yes. But that doesn't matter. I can let you in. Terry's there."

"What about your new tenant?"

"Mike'll be at work. Mrs Finch will be there. I'm sure she'd let you into her flat."

"I think it would be better if you were there," said Fran. "Would it be convenient if I popped round this evening about eight?"

"Yes, of course," said Jane. "Then I could explain to the other tenants what was going on."

"Not too much," said Fran. "They'll laugh at you. And me," she added as an afterthought.

"That's great." Jane stood up. "Thanks for the drink, Libby. Will you come tonight too?"

"That depends on Fran," said Libby.

212

"I don't think I could stop her," said Fran, looking amused.

"Do you think it will work?" asked Libby when Jane had gone.

"It's the only thing other than the boat moment that has got the antennae twitching for ages, so it might. Funny." Fran looked out of the window at the sea. "Just those two."

"And the farm."

"That wasn't connected."

"And you think the other two are?" Libby's voice rose in amazement.

"I haven't got a clue," said Fran, looking back at her with a smile. "It just feels right, somehow."

"Well, look what happened when you tried to connect all those other bits and pieces," said Libby. "You said yourself it was a dismal failure."

"Mmm." Fran's gaze returned to the sea. "I think I'm going to have to sit down and work things out a bit better."

"How?"

"Write them all down, then concentrate on them and see what happens. I can do it with photographs, now, can't I?"

"Yes." Libby looked at her watch. "Ben'll be here in a minute. Shall I send him away? Then I can spend the afternoon helping you before we go to Peel House."

"If you send Ben away now he'll probably never come back," laughed Fran, "and anyway, I'd prefer to be on my own while I try this."

"OK," said Libby, peering out of the landward window. "Here comes Ben. I'll see you at Jane's at eight, shall I?"

"Come to me and we'll go together," said Fran, getting to her feet and joining Libby at the door. "Although I don't know why I'm doing this. It's certainly not to help the police, is it? It's just sheer nosiness."

"We helped Bella when it wasn't anything to do with the police, too," Libby reminded her, "but I know what you mean. Oh well, just call it a hobby."

Ben was placated by the promise of a meal in The Swan, after grumbling most of the way back to Steeple Martin. Libby called Fran and suggested she drop Ben off with Guy first and then meet them when they'd finished at Peel House.

"It'll give us an excuse to get away if we need one," said Libby. "And I've promised to drive."

At ten to eight, Ben was knocking on the door of the flat above Guy's gallery and Fran was climbing into Romeo the Renault.

"Still plenty of people about," said Libby, avoiding a family with young children strolling along Harbour Street with ice creams.

"They might as well make the most of it if they've got young children," said Fran. "When they get back to their hotels or flats they can't do much else, can they?"

"No," agreed Libby. "We always let ours stay up when we were on holiday."

This time, there was space to park almost in front of Peel House. Jane must have been watching for them, as the front door opened almost immediately.

"Where do you want to start?" she asked.

"Which flat was Aunt Jessica's?" said Fran. "This ground floor one, wasn't it?"

"If you can call it ground floor," said Libby. "It's first floor at the back, isn't it?"

"Yes, because we're built on a slope away from the cliff. That's why Mrs Finch has her own front door at the back."

"Is Mike in?" asked Fran. "I don't want to disturb him."

"I've already asked him if he minded if you came in. He doesn't, but says he's going out soon, so perhaps we'd better go in to him first," said Jane, lifting her hand to knock on the door.

Mike, as good-looking as Libby remembered him, opened the door with a smiling but watchful face.

"And this is the clairvoyant lady?" he asked, as Jane made introductions. Fran looked surprised.

"Oh, I don't think I'm clairvoyant," she said. "I just pick up things, now and again."

"I shall have to watch the silver, then, won't I?" he said with a short laugh. Jane looked at the ceiling and Libby stared. Fran smiled.

"Shall we leave you alone?" asked Jane.

"No, I'm fine. If you wouldn't mind me wandering round a bit?" Fran turned to Mike.

"Not at all," he said, sitting on a chair at the table and indicating that his guests should do so, too.

215

So, they sat and watched Fran walking round the room, occasionally trailing her fingers over a surface. She stood still by the window with her head bowed.

"Was this Jessica's bedroom?" she asked suddenly.

Jane looked surprised. "Yes, it was. I thought it ought to be the sitting room because it has a view of the sea."

Fran turned back to Mike. "Would it be a terrible imposition if I asked to see your bedroom?"

He smiled, shrugged and stood up to lead the way. Fran simply stood in the doorway, then, shaking her head, had a quick look in the kitchen and went back to the sitting room.

"Thank you, Mike," she said. "I'm sorry to have been so intrusive, but it was on your landlady's behalf."

"And Terry's," said Mike. "To get to the bottom of his attack."

"Oh, yes, of course," agreed Fran quickly.

With renewed thanks, they left the ground floor flat and Fran asked if she could go down to see Mrs Finch.

"Do you want me to come with you?" asked Jane.

"If you like," said Fran. "Do you think she'd be more comfortable?"

"Not really," said Jane ruefully. "I think I told you, she thinks of me as a sort of interloper. You'd do better on your own. She does know you're coming."

"What did she say about it?" asked Libby.

"Not much. It was a bit like asking if she'd let the plumber in."

"And what did Mike say when you asked him?" said Fran.

"I told you, he was fine. It's just that he was going out."

Fran nodded. "OK, then, we'll go round to Mrs Finch's front door. Coming, Libby?"

Mrs Finch was small and thin, with abundant white hair and a Crimplene suit in pale green.

"What's all this about then?" she said, as soon as they were in her small, overcrowded front room.

"Jessica Maurice," said Fran bluntly.

"Hmph," said Mrs Finch, sitting down abruptly in a tapestry-covered armchair opposite the large television.

"You knew her well, I believe?"

"I knew her. Used to come on our 'olidays. Good little guesthouse, this was." She looked round the room. "This was the dinin' room."

"When was that?" asked Libby.

"In the fifties. Come every year, we did, even after the kids had grown up. Then the old man died and Jess turned this place into flats. So I moved in."

"The old man?" asked Fran. Libby frowned at her.

"Your husband, Mrs Finch?" she said.

Mrs Finch looked at Fran in surprise. "That's right, o' course," she said. Fran blushed.

"And did you ever know what Jessica had done before she ran a guesthouse?"

"Did some sort o' war work, like most of us," said Mrs Finch with a sniff. "Munitions, I was. She was in some sort of govn'ment office. Quite posh, she was." She looked up at the ceiling. "That niece of hers is the same."

Libby hid a grin.

"And that's all you know about her?" persisted Fran. "Did she ever have any visitors?"

"Whatcher talking about, gal? O' course she had visitors! A dozen every week through the summer!"

"Come on, Fran," said Libby, getting to her feet. "I think we ought to leave Mrs Finch, now."

Fran reluctantly followed suit.

"O' course," said Mrs Finch, just as they were opening the door, "there were always them foreigners who came to see her. Every couple of years they'd turn up for a couple o' days and go off again."

"Foreigners?" Fran turned back eagerly.

"Yeah. Dark, they was. Every year. Eyetalians."

CHAPTER
TWENTY-TWO

"So where does that leave us?" asked Jane after Libby had related the story of the visit to Mrs Finch.

"I'm not sure," said Fran. "They could have been friends from the war, couldn't they?"

"There were lots of Italian prisoners of war," said Libby. "And Italians who were already over here were interned. Some of them were deported."

"Why do you need to know?" asked Terry, who had now moved upstairs to Jane's flat and lay in state on the sofa.

"It was unexpected," said Libby with one eye on Fran, who was looking distracted.

"So did you get anything about the house?" asked Jane.

"Only really in Mike's sitting room," said Fran slowly.

"You thought that had been the bedroom, yes," said Jane eagerly. "Then what?"

"I'm not sure," said Fran, and looked up, meeting Jane's eyes. "You're going to have to let me think about it. Whatever it is, I don't think it's anything to do with Terry."

"Or his attacker?" asked Libby.

"Yes," said Fran. "Or rather, no. It isn't."

"Oh." Jane looked disappointed. Terry, unconcerned, reached out and patted her hand. "Don't worry, doll," he said.

"Doll?" muttered Libby. "What decade does he think this is?"

"We're back to the fifties," grinned Fran in response. "Come on."

"Jane, we've got to go now. We're meeting Ben and Guy in The Swan for a meal," said Libby.

"I promise I'll think about the impressions I got from this evening," said Fran, "and I'll give you a ring tomorrow."

"I'll be here all day if you want to come back," said Terry, fixing his eyes on Fran.

"Right, thank you," said Fran. "Come on Lib, we'll be late."

"So what was that all about?" asked Libby, as they got into Romeo.

"What was what?"

"That look Terry gave you."

"He was trying to tell me something," said Fran, "I'm sure of it."

"About the house?"

"I don't know. Possibly. Or perhaps he was trying to warn me off."

"Why would he want to do that?"

"Because he doesn't want Jane involved? Maybe he knows who it was after all?"

"Hmmm." Libby turned the car round in The Tops car park and started back towards The Swan. "So what about Aunt Jessica's bedroom?"

"Yes." Fran stared out of the windscreen. "I'm going to have to think about that, too."

Libby parked in The Swan's car park and turned to face her friend. "Look, this isn't important, you know. This was just to oblige Jane and because you had a feeling about the house. You don't have to get worked up about it."

"I know, I know. But now I'm hooked." Fran gave Libby a small smile. "I know I'm inconsistent and a damned nuisance, but there it is."

Guy and Ben were waiting for them in the bar.

"How did it go?" Guy pulled out a chair for Fran.

"So-so," said Fran.

"I still don't know why you're bothering," said Ben. "This isn't a murder investigation, is it? Are you just keeping your hand in?"

"Fran says she's hooked," said Libby. "I think she's peeved because the body on the island turned out to be a dud."

"Libby!" Fran frowned.

"Anyone know how that investigation's going?" asked Guy. "There hasn't been anything in the paper."

"Don't know. When you phoned Ian did he say anything, Fran?" Libby said.

"Phoned Ian? What about?" Guy looked sharply at Fran.

"I didn't phone him." Fran looked away. "He isn't in charge of Terry's case, so it was pointless."

"And you don't think your feeling about the house is relevant anyway?" Libby leant forward to try and catch Fran's eye.

"No." Fran looked back at them all. "Have you asked for the menu?"

The other three looked at one another and Libby sighed. "That's that, then," she said.

"So, come on then," said Libby the following morning. "What's going on?" She perched on the edge of the garden chair clutching her phone. "God, I wish you still lived round the corner. I'd much rather talk to you face to face."

"Then it's a good job for me I don't," said Fran, sounding amused. "And nice though living in Steeple Martin above The Pink Geranium was, Coastguard Cottage is a darn site better."

"I know, I know," sighed Libby. "Go on then, tell me all."

"Why do you want to know?"

"Because I'm nosy," said Libby. "And we've always done these things together."

"Always? For the last eighteen months, maybe."

"You know what I mean. Come on, there was something there, wasn't there?"

"Honestly, Libby, I'm not sure." Fran was silent for a moment. "Something happened in what was Aunt Jessica's bedroom. I saw a bed, and a woman, and then it all went black."

"You didn't show it," said Libby.

"No. I wasn't facing any of you just then, and because I recognised the feeling, I just closed my eyes and waited until it had passed. She was probably Aunt Jessica."

"So not Simon Whatsit?"

"I don't know. I don't think so. And I have no idea when it was. It wasn't during the war, because she wouldn't have been using that room as a bedroom, would she? Not when she lived in the whole house. So it must have been after she turned the house into flats. Unless she used that room as a bedroom when the house was a B&B, too. Anyway, that's all I got. Nothing from anywhere else in the house, not even Mrs Finch's. So there's nothing to tell Ian. He's not a cold case unit, after all."

"No, I suppose not. What will you tell Jane?"

"The truth, I suppose. There's nothing to connect Terry's attack to Peel House, and no more to be found out about Aunt Jess."

"Shame," said Libby. "What about the Italian connection?"

"Again, no idea. You were right, they were probably friends she made during the war. Perhaps internees who were let out to work on the farms, or something. Lots of them did that, didn't they?"

"Some of them stayed here, after the war, too," said Libby. "I hope they were happy. They had a terrible time at first. People who'd lived here for years with their families and had businesses, ice cream shops, barbers and restaurants, had their businesses smashed up by ordinary people, and then they were just rounded up and interned. Dreadful."

"Terrible," echoed Fran at the other end of the phone.

"Well, we don't know who Aunt Jessica's friends were, so it's no use speculating," said Libby.

"No." Libby heard uncertainty in Fran's voice.

"What?" she said. "Come on, out with it. There's something else, isn't there?"

"No, not really, just a feeling."

"About the Italians?"

"Yes."

"But you said you had no idea about them?"

"I know, and I don't. There's just a sort of muzzy aura around them."

"Well, don't force it. Perhaps it'll come to you," said Libby.

In Coastguard Cottage, Fran clicked off her phone and went to stand at the window. The view across the bay to the lighthouse always soothed her, and today, with the sun shining and seagulls swooping in the sky, it was as idyllic as a postcard. In fact, Libby's paintings of this view sold well as postcards.

Her phone rang again.

"Mrs Castle? Fran?"

"Yes? Who is this?"

"Campbell McLean. How are you?"

"I'm fine, how are you?" said Fran, frowning at the handset.

"I had to tell you, your instinct about Budgen was right."

"Illegal pickers?"

"Exactly. A triumph! And all thanks to you and Mrs Sarjeant."

"Well, not quite," said Fran. "You picked the farm."

"Yes, but Mrs Sarjeant was the one who made the connection."

"Not that it turned out to be the right connection," said Fran.

"I don't know about that," he said. "Look, I'd like to tell you about it. Could I buy you both lunch?"

"Certainly," said Fran. "Where and when?"

"Shall I come to Nethergate? There's that nice little Italian restaurant in the High Street, isn't there?"

"Luigi's, yes," said Fran. "I'll call Libby — Mrs Sarjeant — and ask her to meet us there, shall I?"

"I'll book a table for one o'clock," said Campbell McLean, and rang off.

Libby was as excited as Fran expected her to be.

"Do you think it's something to do with the body?"

Fran groaned. "Please, God, no," she said.

"Why not? That's what you were supposed to investigate in the first place. And now Jane's aunt's gone out the window you haven't got anything else to do."

"I was supposed to be taking up a hobby, remember?" said Fran.

"Oh, the writing. Well, think about how much more you'll have to write about," said Libby gleefully. "I might go into Canterbury and get the train down to Nethergate. Then I can swell Campbell McLean's expense budget on red wine."

The journey involved a long and tortuous bus ride through the villages on the way to Canterbury, but it was a beautiful day and Libby sat on the top deck enjoying the view. Then there was short walk from the bus station to the railway station (Libby still hated the way the younger generation said "train station") and a slow rattle through more villages to Nethergate.

The walk down the hill in Nethergate to Luigi's was probably the most difficult part of the journey, dodging holiday makers who seemed unable to grasp the concept of forward movement, or even staying on the pavements.

"Tourists," she gasped, subsiding into a chair between Fran and McLean. "How annoying are they?"

"Libby, you were a tourist here once. Don't be horrible."

"I bet I wasn't as bad as they are," grumbled Libby, pushing her basket under her chair. "Think they own the place."

Campbell McLean chuckled. "There probably wouldn't be a Nethergate without tourists," he said.

"True," Libby sighed. "Oh, well, I shall have to be more tolerant. Now tell us what's been going on."

But McLean insisted on providing them with a drink first, and then ordering lunch. After which, he sat back and surveyed the two women.

"Well, you know I wasn't too pleased about our investigation into the body on the island being scuppered, nor was I too pleased about the farm investigation, but we were co-operating with the police, so I went along with it."

"And?" prompted Libby.

"As we talked about last Monday, we arranged for another reporter — no one who normally appears on screen — to apply for work at the farm with a hidden camera and microphone. To cut a long story short, it turns out Budgen is part of a scam still working to bring in illegal workers. Who was it mentioned all those strawberries left to rot?"

"Me," said Libby.

"Farmers are really worried about it, apparently. So those that were in on a scam stayed on it. But among the people they're bringing in now are Moldovans and Transnistrians. Remember Transnistria?"

Fran and Libby both gasped.

"Mind you, there are still people from Eastern Europe who can come in legally, but can't work. So there are some of those, too."

"So have the police arrested anyone?" asked Libby.

"Budgen and two of the people running the so-called 'agency'. They're chasing up other leads to the suppliers of the false documents, and many of the workers have been taken to a holding centre."

"Oh, poor things," said Libby.

"I know," said McLean. "And when you look round Nethergate and see how many foreign workers are here doing all the jobs the British don't want to do, you'd think these people would be welcome, wouldn't you?"

"The same as the Italians," murmured Fran.

"Italians?" McLean looked puzzled.

"The war-time interned Italians," said Libby. "We've been talking about them recently."

"Oh." McLean looked up as a waiter arrived bearing plates. "Thank you."

"Do you think he's one?" asked Libby in a stage whisper.

"Ssh!" said Fran. "One what?"

"A migrant worker. He's a very dark-looking Italian."

"A lot of them are," said McLean, amused.

"I only ask, because —" began Libby, until Fran trod on her foot. "The Italians look a lot like the Eastern Europeans, don't they?" she finished lamely.

"The Romanian language is a lot like Italian," said McLean, "and apparently Moldovan and Transnistrian are very like it, too."

"Anyway," said Libby, "what happened next? Has Budgen been talking? How long had he been involved?"

"Oh, some years," said McLean. "In fact, it turns out that he has a connection to another case, very loosely." He suddenly sat up straight in his chair. "Which, of course, is the one I told you about before." He beamed triumphantly.

"What?" Libby and Fran looked at one another.

"Lena Gruzevich. Who borrowed a false Italian passport to get her a job and is now in an Immigration Centre awaiting deportation. Remember?"

CHAPTER
TWENTY-THREE

Taking Libby's and Fran's open-mouthed astonishment as agreement, McLean went on.

"It turns out that it was Budgen's farm Lena was sent to. The conditions were appalling, but she saw enough of life outside to want to stay here, but couldn't work out how. They were kept almost as prisoners, of course. But when that case came up — you know, the one we talked about before — and Budgen's farm was investigated, he got rid of the workers as quickly as he could, which meant they were packed into lorries and transported like sheep."

"How ghastly," said Libby, her eyes wide.

"Lena, apparently, managed to escape and went in search of her brother, whom she knew was in the country having come over with a previous wave of smuggled migrants. She says he had got work in a bar in London, and when she found him, he introduced her to this Italian woman, who Lena says he was having an affair with. Anyway, Lena stayed in the flat the woman was renting and eventually got the job using her passport."

"But the reports say the Italian girl was never found?" said Fran.

"No, and neither was the brother, Andrei, apparently. Lena gave the police all the details, but although they found the bar and people remembered Andrei and the girl, no one had seen either of them for a couple of years."

"How do you know all this?" asked Libby. "We couldn't find it out, even when Fran asked Inspector Connell."

"Friend of mine on the network I used to work for covered it," said McLean, looking smug. "That's how I found out about it in the first place and told Fran."

"So Andrei and the Italian girl did a bunk. Back to Italy, do you think?" said Libby.

"The police tracked the false passport back to Rome, so yes, that's what it looks like. After that, nothing."

"Hang on," said Libby. "I've just realised you said *false* passport. You didn't say that in the first place. You just said the police had tried to trace her family and had no success."

"The Italian authorities eventually came up with the fact that it was false. I told you, it takes months sometimes."

"So a complete dead end?" said Libby.

"That part of it, yes."

"Nothing to do with your body on the island anyway," said Fran. "Sorry you got talked into this one instead."

"I'm not. The police are very grateful, we get an exclusive, and if I'm allowed to," he inclined his head towards Fran, "we shall perhaps do a mini-feature on the help psychics can give the police."

230

"I didn't give you much help, Libby did," said Fran.

"Doesn't make such a good story, though, does it?" said Libby. "Glad you got that awful Budgen though. What about his animals? I know that dog wasn't very friendly, but they can't leave it on its own."

"He might have a wife," said Fran.

"I hope not!" said Libby.

"Divorced years ago, apparently," said McLean. "And the police always bring in appropriate services to deal with anybody or anything left behind in these cases."

"What about the workers he was using now?" asked Fran.

"Immigration Centre, I told you."

"So there was a new operation going on after the collapse of that one four years ago?" asked Libby.

"There are always operations going on. This particular one is based in Moldova, but I should imagine it's closed off lines of communication for the time being now Budgen's been arrested."

"How would the people in Moldova know?" asked Fran.

"There are people watching all the time. Usually the most innocent-looking people, too."

They all turned their attention to the food, until Libby looked up and said, "Isn't it possible that the body on the island was one of Budgen's workers?"

"It is, of course, but Budgen wouldn't identify him even if it was," said McLean.

"And it doesn't answer the question of why he was on the island, does it?" said Fran.

"Hmmm." Libby pushed her remaining pasta around her plate. "That does seem to be the main problem. Why *and* how."

"Do you think," said Fran after Campbell McLean had left them and they were walking down to the sea front, "that there's a connection between Lena and the body on the island?"

"Do you?" Libby narrowed her eyes at her friend.

"I feel as though there is," said Fran.

"You thought that before and you admitted you were wrong."

"But suppose I wasn't?" Fran stopped at Lizzie's ice cream shop. "Want one?"

"Strawberry, please," said Libby. "And why do you suddenly think you might have been right?"

"It's all these coincidences," said Fran, handing Lizzie some coins. "They're piling up. I don't believe in coincidences."

"What coincidences?" asked Libby dubiously, taking her strawberry cornet from Lizzie.

"The Transnistrian one, for a start. Lena turns out to be one of the workers from Budgen's farm."

"That's McLean's coincidence, not yours. He brought up Lena Gruesome's case in the first place as a hook to hang something on. It just turns out that his own investigation has turned up trumps. After all, you didn't even pick Budgen's farm."

"I didn't even suggest going to *see* a farm," said Fran gloomily, taking a cautious lick at her chocolate cornet. "That was you."

232

"Well, there you are then. It's McLean's triumph, nothing to do with you, and even if the body on the island turns out to be Transnistrian, it will still be nothing to do with you." Libby perched on the sea wall and squinted up at the sky. "Lovely day, isn't it?"

But Fran wasn't satisfied. Later that afternoon, she took a deckchair over on to the beach, followed by Balzac, and sat down in the lee of the wall to watch the holidaymakers and the sea. Hovering on the horizon, shimmering in the heat haze, sat Dragon Island, and as she watched it, she felt a cold sensation in her veins, almost, as she described it later, like an anaesthetic injection.

There was something, she was sure. Even though Libby, and she herself, had pooh-poohed the idea, there was a feeling lurking in her mind that all the images that had been floating there since Ian's request were somehow connected. Except possibly, she acknowledged, the rather muddled affair of Peel House. That was a diversion her strange brain had created for her and had served only as a red herring. How, she wondered, watching Balzac picking his way fastidiously across the pebbles, could she marry them up and see if there really was a connection? She had asked Ian about the Transnistrian girl, whose name they now knew was Lena Gruzevich, but that had turned into a dead end, as Libby had said at lunch time.

Perhaps, she thought, sitting upright in the deckchair as an idea struck her, even though Ian was not particularly pleased with her, he might just do her a favour if he thought it might serve him a good turn.

233

And he surely couldn't be too cross with her after McLean's successful uncovering of Budgen's illegal farm workers, even if, in the end, it had been nothing to do with her. She leant back in the deckchair once again, sighed, and closed her eyes.

Later, when the sun had deserted the beach and remained shining only on Cliff Terrace and The Tops car park, Fran went back inside Coastguard Cottage and made herself a cup of tea, which she took out into the back yard. Balzac, ever companionable, came too. After a couple of false starts, she finally pressed Call to Ian Connell's mobile number and waited.

Half to her annoyance and half to her relief, it went straight to voicemail.

"Right," she said clearing her throat. "Ian. It's Fran. I know I said I was bowing out of your investigation, but there is something that keeps niggling away at me. You remember I asked you about that Transnistrian woman? Could you somehow arrange for her to see a photograph of the body on the island? Don't know whether it's possible for you to do that, but I think it might be worth it." She cleared her throat again. "That's all. Bye."

She looked down at Balzac. "Well, that's it," she said. "I've done it. It's up to him now."

Meanwhile, in Steeple Martin, a panic meeting was being held in The Pink Geranium about the entertainment for Hetty's birthday party. No pianist had been found, despite the best efforts of everyone involved, and the best alternative had been a couple of

234

old vinyl long-playing records called "Honky-Tonk Party" and "War-Time Favourites" produced by Lenny and Flo.

"I'll have a look online for some CDs," said Libby. "I'm sure I bought my mother a boxed set of 40s and 50s hits a couple of Christmases ago."

"Well, if that's all we can get, that'll have to do," said Ben.

"What about bands that play that sort of stuff?" asked Harry.

"They'd cost a lot of money," said Libby. "I know. I went to a wedding once where they had a 40s dance band in white DJs with a girl singer and I know just how much it cost the groom."

"There must be local bands that do it, though? Flo, what about those tea dances they have in the village hall?" said Peter.

"Records, love," said Flo. "No real people now."

"Libby?" Ben reached across the table to tap Libby's arm. "Have you gone into a trance?"

"Nooo," said Libby slowly, "but I just had an idea."

To their collective credit, no one round the table groaned.

"You know little Jane Maurice who came along to the audition?"

They all nodded, except Flo and Lenny.

"Well, she works for the *Nethergate Mercury*. She probably knows all the local bands and things, doesn't she? She might even know a pianist. One that plays in a hotel bar, or something."

"Do they do that any more?" asked Peter.

"Ring her," said Ben. "What have we got to lose?"

Libby fished her mobile out of her basket and found Jane's number.

"Oh, hi, Jane," she said when Jane answered. "I've got a question for you. Not disturbing you, am I?"

Grinning at the rather breathless reply to this innocent question, Libby went on to describe the problem.

"She'll get back to me," she told the waiting group, who let out their collective breath and picked up their wine glasses.

The other arrangements for the party were going well it seemed. The local brewery were providing barrels and some memorabilia, the wardrobe at the theatre had been raided of all the costumes that had been assembled for the production of *The Hop Pickers*, and the set builders had done wonders. Everyone was congratulating themselves and casting darkling looks at Libby, the only failure among them, when her mobile rang.

"Libby," said an unfamiliar voice, "it's Terry here."

"Terry? Good heavens! How are you?"

"I'm fine. Look, Jane's just told me about you wanting a pianist."

"Has she?" Libby frowned.

"1940s stuff? Singalong?"

"Yes," said Libby cautiously.

"Well, if I offer to babysit, I might be able to help," said Terry.

"Eh?"

"Oh, sorry. What I meant was, my sister might do it if I babysat her little girl. With Jane."

"Your sister? Does she do that sort of stuff?"

"Oh, yeah. She's a professional, but she's not working much since she had the baby. Been on the radio and everything."

"Really?" Libby's face broke into a huge smile. "But how much would it cost?"

"Oh, just her petrol money. She'll be glad to get out. What d'you reckon?"

"It sounds fantastic," said Libby. "When can you ask her?"

"I'll do it now," said Terry. "Ring you back in five."

In fact, it was ten minutes before Libby's phone rang again.

"Yeah, love to, she said. Just tell me where it is. And she said have you got a piano, or should she bring hers?"

"Hers?"

"Electronic."

"Oh, no, we've got a proper old upright."

"And she says she'll come in her stage gear. She sings as well. Do a good job for you, she will."

"Oh, Terry!" said Libby, feeling almost tearful. "I don't know what to say. I can't thank you enough."

"S'nothing," said Terry. "Glad to help." He paused. "And would you get Fran to ring me? I thought she might want to come back and — er — carry on looking."

"Yes, she thought you wanted to see her again," said Libby. "Want to give me a clue?"

237

"Um — no. She'll tell you. Got to go. Bye."

Ringing off, Libby turned to the expectant faces round the table. "Sorted!" she said.

CHAPTER
TWENTY-FOUR

Wednesday morning found Libby at the theatre in order to let in a hastily summoned piano tuner. The upright piano given to the theatre a year ago had been lifted and dragged onto the stage, and Libby knew enough about pianos to realise that this wouldn't have done the tuning much good at all. Resigning herself to a long wait, she wandered round checking bar stocks, clean tea towels, spare lamps for the lighting rig and various other essentials of theatre life.

She had finally gone outside to the little garden for a cigarette when her phone rang.

"I've got some news," said Fran.

"Good news?"

"Gratifying for me, anyway."

"What is it?"

"What are you doing? Shall I come over? I haven't seen Sidney for a week or so."

"I'm at the theatre at the moment while the piano tuner's doing his stuff."

"How long will he be?"

"Come here anyway and I'll wait for you," said Libby. "Aren't you going to give me a hint?"

"No," said Fran, and Libby could hear the mischief in her voice. "I'm going to keep you in suspense."

Half an hour later, the piano tuner's car passed Fran's roller-skate on the Manor drive.

"Where are we going?" asked Fran.

"Don't mind. Do you want to go to Harry's?"

"I think I'd rather go to yours."

"OK," said Libby, and climbed into the passenger seat after checking the lock on the theatre door.

Sidney greeted Fran like a long lost friend and led her out into the garden while Libby put the kettle on.

"Come on, now," she said, following them outside. "What's the news?"

"Yesterday evening I left a message for Ian," said Fran, lifting an unprotesting Sidney onto her lap.

"Yes?"

"And asked him if it would be possible to show the Transnistrian girl a photo of our body."

"And?"

"He called this morning — very early — to ask why. So I told him I thought there was a connection. As I'd mentioned the case to him before, he accepted that and said he'd find out."

"Hang on, kettle's boiling," said Libby and dashed back into the kitchen. A few minutes later she came out with a teapot, mugs, milk and sugar on a tray.

"There's posh," said Fran, raising her eyebrows.

"Saves me going back in when it's brewed," said Libby. "Go on. What happens next?"

"It's happened," said Fran with a smile. "He already did it."

240

"Golly," said Libby. "How quick is that? How did he manage it?"

"He said he took an executive decision." Fran laughed. "Not like Ian, really, is it? He's not usually impetuous. But apparently the Transnistrian girl —"

"Lena," put in Libby.

"Lena," nodded Fran, "is in a centre near Dover, so he just took the file over and asked to see her."

"And?"

"It's her brother."

"No!" squeaked Libby. "Blimey! So he didn't do a bunk with the Italian?"

"He might have done. It's a couple of years since Lena saw him, she says, after she gave back the passport to the other girl. They didn't keep in touch deliberately."

"Wow." Libby poured tea. "So where does that get us?"

"It gets Ian an identification, so he's over the moon."

"But no nearer finding out who dunnit?"

"I suppose an identity must make it a bit easier."

"But they'll have to find out where he's been for the last two years."

"They've got the address of the flat the Italian was living in, and which Lena stayed in, and the address of the club."

"They had that before, though, didn't they?"

"Yes, but that was another investigation, wasn't it? Ian's team will go in, now. Thanks." Fran picked up her mug carefully, without disturbing Sidney.

"Is she upset?"

"I don't know. Ian didn't give me that sort of detail. Just phoned me from the car to give me the outline and say thanks. I asked him to let me know what happens, but when and whether he'll do that, I've no idea."

"So Lena and — what was his name?"

"Andrei?"

"That's it, Andrei. They both came out from Transnistria; at the same time do you think?"

"It doesn't sound like it."

"Well, anyway, out they come, and then he gets murdered."

"Not quite right away," said Fran, in an amused voice.

"No, I know, but doesn't it seem like there was a connection? With the Italian girl, probably. They'd found out that passport was false, supposing *she* wasn't Italian after all?" Libby sat back in her chair looking triumphant.

Fran stared in astonishment. "Goodness!" she said. "Of course! She could have been Transnistrian, too. Or any nationality, come to that."

"I expect," sighed Libby, picking up her mug, "the police have figured that one out anyway."

"I expect you're right." Fran frowned. "But will it do them any good? She's disappeared off the face of the earth."

"She went back to Italy," mused Libby, "so she vanished from there. Or — she took up her normal nationality."

"In that case, why did she need a false passport over here?"

"Because she didn't want anyone to know who she was, durr!" said Libby. "Either that or she needed an identity the same as the other girl."

"Well, I'm just pleased to be vindicated." Fran stroked Sidney's head. He flattened his ears.

"Yes. It proves that you weren't trying too hard after all, doesn't it? And you still get things right."

"It's just a question of interpretation, really," said Fran. "I knew there was a farm involved somewhere, but it was pure luck when McLean turned up the information on Lena."

"But even then it didn't connect openly with Andrei," said Libby.

"No, but the connection must have been there in whatever bit of my mind I use for this. Or whatever power uses it," Fran made a face.

"Don't scoff," said Libby. "It works. And I reckon he was killed on a boat taking him to the island."

"Because of what happened on our boat trip?"

"Yes. And just suppose," said Libby, warming to her theory, "that he was actually being transported out of the country and something went wrong?"

"Why not, in that case, just dump him overboard, as we've said before?"

"Ah." Libby nodded. "That is the sticking point, isn't it? There has to be a reason."

"Someone knew who he was," said Fran.

"The killers?"

"Of course, the killers, although even that isn't certain. Suppose he'd got involved in something —

drugs, say — under his false name. This could be a drug-related killing."

"What was his false name, did Ian say?"

Fran shook her head. "Lena identified him with his real name. Poor girl. What a life."

"Will they make her go back, do you think?"

"She'd been living quietly in a rented room and was good at her job, Ian said, but that's no guarantee. They split up husbands and wives without compunction, even children, and Lena has none of those."

Libby sighed. "We don't realise how lucky we are, do we? Did you read all that stuff on the internet about Transnistria? It's becoming a centre for every sort of criminal activity."

"I know. Perhaps the authorities will realise that and let her stay."

"But she's already got two strikes against her," said Libby. "She came into the country on a false passport, then obtained a job with another one. Why did she borrow the other one, by the way? The first one must have got her into the country."

"No, it didn't," said Fran. "She was smuggled in."

"Oh, God, even worse." Libby shook her head. "She hasn't much hope has she?"

"And think what will happen to her if she goes back."

"I doubt if she'd get that far," said Fran.

They sat in silence for a few moments, until Sidney, impervious to atmosphere, sat up suddenly and began to wash.

"Well, it isn't our — I mean, your — problem any more. You got Ian his identification, so you can relax."

Fran was staring up into the cherry tree.

"Fran? Hoy, anyone home?" Libby clicked her fingers in front of her friend's face.

Fran blinked. "Oh, sorry," she said. "I was just thinking."

"Oh, dear." Libby sighed again. "What is it this time?"

"I don't know why you say that," said Fran. "You're the one who always wants to go haring off detecting as soon as I think of anything."

"I know," said Libby, "but this last couple of weeks has been so muddled, and you haven't been happy."

"I am now," said Fran. "Things linked up. But something else . . ."

"Something else?" asked Libby after a moment.

"Not sure. Italians. They've come up in both Ian's body and Jane's house."

Libby giggled. "That's a funny way of putting it."

"You know what I mean."

"Surely you don't still think they're connected?"

Fran looked at Libby intently. "And what about that Italian who went to Bruce's firm?"

"He's just a random bloke. Nothing to do with this at all."

"How do we know?" said Fran. "We still don't know how Andrei was killed. That Italian could have been looking for him."

Libby puffed out her breath. "Cor," she said. "Talk about building castles out of sand."

"I know, I know. But there's something else here, I'm sure of it." Fran stood up. "I'd better go home and think about it."

"Don't get too wrapped up in it, Fran." Libby stood and picked up the tray. "You're usually the one who doesn't want to get involved. Don't go against type."

Fran smiled. "I don't think I can help it, Lib. These pictures keep coming into my brain, and until I find out what they mean, they won't leave me alone."

"What are they now?" Libby followed Fran into the house.

"Mainly, I keep seeing a figure in Jane's house, looking for something."

Libby looked dubious. "That's simply because Italians have been popping up all over the cases. Auto-suggestion."

"No. I must find out about Simon Madderling. He's the key to all this."

"To Peel House?"

"And Andrei's murder," said Fran.

"Oh, don't be daft," laughed Libby. "Simon's been dead since 1943."

"I know. It's what happened then, I'm sure."

"Oh, dear, not another Buried In The Past murder," said Libby.

"Why are you being so negative all of a sudden?" Fran rounded on her. "If you don't want to know any more about it, you can opt out. I won't bother you any more." She turned towards the front door and picked up her bag.

Libby shut her mouth, which had fallen open in amazement, and hurried after her.

"No, Fran, don't! I'm not being negative, I promise. I just don't want you to get all tied up in this and feel pressured, like you did a couple of weeks ago. I'm sorry, I'll shut up."

Fran turned back and sighed. "All right, I'm sorry, too, but Lib, you must let me do what I think is right. It isn't your investigation. It isn't even mine, but I need to find out what it is I'm being told without interference."

Libby looked down at her feet. "Was I doing it again, then?" she said. "Trying to take over?"

"A bit," said Fran, smiling. "Just telling me what I ought to do, that's all. Come on, friends again. I'll go home and have a think, and perhaps do a bit more research. Then I'll tell you what I've found out."

"OK." Libby nodded. "Could I help a bit with the research?"

"If you want to. This is only for my own satisfaction, nothing to do with the police case."

I believe you, thought Libby, as she waved her friend off. But thousands wouldn't.

CHAPTER
TWENTY-FIVE

Libby realised she hadn't told Fran about Terry's phone call ten minutes after she'd left. Knowing Fran wouldn't answer her mobile while driving, she had to wait.

"I can't think why I didn't remember while we were having our row," said Libby.

"We weren't having a row," said Fran, "it all comes down to me being ambivalent about these bloody visions, or what ever they are. I thought about it on the way home, and how anyone puts up with my shilly-shallying I don't know."

"You're doing it now," said Libby with a laugh. "You were so certain half an hour ago."

"I know, I know." Fran sighed. "So what did he want me to do? Did he tell you?"

"No, he said you would. He was so helpful about his sister; that's really all I was concentrating on." Libby paused. "Do you think I should ask him and Jane to the party? Would he be well enough, do you think?"

"I thought he had to babysit for his sister?"

"Oh, bugger. Well, perhaps he won't have to, or his sister might think he wouldn't be capable with all his injuries. Anyway, I'll ring him later, or perhaps I'll ring

Jane. Anyway, you call him now. And I'll start digging into Simon Madderling on the computer."

The problem with research, Libby found, was the interesting byways that beckoned. She had been the proud owner of a computer for less than a year and it was still fairly new and exciting. Obviously she'd used them before, but since her marriage broke down, she hadn't had access to any other than Peter's. Now she could email her children and old friends and feel that she was in touch with the real world.

But research — that was something else. Every time she clicked on a vaguely relevant site another link would show up, and off she would go after it like a rabbit down a hole. However, it did come up with some interesting facts, and on this occasion was actually leading her to more information on the elusive Simon Madderling.

The phone rang.

"Terry wants to see me," said Fran. "While Jane's at work."

"Coo!" said Libby. "Does he fancy you?"

"Don't be sillier than you can help," said Fran. "He's got something to tell me. And show me."

"Right. When are you going?"

"Now," said Fran. "I'll ring you later."

"Shall I come over later?"

"No, Bruce is in the area and announced he would take me out to tea this afternoon. There must be a hidden motive, but for Chrissie's sake I suppose I'd better go."

"Rather you than me," said Libby, who had met Bruce once. "I'll look forward to hearing from you, then."

After ten more minutes clicking her way through a trail of links, she came across an official-looking site with many blue underlined sections, indicating further links, which appeared to make particular reference to Simon Madderling. After a few minutes, she realised that it was, in fact, a link she had ignored from another site, but that didn't matter, she told Sidney, who had come in to help, she was there now.

Simon had been born to an English mother and a Belgian father as Simon Maeterlinck, which he had anglicised, the article postulated, in order to quell any rumours of sympathising with the Allies, or later, the Resistance movement. He spoke fluent German and French, and perhaps surprisingly, Italian. Libby raised her eyebrows at this.

The family lived in England and Simon had attended a famous public school and gone on to Oxford, where, it appeared, he had been recruited into MI5. So far, so normal, thought Libby. Then, it appeared, he'd become part of a subdivision of the organisation that monitored all kinds of underground activities. He surfaced now and again as a member of the infamous Right Club, but faded away, only to reappear later when suspicious deaths occurred. How, wondered Libby, did you know which were suspicious deaths in wartime? There was an obvious connection to someone in the Italian embassy who was able to pass messages to the Abwehr (Libby had to look that up: it had been the German intelligence-gathering agency) and to Lord Haw-Haw. During the war, Simon's name had leaked out to the British public and he was branded by them a traitor. In fact, he was a loyal British subject and had been infiltrating subversive organisations and passing on, with great skill, false information.

In 1943 he had disappeared and was never heard of again. His name had been cleared in time, and all his wartime connections investigated. Some had subsequently been tried for war crimes. Another link took the trail to Jessica Maurice, also an employee of MI5 (Yes! thought Libby), with whom Madderling lived in Peel House, which he had bought in 1942. Jessica had continued to work for MI5 until after the end of the war, when she eventually opened Peel House as a guest house. There had been speculation that this had been to provide cover for ongoing operations, but, try as she might, Libby could find no more information about this theory.

Eventually, she sat back and stretched. It didn't seem as though there was any more to find out about Jessica or Simon, or at least, nothing that was in the public domain. She wondered how Fran was getting on with Terry.

Terry was in his own flat when Fran arrived, and made it slowly to the front door and back up again.

"It's the ribs," he confessed. "You wouldn't believe how much they hurt when I move about."

"What about the head?" asked Fran, following him up the stairs.

"Not too bad," he said. "Lucky I've got a thick skull."

"Now," said Fran, when they'd seated themselves in Terry's rather spartan sitting room. "What did you want to tell me?"

He looked away. "It's a bit difficult," he said.

"Why?"

"Because I don't think it's me they're after."

Fran stared at him. "OK," she said finally. "You must have a reason for that."

Terry fished awkwardly in the pocket of his jeans.

"I found that," he said, handing over a crumpled piece of paper.

"It's Jane's name and address," said Fran. "What about it?"

"I found it in here when I got back from hospital. Monday. The day you came round."

"Well, Jane could have given it to anyone, couldn't she? Is it her writing?"

"I don't think so," said Terry. "But, look here, this was on the floor in the bathroom, and I swear it wasn't there before."

"Did the police look round when they came to take their tape off the door?"

"Yes, that's how we knew someone had been in during the week."

"But they didn't find this?"

"No." Terry looked at her with spaniel eyes. "I don't want to scare her, but I'm worried."

"Could *she* have dropped it?" asked Fran. "While she was looking after you?"

"She could have done, but it was stuck, almost hidden by the bath panel."

"What do you mean?"

Terry took a deep breath. "As though someone had taken the bath panel off and dropped the paper before they put it back."

"Looking for something?"

"Yeah." Terry looked down. "I don't know whether I'm making sense."

"You think this is something to do with what I've been looking into?"

He shrugged. "Could be."

"Why didn't you show her?"

"I didn't want to worry her."

"I think you ought to, then if it was hers, she can put your mind at rest. It is only her name and address, after all."

"Yeah, but it could mean someone was looking for her."

"Well, they know where she is now, don't they?"

"What shall I do?" Terry looked at her pleadingly.

"Tell her." Fran stood up. "Show her this and see what she says."

Terry stood up slowly. "Sorry I dragged you over here. I thought perhaps — if I showed you —"

"I might suddenly come up with a reason?" Fran smiled. "I wish I could. I got nothing at all from that piece of paper. Ask Jane when she comes in, and ring and tell me what she says."

Fran was thoughtful as she walked back along Victoria Terrace towards Harbour Street. Terry obviously thought his find was significant, yet to Fran it seemed such a normal thing to find. The name and address of the owner of the house, actually inside the house. Why did it worry Terry so much? Fran stopped dead opposite The Alexandria. Was there another reason? What did Terry know that he wasn't telling anybody? And if he did know something, why had he confided in Fran?

She walked slowly to the railing and looked down on the beach. The obvious reason was that he expected her to be able to tell from just looking at the paper where it came from. Did he suspect he knew where it came from? And if so — how? This led to another question. If he thought he knew where the paper came from, that argued that he might know who had attacked him — and why.

Suddenly, Fran remembered that her son-in-law was taking her to tea. Looking at her watch, she realised that he'd probably been waiting for her for the last ten minutes, and began to run the rest of the way down Victoria Terrace towards The Swan, the only hostelry in the town that Bruce would deign to patronise.

"Thought you'd got lost," he said pushing back his chair and standing up to kiss the air somewhere near her left cheek.

"Sorry," said Fran. "I had an appointment which took longer than I'd anticipated."

"An appointment?" Bruce looked at her in surprise.

"Yes," said Fran, failing to gratify his curiosity. "How's the new house?"

"Oh, fine. Loads to do, of course."

"But I thought it was brand new?" said Fran, smiling up at the waitress who was proffering a teapot.

"It is, but you have to put your mark on it. The kitchen needs a complete redesign." Bruce nodded grumpily as the waitress offered the teapot to him.

"I thought it was a marvellous kitchen," said Fran. "And how's Cassandra?"

"Three kittens," said Bruce proudly. "Little beauties. Over a thousand pounds' worth there."

"Oh, poor Cassandra," said Fran. "Are you going to take all her babies away?"

Bruce looked surprised. "We didn't have them to keep," he said. "She's a breeder. Got a great bloodline."

"Oh," said Fran, wondering how Cassandra felt about that.

The waitress arrived with a selection of cakes on a tiered stand. Bruce looked them over and took three. Fran sighed and took one.

"Doing any more — er — business?" asked Bruce, with a faint sneer.

"Business?" Fran raised an eyebrow.

"Seeing into people's minds, or whatever it is you do."

"Psychic research," said Fran placidly. "No, not at the moment."

"Not helping the police with their enquiries?" Bruce sniggered quietly.

"Just finished." Fran popped the last piece of cake into her mouth.

"Oh?"

"Rounded up a farmer using illegal migrant workers." Fran wiped her fingers on a napkin and sat back, watching Bruce's face.

"Oh." Bruce looked confused. "Oh, good." He sat forward and clicked his fingers. "Just remembered. Meant to tell you. You know I told you about that Italian you were so interested in?"

"Yes?" Fran felt adrenalin kick through her body.

"Saw him again. Never guess where!"

"No, I'm sure I couldn't," said Fran.

"In the car park at Nethergate Station. This afternoon."

CHAPTER
TWENTY-SIX

Fran couldn't wait to tell Libby.

"I still don't see what possible connection it could have to the body — to Andrei, I mean."

"I don't either at the moment," said Fran, "but I connected it when I first heard about it, didn't I? There must be something in it."

Libby jammed her phone between her ear and her shoulder as she poured tea into a mug.

"Did Bruce speak to this person?"

"No, he was just driving out of the car park on his way to his appointment."

"What was he doing in the station car park in the first place?" asked Libby.

"I didn't ask," said Fran.

"All it proves is that a fly-by-night Italian businessman is in the area," said Libby. "It's got absolutely nothing to do with anything. Only Bruce."

"I suppose so." Fran sat down on her sofa and idly scratched Balzac's head.

"What about Terry? What was his startling piece of information?"

Fran repeated her conversation with Terry, concluding with her own thoughts after she'd left him.

"It does seem a bit odd," said Libby. "Almost as if he was trying to make something out of nothing."

"Or point attention somewhere else," said Fran.

"Omigod, yes!" said Libby. "Exactly! What did you say to him?"

"That he was to show it to Jane and see what she had to say."

"And do you think he will?"

"He'll know I'll ask her, so I expect he will."

"Well, I'm going to ring her in a minute to ask them about the party, so shall I ask her then?" asked Libby.

"Better not. I'll do it. In fact, I might even go round there," said Fran.

"Is that safe, do you think?"

"Of course it's safe. Terry's hardly going to bash me up, is he?"

"Is Jane safe?"

"I'm sure she is. He really does seem to be fond of her."

"That could all be an act," said Libby darkly.

"Well, let's wait and see what she says before we go jumping to conclusions," said Fran, "like I did with the Italian businessman."

"Red herrings all over the place," laughed Libby. "When can I call Jane?"

"Whenever you like, but don't mention the piece of paper."

Libby rang off and went back to her computer, where she had printed off all the relevant information about Simon Madderling and Jessica Maurice. Then she punched in Jane's number and waited for the connection.

"Oh, Libby," said Jane excitedly. "You'll never guess what!"

"No," said Libby, "I won't."

"Terry found this piece of paper here in his flat."

Libby stiffened, gripping the handset. Fran hadn't bargained for this.

"And do you know what it was?"

Your name and address, Libby wanted to say. "No," she said aloud.

"It was my name and address written in my friend Rosa's handwriting."

Libby frowned. What could be more normal than that?

"I haven't seen Rosa since just before I moved down her," Jane went on. "She was going to come down for a long visit, and perhaps move down here, too, but she just vanished."

"Vanished?" Libby was having a hard time staying calm.

"Yes. The owner of the café where she worked said she just didn't turn up one morning, and when I tried to call her the phone was out of service."

"And you never heard from her again?"

"No. To tell you the truth, I thought perhaps she was an illegal migrant worker, and perhaps she'd been found out. But don't you see? This looks like a letter from her."

"A piece of paper, you said? Did it look like an envelope?"

"Well, no, but it could have been, couldn't it?"

"I don't know, I haven't seen it," said Libby. "Where did Terry find it, and when?"

Jane repeated all the information Fran had given Libby only moments ago. So he'd told Jane the truth.

"But why should this appear now? It means someone's been in the house. Again," said Libby. "Jane, you should tell the police."

"Should I?"

"Yes." It put a whole new complexion on the normal incident as reported by Fran, thought Libby.

"This Rosa, how long ago did she disappear?" asked Libby.

"Just before I moved down. Over a year ago."

"And what nationality did she say she was?"

"Italian," said Jane.

Half an hour later, Jane having accepted the invitation to Hetty's party on behalf of herself and Terry, Fran and Libby were once more on the phone to each other.

"It does change things, doesn't it?" said Libby.

"It does, but I want to know why Terry thought it was important when on the surface it didn't look like much at all," said Fran.

"Simply because it hadn't been there before," said Libby. "That makes sense."

"It could have worked its way out from behind the bath panel," said Fran, "you know, like pins you stand on work their way up and come out at your knee."

"Do they? Ugh," said Libby. "Yes, I do sort of see what you mean, but it would be unlikely, wouldn't it. I just think Terry's become a bit paranoid after his attack and what with you thinking there's something in the house, and the fact that someone has broken in twice, he jumped to conclusions. Which are probably right."

"How would they have got in again?" asked Fran.

"Terry was sleeping a lot the first couple of days, also he was in Jane's flat much of the time. Whoever it is has a key — probably the one that was stolen."

"So whoever attacked Terry is trying to get at Jane."

"Not necessarily at Jane, just where she lives," said Libby, "which is what you thought in the first place."

"And you think it's this Rosa."

"Yet another disappearing Italian."

"Or possibly Transnistrian."

"We need to talk to Jane," they said together.

If Jane was surprised to find a deputation on her doorstep later that evening, she hid it admirably. Ben had decided to stay in Steeple Martin rather than accompany Libby on yet another foraging trip, as he put it.

"What did you want to talk to me about?" Jane asked when they were settled in her sitting room with the lights of Nethergate twinkling below them.

Libby cast a swift look at Terry, who was trying to look inconspicuous in an armchair.

"Your friend Rosa," said Fran.

"It's definitely her writing on the piece of paper, envelope, or whatever it is?" said Libby.

"Oh, yes. It's quite distinctive. You saw it, didn't you, Fran?"

Fran nodded.

"Can you tell us how you met her? And when?" said Libby.

"But why? She hasn't got anything to do with what's been happening here."

"Then why did Terry find that piece of paper?"

Jane frowned.

"Look, Jane," said Fran, leaning forward. "I know I told Terry there was nothing suspicious about it, but I really think there is, now. I think the police might pooh-pooh the idea, but unless you yourself put that piece of paper in Terry's bathroom, someone else must have done. And broken in to do it."

Jane looked at Terry, who looked down at his lap. "Have you looked behind the bath panel?" she asked him. He looked up and shook his head. "Should we?" she turned to Fran and Libby.

"I doubt it. If there was something there, it'll be gone anyway, and think about it — when was that bathroom put in?"

"Just before I moved in. I had to update all the flats, or I wouldn't have been able to let them. I think I told you."

"Well, that's all right then," said Libby. "Anything hidden would have been found by now. When Aunt Jessica converted the building into flats, she might have taken care to hide anything previously hidden in a new place, but you wouldn't have done, and your builders, or contractors, or whoever they were, would have told you if they'd found anything, wouldn't they?"

"So who could be looking for something now? And why are you interested in Rosa?"

"Because," said Fran patiently, "whoever it was got this address from her."

Jane thought about this. "I think I see," she said.

"So, where did you meet her, and when?" repeated Libby.

"She worked in a café just round the corner from the office where I worked."

"Newspaper office?" asked Fran.

"Yes. It was a London suburban weekly, part of the same group I work for now. The café was the nearest place to get food, either to eat there or take away. We all used it."

"So you just met her there, as a casual acquaintance?" said Libby.

"Yes, about six months before I came down here. She'd been taken on by the owner as a waitress, but she actually did some of the cooking, too. The owner, Pietro, was an Italian who'd been over here since he was a child, and served a lot of pasta and pizza dishes, so Rosa was ideal to help."

"She was a genuine Italian, then?" said Fran. "You said to Libby you wondered if she was an illegal migrant."

"Only after she disappeared. *Because* she disappeared."

"So you met her eighteen months ago or thereabouts," said Libby. "And then you became friends?"

"Yes." Jane looked down at her hands. "You know me, I don't make friends that easily, but she seemed so nice and very quiet, and she didn't have any friends, either. So she used to come home with me and watch television sometimes, or we might go for a meal — somewhere other than Pietro's — or to a film."

"Were you living at home with your mother?" asked Fran.

"Oh, good lord, no!" Jane laughed. "Can you imagine me taking an Italian girl home to meet my mother? No, I had a little studio flat, rented, of course, not far from the office."

"Where was Rosa living?"

"She had a room in a shared house. She'd never let me visit her there, because she said there was no communal living space except the kitchen, which was always untidy, and her room was too small to get anyone in there except her."

"Did she tell you how she came to be in England?" asked Libby.

"I think she came over with a friend to work for the summer to improve her English. She liked it, so she stayed behind when the friend went home."

"She had no relatives over here?"

Jane shook her head. "No. She never spoke of any relatives except her brother, and I think part of the reason she came over here was to get away from him. He sounded the most interfering and overbearing person. Full of family ideals."

"Sounds like the Mafiosi," said Libby.

264

Jane looked worried. "Oh, I hope not," she said. "You don't think that's why she disappeared so suddenly, do you?"

"I shouldn't think so," said Fran.

"Because she'd been so excited about coming here to stay with me. We thought she might find a job down here, in one of the restaurants or hotels. Then, suddenly, she'd gone." Jane frowned. "I couldn't understand it."

Fran looked at Libby, a look which said, you know what I'm thinking, don't you? Libby gave a slight nod.

"What did Pietro know about her?" asked Libby.

"Nothing much. I asked him, of course."

"He must have had to see her work permit," said Fran.

"I don't think he bothered with any of the legal paperwork," said Jane. "He paid her in cash by the day, and didn't even have an address for her, just her mobile number. That was another reason I thought she might be an illegal worker."

"But not if she was Italian," said Libby. "They've been in the EU longer than we have."

"Really?" said Terry. The other three almost jumped at the sound of his voice. "Sorry," he mumbled. "Didn't mean to interrupt."

Jane, Fran and Libby laughed, breaking the tension.

"Shall I make some coffee?" asked Jane. "Or would you like a glass of wine?"

"Coffee for me, please," said Libby. "I've got to drive. Oh, and by the way, I never got round to asking you, Terry, did your sister get her babysitter if you're not doing it?"

Terry grinned. "She didn't trust me," he said, "so a friend's doing it for her. So Jane and I can come to the party. It's great of you to ask us."

"Least we could do as you've provided the entertainment," Libby smiled back.

Conversation became general until Jane reappeared with mugs of coffee. "Only instant, I'm afraid," she said. "I'm not very into coffee." She sat down. "Funny, that. Rosa was. Pietro had an Espresso machine, and she made all sorts of concoctions on it. People used to say she should work for Starbucks."

"Jane," said Fran, putting her mug back on the tray. "What was Rosa's surname?"

"I never knew," said Jane. "I know that sounds silly, but I never needed to know."

"You never even heard it?"

"No. I suppose Pietro would have known."

"Do you think he'd remember?" asked Libby.

"He might have done, but he's not there any more," said Jane. "The café's closed down."

"Oh." Libby and Fran looked at one another. "And do you know where he went?"

"Back to Italy, someone at the office said." Jane shrugged. "Pity. It was a good café."

"Did you ever get the idea that Pietro might have known Rosa before? Or that they were close in any way?" asked Fran.

"Oh, no. She always called him 'signore', and anyway, Pietro's wife was always there. Big woman with

266

a headscarf." Jane smiled reminiscently. "I think she was of the 'good riddance to bad rubbish' opinion when Rosa went."

"So the Pietros went back to Italy. And they'd been here for years?" said Libby.

"His father was an Italian prisoner of war," said Jane, "and married an English girl. A lot of them did."

"Yes," said Libby. "I was talking about that the other evening."

"What about Mrs Pietro?" asked Fran.

"They met when Pietro went back to Italy to see his family. There were lots of them, I believe."

"Back to Mafiosi again," said Libby, and Jane looked worried.

"So we can't find out anything about this Rosa, where she came from or who she really was," said Fran.

"No," said Jane, "and I did try at the time."

"What did Pietro look like?" asked Libby suddenly. Jane looked startled.

"Well," she said, "he was very dark — hair and skin — about, oh, I don't know, fifty? Very smart when he wasn't in his chef's apron. Well-built, but not fat."

"Good-looking?" asked Fran.

"I don't know." Jane wrinkled her face. "He was a bit old for me, so I never noticed."

Libby and Fran exchanged amused glances.

"Well, that's all for now, Jane. Sorry to have taken so much of your time," said Fran, "but although the police might not take it seriously, we do."

"The break-in?" said Terry.

"Oh, I think they take that seriously, no I meant our famous piece of paper," said Fran. "The police would think what I did at first, but I'm pretty sure now it's the clue to the whole thing."

"Really?" Jane frowned. "I can't see how."

"I can't tell you quite yet," said Fran, "but as soon as I've worked on the details, I'll let you have the story as far as I can see it."

"And what's that?" asked Libby as they went down the steps of Peel House.

"The story? Well, you made the connections the same as I did, didn't you?"

"That Rosa could be the mysterious vanishing Italian of the false passport? Yes."

"And that Pietro could be the mysterious vanishing Italian businessman?"

"Couldn't quite see that," admitted Libby.

"They both worked near Jane's office and had the opportunity to get to know her."

"But Pietro had been there for years before Jane got the job."

"Whoever's behind this might have made use of him and sent Rosa there. I bet she disappeared when Lena was arrested, sent back home probably."

"That makes sense," said Libby, opening Romeo's passenger door for Fran. "But why did Pietro sell up and go back home?"

"If he'd stayed there, I'd not have thought of him in connection with this business at all," said Fran, "but the fact that he disappeared not long afterwards suggests that he's involved somehow. But you had seen it, because you were the one who asked what he looked like."

"Well, yes," said Libby, "because of Bruce seeing this bloke again today. But I didn't seriously believe it."

"Tell you what," said Fran, "I think we ought to ask Ian to show a copy of Lena's borrowed passport to Jane."

"Could he get hold of that?"

"Now that she's involved with his investigation, I should think he'd have access to all her papers, which would include the photocopy taken by the council."

"Would he do that? He's not involved with this case."

"No, but Rosa — or whoever she is — is involved with Lena's."

Libby thought about this while turning Romeo round at the entrance of The Tops car park.

"Are you going to tell McLean any of this?" she asked.

"No. If anything comes of it, Ian can tell him in the ordinary way."

"No psychic investigation, then?"

"It's been guesswork so far, hasn't it?"

"There's a few rather tenuous links that only you could have forged," said Libby, crossing the square to go down Harbour Street.

"You didn't have to drop me at the door," said Fran. "You'll have to turn round again now."

"Doesn't matter, and you shouldn't have to walk home in the dark," said Libby. "Look what happened to Terry."

"I am looking at what happened to Terry," said Fran, as she opened her door. "And the more I look at it, the more it seems to me that the body on the island and the mystery of Peel House are linked."

CHAPTER
TWENTY-SEVEN

Inspector Connell, when appealed to, asked if he might come and see Fran later on Thursday morning to discuss her "theories" on his case. Fran agreed and called Libby.

"Shall I come over?" asked Libby.

"No, I'll manage on my own, thanks," said Fran. "Romeo will know his way over here on his own, soon."

"Oh, I don't mind driving," said Libby. "Before you see Ian, though, I'll email you all that stuff I found about Simon Madderling. Might help."

"Help with what?"

"Convincing him to look into Terry's case as well as his own."

"He'll only tell me he's not a cold case unit," said Fran.

"But it has a bearing on his own," said Libby.

"Yes, I know, and I shall try and convince him of that."

"Why," said Ian later, when he was settled with a cup of coffee in Fran's kitchen, "did you suddenly take everything up again?"

"Because I kept seeing things," said Fran. "I thought whatever it was — is — had gone, and I wouldn't ever see anything again, but all these pictures were wafting about in my brain, so I thought I ought to look into them. Libby thought I was trying too hard and none of them would mean anything, but the most surprising things have turned out to be linked."

"And you're going to tell me about them," said Ian, his lean dark face at its most severe.

"I'll try," said Fran. "I just hope it all makes sense."

She began with her feelings about Peel House, then went on to the farm pictures.

"You know about Lena and her brother," she said, "but not about who we think the Italian woman is."

"Italian woman?" Ian frowned.

"The one who lent Lena her passport. We think she's someone called Rosa who made friends with Jane Maurice in London."

"And why would she want to make friends with Jane Maurice?"

Fran explained about Jessica and Simon Madderling and gave Ian the documents Libby had sent over. He glanced through them and frowned again.

"We haven't got a cold case unit here," he said, as Fran had predicted.

"No, I know, but I'm sure there's something hidden in that house that someone else wants," said Fran.

"After all this time?" Ian raised his eyebrows. "Unless it's a priceless jewel, of course."

"Don't be sarcastic," said Fran. "You've trusted my judgement before. You'll see from that information that Madderling had connections with someone in the Italian embassy during the war, and spoke fluent

Italian. If he had something that belonged to this person, or that incriminated him, he may have asked Jessica Maurice to keep it for him until he returned from wherever he was going. Only he never came back."

"And the descendants of this mythical Italian are trying to retrieve whatever it is by tracking down Jane Maurice and hitting her boyfriend over the head?" Ian shook his head. "Honestly, Fran. If it was an incriminating document it would hardly have any relevance now, would it? Over sixty years after the end of the war?"

Fran sighed. "Look," she said, "do you agree that it's odd that Jane's house should have been broken into and searched more than once recently? Since that body was found?"

"Andrei Gruzevich," put in Ian.

"Him, yes. Well?"

"Not really. It's been broken into because Terry Baker's keys were stolen."

"Why was the body left on Dragon Island? Why wasn't it dumped in the water?"

"Because whoever dumped it wanted it found."

"Why would they do that when they'd removed all identifying marks?"

Ian scowled. "Don't think we haven't been working on this, Fran."

"I'm sure you have, and with the best technology and expertise at your disposal, but just think. Without my suggestion about showing him to Lena you still wouldn't know who he was."

"True," conceded Ian. "We also think we know now where the flat was that Rosa Francini rented."

Fran gasped. "Rosa Francini? That's the Italian woman's name?"

"Yes."

"You see! That proves it. It's Rosa who befriended Jane and then disappeared. And I bet her disappearance coincides with Lena's arrest."

"I'll look into it," said Ian uncomfortably.

"So, did Lena show you the flat?"

"At first she couldn't remember anything about it except that it was obviously expensive and somewhere near Victoria. However, when it was pointed out to her that she must have known the address in order to go out and get back again, she said it was in Lansdowne Square, and she knew how to get there without taking any notice of the number of the building."

"Did she have a key?"

"While she was living there, yes. Not for long, because she got her council job and went off to live in a bedsit."

"And she didn't know what Rosa did for a living?"

"Nothing, she thought. Her brother and Rosa were having an affair, which was why Rosa lent the passport."

"Yes, McLean told us that," said Fran. "And that he — or the television company — had tracked down the bar where Andrei worked. But not the flat."

"Well, we have now. It turns out that it's owned by an Italian company and managed by agents over here."

"So who paid the rent on it?"

"Rosa Francini."

"Who wasn't working, so she must have had plenty of money."

Ian shrugged. "She had a false passport, so whatever she was doing here, there was a criminal element to it, which means there was money involved somewhere."

"Well, will you let Jane see the photocopy of the passport?" Fran leant her elbows on the table and looked earnestly at Ian. "It's important, Ian, it really is."

"All right. Tell her to come to the station and ask for me. If I'm not there, ask for Maiden."

"Oh, I remember him," said Fran. "He's the redhead, isn't he? But I thought he was in uniform, not CID."

"He's recently been transferred." Ian smiled briefly. "Keen as mustard. So ask for DC Maiden."

"I'll tell her. And if it is the same woman, will you look into it?"

"Into what?"

"The break-in at Peel House."

Ian gave an exasperated sigh. "It's not my case."

"But if this is the same woman, it could be connected."

Ian stood up. "I'll see," he said. "But only because it's you."

Fran smiled up at him and saw a flicker of awareness in his eyes. Hastily, she too stood up, and went swiftly past him towards the front door.

"Thanks, Ian," she said as he stepped out into Harbour Street. "I'm sure you won't regret it."

He pulled down the corners of his mouth. "I damn well hope I won't," he said.

As soon as she'd closed the door behind him, she picked up her phone and called Jane.

"There's something I want you to see at the police station," she said without preamble. "I'll come with you, if you like. When could you go?"

"The police station?" said Jane, sounding thoroughly bewildered. "Why? What for?"

"You'll see when we get there. It's a long shot, but it might explain things."

Jane was all for leaving straight away, but Fran knew that Connell wouldn't have had time to set things up at the station, so persuaded her to leave it until after lunch. Luckily, Jane's job as a reporter meant she was free to leave the office at any time.

The police station was at the top of the town beyond the railway station. Jane and Fran met there at two o'clock.

"Is Inspector Connell in?" Fran asked the desk sergeant.

"No, madam, afraid not." He beamed, as though this was the very news she wished to hear.

"DC Maiden, then? Inspector Connell will have informed him."

"Oh?" The sergeant lost his smile. "Who shall I say?"

"Miss Maurice and Mrs Castle."

Fran saw her name make an impression, as he turned away to pick up the phone and mutter into it. They barely had time to sit on the bench seat opposite the desk when DC Maiden, red hair on end and blue eyes bright with enthusiasm, appeared through swing doors.

"Mrs Castle," he said holding out a hand. "Nice to see you again."

"And you," said Fran politely. "And this is Jane Maurice."

Maiden's eyes flitted quickly over Jane and Fran saw the ready colour start to creep up her neck.

"Pleased to meet you," said Maiden. "You wanted to see this photocopy?" He held the swing doors open for them and Jane frowned up at Fran.

"Please. Inspector Connell told you about it?"

"Some of it." He glanced quickly at Fran, and she remembered his open-mouthed astonishment last year when she'd surprised everybody by visualising a scene that proved in the end to have taken place.

Jane was still looking puzzled as Maiden collected a file from an office and showed them into an interview room. Now she looked simply scared. Fran patted her hand.

"It's all right, Jane," she said. "Just a little mystery to clear up."

Maiden turned his bright blue eyes on Jane's pale, scared face. "Have a look at this, Miss Maurice," he said, and pushed a piece of paper towards her.

Jane looked and her eyes widened. She gasped and looked at Fran.

"But that's Rosa!" she said. "What's happened to her? Is she all right?"

"We don't know," said Fran and turned back to DC Maiden. "Thank you, Mr Maiden. Would you inform

Inspector Connell about this? He knows what it's about."

Maiden retrieved the paper and put it back in the file. "Certainly. As I said, he's explained some of it. I believe he said he would be in touch with Miss Maurice later today if she identified the subject."

Jane nodded and allowed herself to be led out of the interview room. Fran said goodbye to DC Maiden and almost pushed Jane out onto the pavement.

"Would you like me to be there when Inspector Connell talks to you?" she said.

"Yes, please. You haven't even told me what this is about. Where did they get her passport?"

"It's a long story," said Fran. "Have you got to get straight back to work?"

"No," said Jane. "It's Thursday, so the paper's gone to bed. I'll have to work on a couple of things over the weekend, so I'm free now. Let's go into Giglio's. I need a hot chocolate."

Giglio's was a nineteen-fifties-style ice-cream parlour, which Fran knew from personal experience hadn't changed since her childhood. Hot chocolate was served in glass mugs with chrome holders and pictures of the island of Giglio, after which the café was named, decorated the walls.

"Now," said Jane, when they were seated at one of the little round, glass-topped tables, "tell me what this is about."

Fran told her the whole story. Apart from slight pique because she hadn't been allowed to interview Fran in the first place, Jane listened intently, asking only one or two questions when the narrative became over-complicated.

"So," she said, leaning back in her chair when Fran had finished. "Rosa wasn't really Rosa any more than this Lena person was?"

"No."

"And you think she made friends with me deliberately?"

"It looks possible," said Fran carefully.

Jane shook her head. "I don't see why you think that. She was on a false passport. When the other girl was arrested it made sense for her to disappear."

"She was living in a luxury flat in Belgravia," said Fran, "not a bedsit in Battersea."

"I still think you're on the wrong track," said Jane. "There's absolutely no evidence to say she was trying to make friends with me in particular, or for any particular reason."

"What about the piece of paper Terry found?"

"I don't know," said Jane testily. "All this passport proves is that she had a kind heart, lending it to her lover's homeless, displaced sister just to help her."

Fran looked at her consideringly. "What about Aunt Jessica and Simon Madderling?"

"What about them?" Jane lifted her chin. "Aunt Jess was obviously a bit of a heroine in the war, and Simon was a hero — even if that wasn't discovered until too late. There isn't anything else."

"OK." Fran sighed. "We'll leave it at that. At least you've confirmed for the police who Rosa was — or wasn't. That's all you need to say to Inspector Connell when he calls you."

Jane wilted a little. "You said you'd be with me."

"He'll call first, and if that's all you've got to tell him he won't need to see you, will he?"

"No, I suppose not," said Jane.

"Tell me, Jane," said Fran, stirring what remained of her hot chocolate. "Why have you changed your mind? Yesterday you were all for finding out all about the piece of paper. And keen to know about your aunt and Peel House."

Jane sat looking at the table top for a long time. "I suppose," she said eventually, "it's because it's suddenly become real and personal."

"It couldn't have got more real than poor old Terry being knocked over the head," said Fran, amused.

"But it wasn't *me*," said Jane. "I was just worried because Terry had been hurt. And even though I knew his flat had been searched, it didn't really feel like anything to do with me. And it brought us together," she added, the familiar colour rising up her neck again.

"But you were quite excited when you thought I might find out something last Monday night."

"I told you, it didn't seem real. It was like a story." She hunched her shoulders. "But now — with the police —"

"I know." Fran picked up her bag. "Come on. You don't still want to be here when the Inspector calls."

"What about Pietro?" Jane asked suddenly as they reached the square. "You didn't mention him to the Inspector."

"There's even less to connect him to anything that's been happening at your house than Rosa. Or whatever her name was."

Jane nodded. "Well, I'll go home and tell Terry all about it. And we'll see you on Saturday at Libby's party?"

"Of course you will," said Fran. "Give my regards to Terry."

And that was that, she told herself, as she walked back along Harbour Street to Coastguard Cottage. If Jane had been frightened off there was nothing more she could do, even for her own sake. Ian had his identification, Jane knew the history of her house as it related to her aunt, the only outstanding mystery was who hit Terry, and why. And unless she had a sudden inspiration about that, it looked likely to remain a mystery for some time to come.

CHAPTER
TWENTY-EIGHT

On Saturday evening at seven o'clock, Ben opened the front door of The Manor and led his parents outside.

"We're picking Libby up at the theatre," he said. "She had to pop in for something."

"Shall we wait here?" asked Hetty.

"No, love, I'd like to see what they've been doing in the theatre," said Greg, who was in on the secret. "Let's go in."

The foyer was quiet. Ben went up to the double doors into the auditorium and gave them a little push as a signal, then stepped back. Suddenly, both doors were swept open, a great cheer went up and the piano struck up "Down at the Old Bull and Bush". Hetty stood, struck dumb, flanked by her husband and son.

When the song finished, everyone in the auditorium cheered and applauded, and Hetty was led down to the stage, where Libby and Peter helped her up on to the stage and presented her with a huge bouquet. By this time, she was looking suspiciously bright eyed, and Ben, after a few words of greeting and explanation, led her and Greg to a table on the opposite side of the stage to the piano, where Peter, James and their mother, Millie, and Susan, Ben's sister, already sat.

Harry presided over a huge industrial barbeque in the tiny garden, and came in to join them as they took their seats.

Members of The Oast House Theatre company manned the bar, and after several more rousing choruses of well known, if ancient, songs, Libby sipped a glass of red wine and confided to Ben that it seemed to be going well and Hetty was enjoying it.

"Told you she would." Ben cast a critical eye over the recreated pub on the stage. "Dad said it took him back."

"I can't quite see him in a public bar during the war," said Libby, laughing.

"Not here, no," said Ben. "I told you, didn't I, there was always trouble between the pickers and the home dwellers, and the Squire's son, as he was known then, wouldn't have got involved. But when he was in the army he could do what he liked."

"Not quite," said Libby, amused.

"You know what I mean." Ben gave her a friendly thump on the arm. "Is that young Jane's Terry over there? I'd like to meet him."

"Come on then, I'll introduce you," said Libby and led him down into the auditorium, where Terry's eyes were fixed on his beautiful sister, who was playing and singing like a demon.

"Good, isn't she?" said Jane proudly.

"Wonderful," said Libby. "We just couldn't have found anyone so perfect. Thank you, Terry."

He dipped his head modestly. "Thanks," he said.

Libby introduced Ben, then went off to find Fran. She and Guy were discovered in the queue for sausages and mash in the garden.

"Fantastic, isn't it?" said Guy. "Well done you."

"Oh, I only organised Terry's sister, and that was by accident," said Libby.

"You helped with the set and the wardrobe, though, didn't you?" asked Fran.

"A bit," said Libby honestly, "but most of it was the others. Peter and Ben, mainly." She looked over her shoulder. "So, have you heard anything from Jane since Thursday?"

Fran shook her head. "Ian phoned and said he'd talked to her and got the same result as I did, but he'd decided anyway to have a look a bit deeper. He said a grudging thank you." She grinned. "I do annoy him!"

"So he's going to look into Terry's attack, is he?"

"I'm not sure, but he intends to follow up on Rosa." Fran sighed. "Nothing more for us to do, though, Lib."

"No." Libby chewed her lip. "Do you think we ought to have asked Mike a bit more about that evening?"

"When he found Terry? He was questioned by the police, wasn't he? I don't think he'd have responded very well to us poking about. Look at how he was when we went in last Monday."

"I just can't help feeling . . ." Libby tailed off. "Especially after Bruce said he saw that Italian again . . ."

Fran's eyes widened. "You think Mike Charteris is the disappearing Italian?"

"He could be, couldn't he?"

"What on earth does a business contact of Bruce's have to with Terry?" asked Guy.

"Oh, that was me in the first place," said Fran uncomfortably. "I was busy making connections all over the place, most of which had no relevance to each other at all."

"I said you were under too much pressure," said Guy, giving her a squeeze. "Oh, thanks, Harry." He handed one laden plate to Fran.

"What about the old trout?" asked Harry.

"I'll have mine later," said Libby, "on the FKO principal."

"FKO?" asked Guy.

"Family Keep Off," said Libby. "If you had guests that's what you said to the children, to allow the guests to have what they wanted before the family got their mitts on it."

"I thought everyone knew that," said Fran, pouring brown sauce on top of her mashed potatoes, while Libby looked on with disfavour.

"Anyway," she said, "I'm still suspicious of Mike. I was from the start. Especially when he kept trying to get into Jane's apartment."

"Well, don't say anything to Jane," said Fran. "She's busy blanking it out at the moment. She'll go to pieces if she starts worrying about Mike as well."

"Ah, but Terry's there to look after her," said Libby. "I bet they move into the one flat, soon."

"When he's strong enough," said Guy, with a wink.

"Cheeky," said Libby and left them to their sausages.

A little while later, the family tucked into their own meals, while Terry's sister took a break.

"Good stuff, gal," said Hetty. "Your idea, the music, was it?"

Libby nodded modestly.

"Lenny's idea to have the party," said Flo, who'd joined them. Hetty raised her glass to him.

"That gal's good, too. Knows all the songs better'n I do."

"She sent us her set list and I downloaded all the words," said Peter.

"That's these, is it?" asked Greg, lifting his song sheets. "Very clever. Not sure I'd know how, but Ben is teaching me his computer slowly, aren't you boy?"

Libby hid a grin at Ben being called "boy".

"It's helping find some of the old army buddies, isn't it, Dad?" He smiled over at his father.

"Fascinating," said Greg, pushing his plate aside. "Do you know, there are more of them still alive than I would have believed."

"There's even talk of a reunion next year," said Ben.

"Later this year," corrected Greg. "More chance of getting there." He twinkled across at Hetty who patted his arm.

When Terry's sister returned to the piano, the lights in the auditorium were lowered and a spotlight picked up Harry, who carried an enormous birthday cake down the central aisle to a deafening chorus of "Happy Birthday To You". Hetty was persuaded to say a few gruff words of thanks, and the party resumed.

By eleven o'clock people were beginning to leave and Terry's sister, with the effusive thanks of most of Steeple Martin, drove back to her babysitter. Terry and Jane came up to thank Libby and Ben for the party.

"It was so good to get out," said Jane, "and do something completely different."

"Yeah, really took our minds off things," added Terry.

Fran and Guy were soon after them, as Guy had been chauffeur for all four of them, and as Libby and Ben waved them off, Libby yawned widely.

"Have we got to do all the clearing up tonight?" she asked.

"No, tomorrow will do. Harry, bless him, is paying Donna and the current boy-in-the-kitchen to collect all the glasses and empties, so all we've got to do is strike the set, so to speak, and clean up."

"Good," said Libby. "Then if you don't mind, I shall say goodbye to your mum and dad and go home."

"I'll have to wait until everyone's gone," said Ben. Libby sighed.

"OK, I'll wait too," she said, "but I'm still going to say goodnight to your parents. They must be whacked."

Hetty pronounced herself delighted with the whole affair and shepherded a quite perky Greg off to The Manor. "Done 'im good, too," she told Libby, as they trundled off.

"All those people who it done good to," Libby said to Ben, as they finally walked down the Manor drive a little later. "Hetty, Greg, Jane, Terry — did it do you good, too?"

"It made me very proud of my family and friends," said Ben, squeezing her arm, "and very pleased that, for a few days at least, we haven't got anything to do at all."

Guy drew up in front of Peel House and switched off the engine.

"Would you like a nightcap?" offered Jane shyly. "It's only half past eleven."

"That's very kind," said Fran, "if you don't mind, Guy?"

"No, that's fine," he said, and stretched. "I can leave the car here and collect it in the morning."

"Thanks for taking us," said Terry, as he clambered awkwardly out of the back seat. "Great party."

"Terry!" Jane's voice was suddenly sharp.

"What?" They all swung round.

"Did you leave my lights on?"

"No." Terry looked up. "It was daylight when we left."

"They're on now."

Fran felt her heart thump hard in her chest, and reached out for Guy's hand.

"Don't go in," she whispered.

Terry looked back at her. "Got to," he said, and took the key from Jane.

The four of them crowded silently into the hall, and Terry began slowly to climb the stairs, the other three following reluctantly. He paused outside his own front door and carefully unlocked it, peering inside. Shaking his head, he waved a hand at the others, indicating they shouldn't follow, but Guy pushed past Jane and began to climb the final flight behind him.

The light went out. Blackness descended on them all, and Fran felt herself suffocating. The silence was absolute. She wanted to call out, but couldn't.

Instead, she found Jane's hand and hung on tight. For a long moment nothing happened. Then came a crash from somewhere above them and a deep groan.

Something brushed past Fran and she screamed. "Stay there." Guy's voice was muffled. Fran found the light switch and they stood looking down at the unconscious form of Mike Charteris on the lower landing.

"Christ," said Guy.

"Where did he come from? Why didn't we see him on the way up?" said Jane. "And where's Terry?"

"He went on up," said Guy.

"So who did we hear?" said Fran, the icy cold invading her again.

"Terry!" screamed Jane and leapt up the stairs with Fran after her. They rounded the last bend and something loomed over them. A black shape that slowly moved to block their way, then, almost in slow motion, toppled towards them.

Fran pulled Jane back against the wall as Terry slid gracefully down the stairs on his front.

CHAPTER
TWENTY-NINE

"Bloody hell," said Guy as he knelt to look at the back of Terry's head. Fran squeezed past and pulling her mobile out of her bag went down to check on Mike, who still lay on the landing. She punched in 999 and called for police and an ambulance, by which time Guy had joined her.

"Mike must have been here when we came up in the dark," said Fran, switching off the phone. "I felt something go past me." She frowned. "But I didn't hear anything after that. I don't get it. Oh, God." She put her hand to her mouth. "That means they're still there."

"Jane!" Guy ran quickly to pull the weeping girl down on to the landing. "There might still be someone here."

Fran crept past Mike, who, she noticed, seemed to be breathing quite normally, and down the stairs. The front door was open. She caught her breath again, then with relief saw the blue light of a police car coming along Cliff Terrace.

The next half an hour was pandemonium. The police herded them all into Terry's flat, and while the paramedics attended to and subsequently removed

290

Mike and Terry, searched Jane's flat. Then they began to take brief statements.

"Are you in trouble again?"

Fran looked up with relief. "Ian!" she said.

"Sir," said both the policemen.

Constable Maiden bounded into the room and beamed at Fran and Jane.

"I suppose we couldn't go up to Jane's flat now they've searched it, could we?" asked Fran. "They'll want to search in here and Mike's flat, too, won't they?"

"Crime scene, sir," said one of the uniforms.

"Well, where can we go?" said Fran.

"It's all right, Constable," said Connell. "I'll take the responsibility." He shepherded them all out.

In the top flat, Fran went into Jane's kitchen and put the kettle on, more because she needed something to do than any real desire for tea or coffee.

"I need to see Terry," Jane was sobbing into Guy's shoulder. Connell was looking exasperated.

"We'll run you to the hospital as soon as we can," he said. "We've just got to establish whether anything's missing or there's any damage."

Reluctantly, Jane got to her feet and allowed Fran to lead her round the flat.

"Nothing," she said, when they came back to the living room.

"Nothing missing?" Connell frowned. "You didn't look very hard."

"I haven't got very much," said Jane.

"Were they disturbed, do you think?" asked Guy.

"They?"

"We think there were two of them," said Fran, and explained.

"So, you think Mr Charteris heard them and came to investigate? Then when you came in they knocked Mr Baker on the head and escaped?"

"Seems like it," said Guy.

"So — what happened?" asked Jane, who had (temporarily, Fran was sure) stopped crying.

"We haven't had much time to work it out, but you said the lights came on again, which was when you saw Mr Charteris?"

"Yes," said Jane.

"I switched them on," said Fran.

"Yes."

"Well, it would appear that Mr Baker came up the stairs, whoever was here switched off the lights and hit him from behind, then ran down the stairs. You felt him go past, Mrs Castle. He must have put Mr Charteris out of action earlier." Connell frowned. "Very quick thinking."

"Will this be your case now?" asked Fran after a moment while they all took this in.

"I'll liaise with the team who investigated the first attack," said Connell, standing up. "Now, we'll get Miss Maurice to hospital and you and Mr Wolfe can go home, Mrs Castle. And please don't even think of poking your nose into this investigation."

Fran bit her lip, and nodded. "Will you be all right, Jane?" she asked. "Do you want me to come with you?"

"Miss Maurice will be fine," said Connell. "Thank you, Mrs Castle. I shall want to talk to you again tomorrow, of course."

"Of course," said Guy and Fran together.

Outside, they had to convince the officers on guard duty that they had permission to drive Guy's car away, then run the gauntlet of interested bystanders and one persistent young man with a camera and a tape recorder.

"I wonder if that was Jane's boss?" said Fran as they finally made it into Victoria Terrace and down to the square.

Guy grunted.

Once inside Coastguard Cottage, he found Fran's bottle of gin and poured them both large measures topped up with tonic.

"So will you?" he said, leaning back in his armchair and watching her quizzically.

"Will I what?" Fran leant her head against the cushion and closed her eyes.

"Poke your nose into this investigation?"

Fran opened her eyes again. "Not if I can help it," she said.

"Libby will."

"Not without me, she can't," said Fran. "And I bet you anything you like Ian will be asking me for 'any thoughts' within a day or so, whatever he says now."

"Why?"

"He asked me about Andrei's body — the body on the island — in the first place. He allowed the Kent and Coast investigation with me along. And he got his identification of Andrei's body through me. He'll ask." She closed her eyes again.

"But this time you're too closely involved," said Guy, leaning forward and grasping her hand. "We all could have been hurt tonight. You're actually a witness."

"I don't think that will make any difference," said Fran tiredly. "Rather the reverse."

Guy sighed.

Libby and Ben, bidden to Sunday lunch at Flo's little house, along with Hetty and Greg, wandered in a desultory fashion round The Oast House Theatre on the following morning. Harry's minions had already done most of the clearing up, and Ben said he refused to dismantle "Hetty's Bar" without the help of his cousins.

At twelve thirty, Flo being insistent that lunch was not lunch unless served at one o'clock, they collected Hetty and Greg from The Manor and strolled down to Maltby Close.

"Hear the news this mornin'?" asked Flo, having provided them all with drinks, and an ashtray for Libby.

"Local, she means," said Lenny. "Radio Kent."

"Don't listen to it," said Ben.

"Some bloke got 'is 'ead bashed in for a second time down in Nethergate," said Flo. "That's where your Fran lives, ain't it?"

"What?" said Ben and Libby together. Libby dabbed at the red wine she'd splashed onto her jeans. "Did it say who? Where?"

"'Is own 'ome," said Lenny. "Wasn't takin' that much notice till they said Nethergate."

"Terry," said Ben and Libby, looking at each other.

"Not that young feller whose sister played last night?" said Hetty.

"Oh, my gawd," said Flo.

"I'd better ring Fran," said Libby. "She might not know."

Outside in Flo's tiny garden, Libby punched in Fran's number.

Five minutes later she was back inside.

"She was there," she announced dramatically. "They all were. Inside Jane's house."

Everyone started speaking at once, but eventually Hetty called order and told Libby to tell her story.

"Are you going down there?" asked Greg.

"No." Libby shook her head. "She and Guy are spending the day quietly. Connell had them into the station this morning to sign statements, and Jane is still at the hospital, apparently."

"How are Terry and Mike now, does she know?" asked Ben.

"Only what Ian told them this morning. Mike was going to be allowed home, he wasn't badly hurt, apparently, but Terry was being kept in. I don't know what state he's in, poor bloke."

"It could be serious, couldn't it?" asked Greg. "If he's only just come out of hospital after a bad bang on the head?"

"And he fell on his front." Libby winced. "That won't have done his ribs any good."

"Nothing we can do at the moment, then?" said Ben.

"No." Libby sighed. "Nothing."

Flo provided, as usual, a splendid traditional roast and wouldn't let anyone help her clear up, especially Hetty. Ben and Libby left the four older people dozing in armchairs and decided to pop in to the pub on the way home.

The afternoon was mild, if cloudy, and they took their drinks into the garden, where children and smokers made an unlikely amalgamation.

"Fran says Mike was already unconscious when Terry was hit, so it couldn't have been him," said Libby.

"Mike? Did you think it could have been him?"

"I told you I was suspicious of him, didn't I? Turning up all pat as soon as Jane advertised the flat. And then being the one to find Terry, when nobody else saw him."

"But I thought he'd been ruled out anyway?"

"Oh, yes," sighed Libby. "He's just an ordinary bloke down here on a contract. His references all checked out. He just seemed very keen on getting into Jane's flat."

"Single bloke — attractive girl — can't see anything suspicious in that," laughed Ben.

"No, I know. Pity, though. At least we would have known who the attacker was then. Now it's just some complete stranger."

"What about this connection with the Italian girl?" asked Ben. "Is it anything to do with her?"

"I can't see how," said Libby. "Although there was the piece of paper. I'm sure Fran will have given Ian all the information by now, so he'll be looking into it thoroughly. Bet he asks for Fran's help."

"Hasn't he already?"

"No." Libby giggled. "Apparently he told her not to poke her nose in!"

Ben laughed. "Doesn't sound like Ian."

"No, but I reckon he's a bit confused at the moment, like the rest of us. Fran's been blowing hot and cold for weeks, and he doesn't know where he is."

"Not blowing hot and cold about him?" Ben's eyes narrowed.

"No, no. She assured me she's over that particular aberration." Libby gazed into the distance. "He is attractive, though."

"Hmm," said Ben. "By the way. Do you remember our conversation about old boyfriends and girlfriends?"

Libby brought her gaze back. "About tastes changing and all that?"

"Yes. Mind you, I'm not sure what this proves, if anything." He reached round into the pocket of his jeans and brought out an envelope. "Have a look at this."

Libby opened the envelope and drew out an obviously old black and white photograph.

"That's me!" she gasped. "I've never seen this before. Where was it taken? Where did you get it?"

"I took it," said Ben.

Libby stared at him with her mouth open. "You what?" she managed eventually.

He laughed. "I knew you hadn't recognised me when we met a few years ago, but when we began to get —

well, better acquainted, let's say — I thought it might click. Never has, though, has it?"

"But Ben, I'd swear I'd never met you before." Libby's eyes were wide with worry. "How could I have forgotten you?"

"Do you remember Tony Bush and Colin Rabson?"

"Yes. From the boys' grammar school."

"I was one of their crowd. I fancied you rotten."

Libby felt herself turning pink. "Oh, God, Ben, I'm sorry," she said. "Why didn't you remind me when we first met?" She looked down at the photograph. "I don't remember anything about this. Where were we?"

"Colin had borrowed his dad's car and six of us went to Box Hill for the day." He smiled ruefully. "I guess I made no impression at all."

"Neither did the day," said Libby. "I remember going to Box Hill several times — my father's boss had a caravan there, of all things, and he used to lend it to us for weekends. And my first proper boyfriend and I used to go there for the day." She looked at the picture again. "So this proves that tastes change. I didn't even notice you then, and now I fancy you rotten, too."

He smiled and took her outstretched hand. "Snap."

"But what were you doing in London at school? You were born and brought up here."

"When do you think this was taken?"

"I haven't got a clue." Libby looked back at the photograph. "I must have been about nineteen, I suppose."

"That's about it. And Tony, Colin and I were students together. Remember I told you I did backstage work in theatres when I was a student?"

"And this was then?"

"Tony and Colin said they had a friend who was a drama student and we'd have something in common." He laughed. "Can't say we did, though. I don't think you noticed me."

"Perhaps you weren't as charismatic as you are now?"

"Charismatic? Moi?" Ben clasped his hand theatrically to his chest.

Libby looked fondly across the table at the closely cropped grey hair and brilliant blue eyes, all wrapped up in a blue shirt and worn jeans. She experienced the same swooping feeling in her stomach that had characterised her first meetings with Ben, a "teenagerish" reaction, as she put it herself.

"You know you are," she said. "And I haven't got a clue what you see in me."

"Stop fishing," he said, leaning across the table and recapturing her hand. "And don't look at me like that, or I shall rush you straight back to your bedroom."

"Wow," said Libby softly.

CHAPTER
THIRTY

Sitting in Jane's flat, Fran heard the slam of a car door through the open window. Looking out, she saw Mike Charteris paying off a taxi before climbing the steps to the front door.

"Who is it?" Jane asked in a shaky voice.

Fran pushed down a spurt of irritation. "Mike. Do you want to talk to him?"

"No." Jane clutched her hands together until the knuckles grew white.

"Don't you want to know what happened last night?" Fran said gently, going over and laying a hand on Jane's arm.

"I know what happened," said Jane.

"We don't, you know," said Fran. "All we've got is speculation on the part of the police."

"Oh, so you're saying Terry hit himself?" Jane's voice rose sharply.

"No, of course not," said Fran, although privately she'd wondered whether that had, in fact, been the case. Mind you, she didn't know how he would have done it.

"I want to go back to the hospital," said Jane, standing up.

"I've only just brought you home," said Fran, barely hiding her exasperation. "And I've got to get back home."

"I'm sorry." Jane was immediately contrite. "I'm being irrational, aren't I? I'm just so worried about Terry."

"His parents are there now, we saw them," said Fran. "They'll let you know as soon as there *is* anything to know." She paused and frowned. "But aren't you worried about the burglar — intruder — or whatever he was? It's obvious he's targeting this house. Wouldn't you be safer moving out for a while?"

"What about Mrs Finch?" said Jane. "I can't leave her here alone."

"You're not exactly much good to her up here," said Fran. "You'd never hear if anyone broke into her flat. And by the way, is there access from her flat to the rest of the house?"

Jane shook her head. "No. It's completely self-contained. The staircase from what's now Mike's kitchen was blocked off when Aunt Jess had the house converted."

Fran was interested. "Is it still there?"

Jane shrugged. "I suppose so, behind the bricked-up doorways."

"Where did it come out in Mrs Finch's flat?"

Jane frowned. "I don't know. Why are you asking?"

"Just curious," said Fran. "Well, if you don't want to see Mike, do you mind if I pop in and see him?"

"Why?" Jane looked frightened.

"To see if he's all right, of course." Fran now couldn't hide her vexation. What the hell was wrong with this stupid girl?

"Oh — oh, of course." Jane relaxed. "Yes, that's a good idea."

"And shall I ask him about last night?"

"Yes. Yes." Jane nodded furiously.

"But you don't want to do it?" said Fran.

"No."

"Right." Fran sighed and stood up again. "I'll get going then, and call in on Mike on the way."

"Thank you, Fran." Jane stood up and unexpectedly threw her arms round Fran. "Thank you so much for everything. I've completely wrecked your Sunday."

"It wasn't your fault Guy and I had to spend the morning at the police station," said Fran, amused.

"In a way it was." Jane stepped back and looked down at her feet. "If I hadn't come looking for you in the first place —"

"Oh, nonsense," said Fran. "Come on, buck up. You can drive yourself to the hospital later on, can't you? And let us know how he is."

Five minutes later she was knocking on Mike's door. He answered promptly, but looking drawn and weary.

"Hi," he said.

"Just wanted to know how you were," said Fran. "We — er — we found you last night."

He nodded, and stopped abruptly, putting a hand to his head. "That was silly," he said with a humourless laugh. "Yes, thanks, I know. They told me at the hospital."

302

"Have you only just got back? I thought they were letting you out earlier today?"

"Yeah, well, I had to hang around until I was signed off." He grimaced. "Then I had to get a taxi."

"Yes, we saw you arrive," said Fran. "That must have cost a fortune all the way from Canterbury."

He grunted. "Well, thanks for asking, anyway," he said. "Bit sore, but Terry's in a bad way."

"Not that bad," said Fran. "I've just brought Jane home. Pity we didn't know you were still there, we could have given you a lift."

"Would have been good." He gave her a small smile. "So he's not too bad, then?"

"He's not too good, either," said Fran, "but he's obviously got a very hard head. His ribs took a bit of a battering, too, but I don't think there are any further breaks."

"His ribs?" Mike frowned. "What happened to his ribs?"

"He slid down the stairs on his front," said Fran. "Right after we found you."

"Ah." Mike stared up at the staircase. "Hope the police take it all a bit more seriously now."

"I think they are," said Fran. "My friend and I spent the morning at the police station."

"Oh? Why?"

"Giving statements," said Fran patiently. Obviously the bang on the head was having an effect. "Can you remember what happened last night?"

"Not much." Mike frowned. "I'd been to The Swan for dinner as usual, then I went to see a band playing at the Carlton. I came home and the house was in darkness. Then I thought I heard something upstairs. I started going up the stairs — and that's all I remember."

"We found you on the lower landing," said Fran. "We must have walked right past you on the way up." She reached out and patted his arm. "I'll let you rest. Just wanted to make sure you were all right. Anything you need?"

"No, thanks. Really kind of you." Mike's voice was gruff, and Fran was surprised to see a tinge of pink in his otherwise unnaturally pale face.

"No problem. I'll be off then." Fran smiled and turned to go.

"Hang on." The gruff voice stopped her. "How's young Jane?"

"Very shaken," said Fran. "She's going back to the hospital later."

"Is she all right? What happened to her?" He looked startled.

"She's fine." Fran was surprised. "She's just worried about Terry — and the house of course. She thinks she's a target." Jane didn't seem to think anything of the sort, Fran thought, but best not to say that.

"Oh." Mike relaxed. "That's OK, then. Thanks."

"Bye then," said Fran, and this time he let her go.

As she drove back to Harbour Street where Guy was cooking a meal for them both, she pondered the odd behaviour of Jane and Mike. Neither had reacted quite the way she had expected, especially Jane. Was she still scared of Mike? It looked like it, yet last week she had reacted perfectly normally in his presence when Fran had been conducting her psychic survey. Perhaps it was simply the fact of being alone in the house with him again. You couldn't count Mrs Finch, as Fran had pointed out herself.

"Do you want to ask her to stay with you?" asked Guy, after he'd provided her with a drink.

"No," said Fran firmly. "I don't want anyone sharing my house."

"I'm aware of that," said Guy with an amused snort.

Fran blushed. "You know what I mean. Besides, she irritates me. Talk about blowing hot and cold."

"You've been doing a bit of that yourself recently," said Guy, returning to the cooker, where he began stirring a large pot.

"Don't remind me," sighed Fran.

"So aren't you feeling anything about this latest attack? Or about Jane? I thought the psychic antennae were twitching again."

"They have been, but all I'm getting now is a replay of what happened last night."

"And Connell hasn't asked you to get involved after all." Guy turned a smug grin on her. So there, he seemed to be saying. Fran scowled.

"He will," she said.

Ben spent the evening stopping Libby from phoning Fran.

"Not a good idea," he said again. "She'll call if there's anything to tell."

"I don't even know if Jane's home," fretted Libby.

"Well, call her, then. Just don't bother Fran." Ben adjusted his towelling robe as he stood up and made for the whisky bottle. "Want one?"

Libby picked up the phone and punched in Jane's number. "Straight to voice mail," she said after a moment. "She's switched off."

"Which means she's either still at the hospital or she's sleeping at home and doesn't want to be disturbed," said Ben, handing her a glass. "Leave it till tomorrow. Then I'll be out of your hair and you can do as you like."

Libby smiled up at him. "Don't I do as I like anyway?" she said.

"Most of the time," he said, sitting down on the creaky sofa next to her. "And sometimes you do what I like, too."

"Do I?"

"I'll show you," said Ben, putting down his glass.

The following morning, as the click of the cat flap signalled Sidney's departure after breakfast, Libby called Fran.

"Sorry, I know it's early," she said, "but Ben wouldn't let me call you last night, and I couldn't wait to hear what the news is."

"It's all right," said Fran. "I was awake. But I don't know what the situation is this morning."

"Well, what was it last night?" persisted Libby.

Fran told her how things had been left the previous evening.

"It's odd, though, Lib," she finished, "but Jane seems to have changed. She seemed really frightened when I brought her home."

"I'm not surprised. I'd be frightened if my home was under attack."

"Yes, but she was fine last week wasn't she? And only too keen for us to find out anything we could about her aunt and Simon Madderling. I mean, letting me go all round the house. And now — she's changed."

"I think this second attack would be enough to unnerve anybody," said Libby. "Weren't you scared?"

"Of course," said Fran.

"By the way," said Libby, "when you told her all about Lena and Rosa's passport, did you mention the fact that the body on the island was Andrei?"

There was a pause. "No," said Fran. "I didn't. I just connected up Lena and Rosa for her."

"And was she surprised?"

"Not surprised, exactly. She was when she first saw the passport. But by the time I told her the story she'd had time to put it all together herself. Why?"

"Oh, I don't know. I just wondered if perhaps Rosa had told her more than she's letting on."

"More about what?" asked Fran.

"I don't know that, either, but Rosa's disappeared, hasn't she? Perhaps Jane actually knows who she is and where she went."

"Now, why on earth would you think that?"

"I just think she's been too innocent about the whole thing," said Libby. "Everything. She hasn't really been bothered by any of it, except Terry's attack."

"Attacks plural."

"Yes, but you said now she seems really scared. Something's registered with her."

"You were the one saying it would be enough to scare anybody, just now," said Fran.

"I know. But it only just struck me. I think we ought to tell her about Andrei and see what the reaction is."

"Who's we, Tonto?"

"Oh, all right, me, then."

"And what are we expecting?" said Fran. "That she's going to own up to his murder?"

"No, of course not. Do you know whether Ian's got any further on that?"

"No, but he wouldn't keep me up to date. And unless he wants to see me again, I can hardly ask him."

"Well, I'm going to call Jane and find out how Terry is and see if I can't slip in a mention of Andrei Gruesome."

"Gruzevich," said Fran.

"And him. And I'll let you know what happens."

"Libby, please don't start poking around too deeply," said Fran.

"I'm only going to talk to Jane," said Libby. "What on earth could happen to me?"

CHAPTER
THIRTY-ONE

Libby pottered around making more tea and some toast, while thinking about her approach to Jane. She wasn't sure what had made her suspicious, even less what she was suspicious of, she was just certain that Jane was keeping something from them. And that could mean she was keeping something from the police which would help them find out who was behind Terry's attacks. And maybe even Andrei's killer.

That brought her up short. Rosa had told Jane a farrago of lies, which didn't include her Transnistrian lover, so Jane wouldn't react to his identity after all. Although Fran had told her about the real Rosa and the connection to Lena, so perhaps . . .

"You silly bugger," she said out loud. "Carried away, that's what you are." Regretfully, she abandoned all reflections on Jane's possible ulterior motives and went upstairs to shower.

Later, she decided it was still a good idea to ask how Jane, and more importantly, Terry, were. There was no reply from her mobile, and the *Mercury* hadn't heard from her. Bob, the news editor, expressed horror at this further attack.

"She hasn't rung in, no, but then she's probably got more than enough on her plate," he said. "Give her our best when you see her, won't you? And tell her she's not even to think of coming back until she's better."

Deciding that Jane was almost certainly at the hospital, Libby thought it would not come amiss if she were to visit the injured party herself. No flowers this time, she thought, but a card, perhaps. She drove round to the eight-til-late and picked the most appropriate of Ali's selection, then set course for the Kent and Canterbury hospital.

She managed to find a parking space outside the gates, thus saving several pounds in charges, and set off for the main block.

She was directed to the right ward, where she discovered, to her relief, that Terry was once again not in intensive care, but in a general ward. She was, however, told that he wasn't allowed any visitors but his parents and his "fiancée".

"Is his fiancée in there now?" asked Libby.

"She's been there all the time," said the staff nurse pulling a face. "Can't get her to go home. His parents tried to persuade her, but she wouldn't go."

"Do you think she would come out and see me?" asked Libby. "Tell her it's Libby."

A few minutes later Jane emerged from a room further down the corridor. Libby was shocked at her appearance.

"My God, Jane. When did you last sleep?" asked Libby, taking her hands and sitting her down on the bench.

310

"I dozed by the bed last night," said Jane in an exhausted voice. "And the night before. I have to be here when he wakes up."

"Hasn't he woken up yet?" Libby felt her heart sink.

"Oh, yes, but only for a little while at a time." She brightened. "The doctors are very impressed with him."

"I'm sure," said Libby, thinking that Terry must be almost superhuman to have survived both attacks so well. "Has he damaged his ribs any further?"

"I don't know. Apparently they don't X-ray ribs these days, but they have to be careful of fluid collecting in the lungs because people don't cough with broken ribs."

Libby correctly interpreted this to mean it hurt too much to cough.

"Does he remember what happened this time?" she said. "Although the rest of you know, so I suppose it doesn't matter that much."

"I haven't asked him," said Jane. "I just can't believe that all this has happened just after we got together."

"It was the body, really, wasn't it?" said Libby cheerfully. "If it wasn't for that, you wouldn't have met Fran and me."

"I suppose it was." Jane nodded. "Have the police made any more progress on that? I'd forgotten all about it."

"They know who it is," said Libby. She watched Jane's tired face carefully. "Your Rosa lent her passport to Lena, his sister. Fran told you about that when you saw Rosa's passport."

"It's him?" If possible, Jane's face lost even more colour. "It's Lena's brother?"

"You didn't realise when Fran told you the story?"

"No."

"His name was Andrei," said Libby gently, "but they still don't know who killed him, or why."

"No." Jane's voice was hardly above a whisper. Libby watched her for a moment.

"Are you sure you wouldn't like me to take you home for a bit of rest?" she asked. "You're absolutely wrecked aren't you?"

"I've got my car," said Jane, rousing herself slightly, "but, no, I don't want to go home."

"Well, how about coming back with me for an hour or so? The spare bed's still made up."

Jane seemed to focus on her properly for the first time. "Yes . . . perhaps that would be better."

"Better?" Libby frowned.

Jane shook her head. "Closer. Sorry. Are you sure you wouldn't mind?"

"Of course not," said Libby. "Go on, get your coat, or your bag, or whatever and let the staff know where you'll be."

"No need to do that," said Jane quickly. "They've got my mobile number. I'll get my bag."

Still frowning, Libby watched her go back down the corridor and wondered if she was doing the right thing.

By the time Libby had navigated out of Canterbury, Jane was asleep and Libby was left with her thoughts. She'd been right, Jane hadn't known who the body on Dragon Island was, and now she did, it was obvious that she knew more than anyone had suspected about Rosa. Certainly more than she and Fran had suspected. She couldn't wait to speak to Fran.

As soon as they arrived at Allhallow's Lane, Libby hustled Jane upstairs into the spare room and went back to put the kettle on. While she waited for it to boil, she called Fran.

"I'll be right over," said Fran. "Don't let her get away."

"Get away? She's not a criminal, you know!" Libby poured water into a mug.

"No," said Fran. "I'll be there as soon as I can."

When Libby took up the tea she'd made, Jane was already out for the count in the spare bed. Libby smiled and pulled the curtains across the window. With a bit of luck she would sleep for at least a couple of hours.

Fran arrived half an hour later, and Libby made more tea.

"She knows," said Fran, accepting a mug.

"Knows about Lena and Andrei, you mean?" said Libby.

Fran nodded. "When I told her about Rosa and Lena and the passport, I realised afterwards she said 'lending it to her lover's homeless, displaced sister just to help her'. I'd said nothing about a 'lover'. She already knew."

"She's a bloody good actress, then," said Libby. "She's pulled the wool over all our eyes."

"But *what* does she know exactly?" said Fran. "She appeared to be completely up front when she told us about the Rosa who worked in Pietro's café and lived in a bedsit."

"But then when you told her about Rosa and Lena, it was obvious she knew about Andrei." Libby pursed her lips in thought. "And when I told her the body was Andrei, it shook her rigid."

"It was also after I'd shown her the passport and told her the story that she began to back off. Before then she'd been happy for us to investigate her aunt and Simon Madderling —"

"And Peel House," cut in Libby. "Exactly. Why?"

"You know what I think," said Fran after a moment. "I think she probably knew most of it. I think her aunt told her about whatever it was that had happened in the past and about Madderling, and I think she was hoping I could find where whatever it was was hidden."

"You mean she didn't know that?"

"It's the only reason she would be happy for me to trail round looking for something, isn't it?"

"Or she knew nothing was there, so had nothing to fear."

Fran looked startled. "But if that was the case, why did I feel there *was* something there?"

"Perhaps she didn't know it was," suggested Libby. "Perhaps she didn't really believe you could see things."

"I picked up enough to convince her, then, didn't I? And do we really believe that a modern young woman, and a reporter at that, wouldn't have done her own internet research on her aunt and the house to have found out about Madderling? That just didn't ring true."

"I wondered about that at the time," said Libby. "Two old birds like us found it within hours. She owns the house. She must have seen the deeds."

"Of course!" Fran slapped her forehead. "God, I'm dim. Of course she would have, and Simon's name would have been there. So she knew all along about the Right Club and the fascist connection."

"And Aunt Jessica working for MI5."

"And we thought we were being so clever," said Fran. "So we come back to the question, why did she encourage us to go ferreting about?"

"Not only that," said Libby, aggrieved, "all that guff about being lonely, and getting us on her side and Terry —"

"Oh, I think that part of it's true," said Fran. "I think she was genuinely lonely and shy. I also think that she met Rosa exactly as she told us, but Rosa probably told her the truth."

"Why?" Libby wrinkled her brow. "Are we saying Rosa was sent to look for Jane? And then told her why?"

"Perhaps Rosa didn't realise how serious it all was. But she *did* make friends with Jane, and she *did* lie about where she lived — her whole lifestyle, in fact — so it looks as though she was looking for Jane. And she was going to come down here and stay, wasn't she?"

"And Jane seemed pleased about that," said Libby, "yet if Rosa had told her the truth about her lifestyle, say, before she had to leave the country . . ." she trailed off. "I don't understand any of this."

315

"And why is she suddenly scared to go back to Peel House?" said Fran. "Yesterday, she wouldn't come and stay with me, said she couldn't leave Mrs Finch, which is a bit mad."

"But she did go straight back to the hospital," said Libby, "and she stayed there all night."

"But she still would have gone back home at some point," said Fran. "It was only after you told her about Andrei that she didn't want to go home."

"Do you know," said Libby, after a pause while they both thought about the situation, "right at the beginning, people were asking if Jane had something to do with it all. The body on the island, I mean. Harry did, didn't he?"

"And now it looks as though she did. But I think it must have gone wrong. Because Jane didn't know who the body was."

"You mean it was deliberately left there so she would see it — or get to know about it, anyway?"

"I think that's what I mean."

"Why?"

"As a warning?"

Libby frowned. "A warning about what?"

"Well, what's happened since, I suppose."

"Look out, we're out to get you?" Libby snorted.

Fran cocked an eyebrow at her friend. "I did try and say that Peel House and the body were connected didn't I? Perhaps my inner workings weren't quite so off-beam as we thought."

Libby looked shame-faced. "As I thought, you mean."

"No, I thought the same. So did Guy. I just haven't learnt how to manage it yet."

"What about your sea moment?" said Libby suddenly. "What was that about?"

"As I said before, I think that was where he was killed. On the boat. Then he was dumped."

"They must have been good sailors," mused Libby, "with all those rocks. And it was at night."

"But who were they?" said Fran. "And where are they now? They're obviously the ones who attacked Terry the first time and who broke in on Saturday."

"How about," said Libby, "and this is only a guess, mind, that Pietro? He went back to Italy, Jane said. Well, perhaps he didn't."

"We've already considered him," said Fran.

"Before we knew the full story," said Libby.

"We don't know the full story yet, Libby," said Fran. "All we've got is speculation, as usual. I have a feeling the worst is yet to come."

"And I have a feeling you're right," said Jane.

CHAPTER
THIRTY-TWO

Fran and Libby gasped simultaneously and turned to the door.

Jane came into the room looking only slightly less rumpled and weary than she had an hour ago.

"You should still be asleep," said Libby, when she'd found her voice. "What are you doing up?"

"I woke up when I heard Fran arrive," said Jane, sitting on the chair by the table. "I decided I ought to listen to what you were saying."

Libby risked a glance at Fran, who was sitting staring rigidly ahead. She cleared her throat. "Er — would you like a fresh cup of tea?" she asked. "You were asleep when I brought the first one up."

Jane nodded. "Yes, please."

Well, she didn't look capable of attacking anyone, thought Libby, whatever she'd been concealing. She went into the kitchen, where the kettle was still simmering on the Rayburn and put a teabag into a mug. Her brain was almost in suspended animation, not knowing quite what to think or what to feel. Fran, it appeared, was in the same position.

"So you heard what we were saying," Libby said, taking the bull by the horns. "And were we right?"

Jane took a sip of her tea and nodded. "I didn't think for a moment anyone would know what was going on," she said wearily, "and I didn't really believe in Fran's psychic ability at first."

"But she convinced you?"

Jane nodded again. "And once you'd got on to Aunt Jess and Simon Madderling I got worried."

Fran seemed to come awake. "So you knew all about it?"

"Aunt Jess told me years ago. Since I was a child she'd shown me pictures of Simon and told me about what they did in the war. She always said someone would come looking one day."

"Looking? For what?" said Libby.

"For some documents Simon had left with her. Only he hadn't."

"He *hadn't*?" said Fran.

"So she said. But then I met Rosa."

"Ah, yes. Rosa," said Fran.

"What I told you was true," said Jane with a sigh. "Everything. But then she heard from Andrei that Lena had been arrested. And her family wanted her out of the way quickly. Apparently they were very angry at what she'd done. So she told me all about it."

"Go on," said Libby, when it appeared that Jane had fallen into a trance.

"Her family had kept track of Aunt Jess ever since the war."

"The Italian visitors," said Fran, "that Mrs Finch told us about."

"Yes, them. They were supposed to be friends of Aunt Jess's. And others, from a distance. She said they thought she would never do anything with these documents because they would ruin her reputation, let alone Simon's."

"They didn't know she and Simon were working for MI5?" said Libby.

"No, they thought Simon was a traitor." Jane made an attempt at a smile. "Funny, really, wasn't it?"

"Then what happened? The fifty-year rule?" asked Fran.

"And they discovered what the real state of affairs was," said Libby.

"So what did they do?" asked Fran.

"It wasn't until about three years ago that they discovered all this," said Jane. "Then Aunt Jess went into a home and then she died. They found out that the house had been left to me. They tried to break into the house, but didn't manage it, perhaps they didn't realise there were tenants there. So Rosa was sent over to make friends with me."

Libby and Fran watched as Jane's face crumpled. Fran got up and went over to her, putting an arm round her and leading her from the upright chair to the creaky sofa. Libby got up to make room for them and sat down in Fran's abandoned armchair.

"What happened next?" asked Fran after a decent interval.

"What I told you. She worked for Pietro and we became friends. Now I know why she didn't ever invite me home, of course." Jane sniffed and sat upright.

"Anyway, you know the rest. She told me everything and disappeared."

"Did you meet Andrei?" asked Libby.

"Once. Rosa gave him my mobile number and he rang me to tell me she'd gone back to Italy. I went to meet him in a bar in London. He said it was safer not to be near either of our places of work."

"Did he say why?" asked Fran.

"Her family were dangerous, he said." Jane sniffed again. "He was nice."

"Who were they? The family. We know Francini wasn't her real name." said Libby.

Jane shook her head. "I don't know. And I don't know why these documents are so important to them, either."

"Inspector Connell said he couldn't see why anything would be so important after all this time," said Fran. "It's over sixty years since the war ended. Anyone exposed now would either be dead or very old. Would it matter?"

"I've been thinking about that," said Libby. "There've been at least two fairly high profile cases with very old people being put on trial for war crimes. There was a woman in London and a bloke in Kent, I'm sure."

"So would Italy put someone on trial if they were exposed now? That's presumably what they're worried about," said Fran.

"No idea," said Libby. "What do you think, Jane?"

"I don't know," said Jane with a sigh. "And why would they murder poor Andrei? And was it a warning for me?"

"Very clumsy if it was," said Fran. "You didn't see it properly and were never told who it was. It took long enough for the police to find out."

"And that was only because of your suggestion," said Libby.

"As for murdering Andrei, I suspect they thought he knew too much as he'd been Rosa's lover," said Fran.

"Don't you think you ought to tell Inspector Connell everything you've told us?" asked Libby.

Jane looked frightened. "They'd find out," she said.

"How?" asked Fran.

"I don't know. But if I go home they'll know where I am. If I talk to the police they'll find out."

Libby and Fran looked at one another.

"How about if I ask Ian — Inspector Connell — to come here to Libby's house? You wouldn't mind, would you, Lib?"

"Of course not. That's a really good idea," said Libby. "Don't you think, Jane?"

"He'll be cross with me," said Jane, hanging her head. Fran let out a tut of exasperation.

"Yes, I expect he will," she said, "but what choice do you have? Two of your tenants have already been attacked, your house has been broken into several times — what about old Mrs Finch if you won't think of yourself?"

"I was," she said. "That's what I said yesterday, but when Libby told me about Andrei this morning —" She let the sentence hang.

"The police are the best people to deal with this sort of situation," said Fran decisively. "I'm going to phone Connell now." She got up and went to her bag. Jane just sat on the sofa looking scared.

"Cheer up, Jane," said Libby. "Terry's going to get better, the police can find out who's been doing this and maybe," she paused as a thought struck her, "just maybe, they can find some other top secret information about Simon Madderling. Somewhere there must be a record of what he was doing and who his contacts were. Bingo!"

She looked proudly at Fran and Jane. Fran shook her head before speaking into the phone. Jane looked puzzled. "But if there were records," she said, "why did Simon hide those documents in the first place. Or say he had."

"Because — oh, I don't know." Libby frowned. "MI5 would have known about his contacts, though. He wouldn't have wanted the Italians, or whoever they were, to know he was MI5."

"But why," said Fran, clicking off her phone, "did he say he'd hidden documents when he hadn't?"

"That's what Aunt Jess said. She was never given anything to hide, or told where anything was. She thought it was all a bluff on Simon's part to keep him alive."

"Well, he got that wrong, didn't he?" said Libby. "Did you get through, Fran?"

"I spoke to Constable Maiden. He'll get through to Ian and presumably he'll phone here."

"I ought to get back to the hospital," said Jane.

"You haven't had enough sleep yet," said Libby, "and I refuse to drive you until you have. We'll wake you when we hear from Inspector Connell."

"Well," said Fran, when Jane had been persuaded back up the stairs. "What about that."

"You got nearly all of it right," said Libby.

"Except the killer. We still don't know who that is." Fran sighed.

"It's got to be one of the Italian family," said Libby.

"Or someone they've hired."

"To get close to Jane again?"

They looked at each other in horror.

"It can't be Terry," said Libby in a small voice. "He's been attacked twice."

"And survived twice," said Fran grimly.

"But what about the first time? They said he'd been attacked in the hall first. They found blood."

"Easy enough to shed a bit of your own blood," said Fran. "And they never found the weapon, did they?"

"Well, how on earth could he have concealed the weapon if he'd knocked himself out?" said Libby.

"How about a deliberate fall? That would have broken his ribs as well."

"He was in the army, wasn't he?" said Libby. "Grenadier Guards, Jane said."

"Suppose it was something else? Like the SAS?" Fran looked out of the window and sighed again. "I think we're out of our depth, Lib."

"Well, he's safe enough in hospital at the moment," said Libby, "and Ian can take over now."

324

"Thank goodness." Fran leant back in the armchair and stretched. "This is all a bit draining, isn't it?"

"By the way," said Libby, "why did you shake your head at me when I said Ian could get into the MI5 records?"

"Because I doubt if he could. Anything that's going to be released already has been. They wouldn't let anything else out unless it was of national importance. And I doubt if the murder of an illegal migrant worker is that."

"What do we do about Jane?" said Libby, standing up and going on a cigarette hunt. "We can't tell her what we think about Terry."

"No." Fran rubbed her temples. "I suppose we tell Ian and leave him to sort it out. God, I don't want to think about what will happen when she finds out."

"You don't suppose we're wrong, do you?" asked Libby, sitting back down with her cigarette. "It isn't Terry?"

"Who else?" asked Fran. "He's the only one who's got close to Jane except you and me and the two old boat boys."

"And he would have known about Jane's trips out with them," said Libby. "He's the only one who would. Oh, dear."

"I wonder if he's got an alibi for the night before the body was found," said Fran.

"Whether he has or hasn't," said Libby, "how would he have got a boat out from Nethergate with a body on it?"

"It didn't come from Nethergate," said Fran. "It came down the river to the estuary and round the coast."

She sat up and looked as surprised as Libby did.

"Well!" said Libby. "And where did that come from?"

"Where do you think?" said Fran. "It's nice to know it's still working. Although whether Ian will give it any credence I don't know."

"Even if he does, he can hardly order forensic examination on every boat within here and Tilbury," said Libby.

"Docklands," said Fran.

"Oh, right," said Libby. "Any more?"

"St Katherine's, I think," said Fran.

"Good heavens, that's a bit specific," said Libby.

"It just looks like it," said Fran. "I'll tell Ian."

"Well, it'll narrow down the search," said Libby, "if that's where it is now."

"I doubt it," said Fran. "I should think it's been shipped off — oh, dear, didn't mean that — somewhere else by now."

Libby's landline phone rang and made them both jump.

"Mrs Sarjeant," said Ian Connell. "Is Mrs Castle there?"

"Yes," said Libby, pulling a face at Fran. "I'll hand you over."

"Why didn't he ring your mobile?" she whispered.

"Because Constable Maiden said you were there," Ian, who had obviously heard, told Fran. "And I just thought before you tell me all the information you've wheedled out of Jane Maurice, you ought to know that we've got Terry Baker under guard at the hospital."

CHAPTER
THIRTY-THREE

"Under guard?" gasped Fran.

Libby's eyebrows shot up. As she watched, Fran's expression changed from astonishment to puzzlement and finally, she looked up at Libby and just shook her head. Eventually, she spoke, telling Ian what Jane had told them and then ringing off.

"Who's under guard?" said Libby immediately.

Fran laughed, a little hollowly. "Terry, would you believe."

"We were right!" said Libby.

"No, we weren't. Apparently, from their own investigations, they decided Terry was in danger, so they've put a policeman on duty by his bed."

Libby frowned. "You didn't tell him what we thought about Terry."

"Well, no. If there's policeman by his bed he's hardly going to get away, is he?"

"So what did Ian say about our news?"

"He wants to see Jane as soon as possible. I said she was asleep — which I hope she is — so I'm afraid I volunteered us to take her into the police station."

"Why not here?" asked Libby.

"I didn't ask him. He just said would I phone when we're on the way."

"At some point she's got to collect her car from the hospital," said Libby. "I just hope she didn't park it in the car park. It'll be clamped."

"Should we let her go back to see Terry?" said Fran.

"As you said, there is a policeman there."

It was mid-afternoon when Jane came downstairs, looking slightly better than she had earlier. Fran told her about Ian's call.

"But I wanted to get back to Terry," she said plaintively. Libby and Fran exchanged looks.

"I think we ought to take you to the police station first," said Libby. "Then I'll drive you back to Canterbury. Where did you park?"

Looking rather taken aback, Jane revealed that she had, indeed left her car in the car park.

"I'm sure Ian will be able to do something about that," said Fran. "We can ask him when we see him."

After Libby had persuaded Jane to eat half a sandwich and drink half a cup of tea, Fran opted to take her back to Nethergate and then deliver her to the hospital. "You've done enough running around today," she said to Libby. "I'll come back here after I've dropped Jane."

Frustrated, Libby waved them off, but respected the fact that neither Jane nor Ian would want them both cluttering up the police station, and he would certainly not let them both into the interview room, even if he could be persuaded to let Fran in.

By the time Ben arrived at a quarter to six, as he usually did after going back to The Manor to change if he'd been out on the estate, Libby had still heard nothing.

"I can't go out, Ben," she said. "I'll have to wait for Fran."

Ben frowned. "She could be ages."

"That's all right. I'll cook us something, and we can have a drink here. Then when she arrives you can go off to the pub if you want to."

"Trying to get rid of me, are you?" he said, sliding his arms around her waist.

Libby was just reassuring him that this was far from the case when her phone rang.

"Fran," she told him, switching off. "She's on her way."

"We've got twenty minutes, then" said Ben, a wicked look in his eye.

"Yes," said Libby, giving him a push. "Twenty minutes for me to cook something quick."

In fact, it only took ten minutes for Libby to serve up a stir-fry with noodles, of which she had made enough for Fran should she want it. She did.

"I'm starving," she said, sliding in to a chair at the kitchen table. "Hello, Ben."

"Hi." He stood up and gave her a kiss on the cheek. "Look, I've finished, so I'll nip down and see if I can get Pete to come for a drink. Join us later if you want to."

"Right," said Libby, pouring two glasses of wine. "Tell all."

"I shouldn't really drink if I've got to drive," said Fran, eyeing the glass warily.

"You're eating with it, and you won't be going yet," said Libby.

"You're right," said Fran, and took a healthy swallow. "That's better."

"So what happened?" said Libby, placing a laden plate on the table and sitting down again.

Between mouthfuls, Fran explained.

"Ian wouldn't let me into the interview room —"

"I thought he wouldn't," said Libby.

"So I waited outside. They weren't as long as I'd expected, and when they came out he asked if he could have a word with me, and asked me what I had thought of her story. I told him we'd sort of worked it out — well, some of it — and he grumbled a bit, then I told him what we'd thought about Terry. He didn't like that at all. I asked if he could look into the Simon Madderling business, and he said that was very doubtful, so I asked him about the boat. As you can imagine, he was very dismissive of that, but once I'd reminded him of a few things, he said he would look into it. I don't know how *well* he'll look into it, but it's a start."

"So then you took Jane back to the hospital?"

"No, she wanted to have a shower and change, which was fair enough, so I took her back to Peel House. She was scared, though. She insisted I stayed with her. I was going to pop down and tell Guy what was going on, but in the end I just phoned him."

"What exactly is she scared of?"

"Someone attacking her in the house. I went down to see Mike while she was in the shower and put him in the picture —"

"What? You told him everything?"

"No, silly. Just that she was going back to the hospital and she and the police were worried about another attack. He said he'd go down and check on Mrs Finch and keep an eye on things."

"Nice of him," said Libby, "especially as he's been a victim as well. How is he?"

"Oh, back to normal, he said. Just a bit sore."

"So then you went back to the hospital?"

"Yes. And I told Ian about the car, and bless him, he'd sorted it all out, and when we got to the car park it had a big 'Police Aware' notice on it."

"Did you go up to the ward with her?"

"Yes. I said I'd like to say hello if he was awake."

"And was he?" asked Libby.

"Yes, he was. Delighted, as far as you could tell, to see Jane, and quite pleased to see me. Not saying much." Fran sighed. "I must say, I don't like to think of him being a villain."

"Neither do I." They sat in silence for a while and Fran finished her meal.

"What do we do now?" said Libby, as she cleared plates into the sink.

"Wash up?" suggested Fran.

Libby poked her tongue out. "No, what do we do about Jane. And everything else."

Fran shrugged and led the way into the sitting room. "Nothing. We've told Ian everything we know, or rather,

332

Jane has, so it's up to him. I suppose we provide support for her, which she's going to need."

Libby sighed. "Oh, God, I suppose so. Nasty." She looked at the clock. "Are you going to come for a drink? Or would you like a cup of coffee here?"

"Cup of coffee, then I'll go home. I've been out since lunchtime, after all."

Libby had just provided her with a mug of coffee when Fran's phone rang.

"Oh, Bruce. Hello," she said and made a face at Libby. "No, I'm not at home, I'm sorry. Pity."

Libby giggled.

"Sorry — what was that?" said Fran, frowning. "You did — what? Where?" She looked at Libby and mouthed something. Libby shrugged and shook her head.

"OK, Bruce," Fran went on. "Well, good luck with it. Yes. Love to Cass — I mean Chrissie." She rang off. "You'll never guess what," she said to Libby.

"No," said Libby. "I'm not a lip-reader."

"Bruce has seen his Italian businessman again — in Nethergate."

CHAPTER THIRTY-FOUR

"Pietro?" said Libby. "In Nethergate?"

"We don't know it's Pietro. We're still jumping to conclusions." Fran stood up and began pacing, as far as Libby's cluttered sitting room would allow.

"Why did Bruce tell you?"

"He's in Nethergate and decided it would be handy if he could pop in and see me. I expect he hoped I'd feed him."

"He's been in Nethergate a lot, hasn't he?" said Libby.

"His firm have got a contract with someone there," said Fran. "I don't think it's another woman, Lib."

"Sorry," said Libby. "So where did he see Pietro this time?"

"I wish you'd stop calling him that," said Fran. "It probably isn't him."

"Well, where was he, anyway?"

"In The Swan."

"The Swan? That's a bit close to home," said Libby, looking worried.

"Exactly. Do you think I should phone Mike?"

"And tell him what?" said Libby. "There's a strange Italian businessman in The Swan who just might come up and try to break into Peel House? You were the one saying don't jump to conclusions."

"I wish I could get a look at him," said Fran. "Then I'd know."

"If it was Pietro?"

"No, if it was the killer."

"Well, why don't we go down now?" said Libby. "He might still be in The Swan. Did Bruce say he was still there?"

"Yes. He said he was going over to speak to him. I wished him luck."

"Quick, ring him back!" said Libby. "Find out what's happening."

But Bruce wasn't answering his phone.

"I hope he hasn't been bashed over the head," said Fran gloomily.

"Come on, let's go," said Libby, grabbing her basket and stuffing her arms into a long cardigan.

"How are you going to get back?" said Fran.

"I'm driving. I've only had a glass and a half of wine. I'm safe."

Within minutes, after Libby had called Ben and told him where she was going, the little convoy was out on the road to Nethergate. As they drove past the turning to Steeple Mount, Libby couldn't resist a swift glance into the darkness on her right, where she knew, beyond the trees, stood Tyne Hall, now closed and boarded up, but once the scene of some very unpleasant, not to say murderous, deeds. She shivered and hoped she and Fran weren't driving headlong into more of the same.

They wound down the hill into Nethergate, through the square and into Harbour Street, where they both parked.

"The Swan?" said Libby.

"I'll just go in and tell Guy where we're going," said Fran. "I promised I'd call him."

Guy offered to come with them, but Fran thought a third party in their rather haphazard exploration would increase the embarrassment factor.

"I'll feel enough of a fool if we're making a mull of this without Guy looking on," she confided to Libby as they walked along Harbour Street towards The Swan.

The Swan was busy, but neither Bruce nor an unknown Italian could be seen, either in the bar or the restaurant.

"Mike's just come in, though," said Libby, pointing to the door. "He might have seen Bruce."

"Not if he's only just come in," said Fran. "Worth a try, though."

"No, I've been here a while," he said, when they joined him at the bar. "I eat here most evenings. Can I get you a drink?"

"No thanks. I thought I saw you coming in, that's why we asked," explained Libby.

"I went outside to take a call," said Mike, raising his eyebrows. "Is it important?"

"It's like this," said Fran hastily. "You remember what I said when I saw you earlier? Well, we thought someone might be lurking around here."

"Lurking? In The Swan?" He laughed. "How would I know if anyone was lurking? I only know the regulars who come in. Anybody could be a criminal as far as I know. What does this person look like?"

"My son-in-law was in here," said Fran. "Tallish, brown hair, a little thinning on top."

"Take a look." Mike waved his hand. "Half the customers answer that description."

"But my son-in-law knew this person. He was an Italian businessman."

"And what did he look like?" Mike's eyes narrowed. Fran and Libby looked at each other.

"Italian?" said Libby helplessly.

Mike threw his head back and laughed. Fran went crimson, and even Libby felt a little hot under the collar. "I must say," he said, "you ladies have enlivened my stay in Nethergate."

"Glad to have been of service," said Libby and turned on her heel. "Come on, Fran."

"Hey, wait," said Mike, stopping her with a hand on her arm. "Sorry, I shouldn't have said that. I checked on old Mrs Finch before I came out, just as I said I would, but young Jane isn't home yet. I'll check her out as soon as she gets there."

"She's still at the hospital," said Fran. "Thanks, anyway."

"Berk," said Libby as soon as they got outside.

"You must admit we appear a bit odd," said Fran with a sigh. "He must have been laughing up his sleeve every time we turned up."

"Except when he got bashed over the head," said Libby.

"He probably blames us for that, too," said Fran. "Ah well." She set off back down Harbour Street, punching a number into her phone.

"Bruce still has his phone off," she said, switching off. "Wonder where he's got to?"

"Gone off with the Italian businessman?" said Fran. "I do hope not, if it's who we think it is."

"It could be perfectly innocent, you know, Fran," said Libby. "Maybe it is just a businessman who reneged on a deal. And Bruce finally managed to buttonhole him."

Fran sighed. "And we've built it up into something it isn't — again. I'd still like to know where he is, though."

When she passed Coastguard Cottage and carried on walking, Libby turned and looked at her. "Where are we going?" she said.

"There's a new boat," said Fran. "The other side of the hard." She led the way across the hard in front of The Sloop, past the *Dolphin* and the *Sparkler* rocking gently at their moorings, and sure enough, tied up on the other side, a sleek dark launch skulked in the shadows.

"How did you know?" whispered Libby.

Fran gave her a look, even as she was dialling Ian's number. For once she got straight through.

"It's called the *Ladana*," said Fran. "Is that enough to check on?"

Ian obviously asked a few more questions and Fran switched off.

338

"Is this it, then?" asked Libby, as they began to walk slowly back to the cars.

"I'm sure that's the boat Andrei was killed on," said Fran. "As we left The Swan it just came into my head. If we can check who it belongs to — well, we'll be a step nearer."

Fran's phone rang.

"Yes, Ian?" she said. A minute later she switched off and relayed the information to Libby.

"He'd actually checked up on the marina or whatever it is at St Katherine's Dock and got a list of boats moored there around about the time when Andrei died. When I gave him the name of the *Ladana*, he looked, and there it was. And —" she paused for effect "— owned by Massimo Berini."

"Who?" Libby wrinkled her brow. "Do we know him?"

"No, idiot! Berini! Get it?"

Libby shook her head. "No."

"Berini is one of the so-called great reformers of Italian politics," said Fran.

"Is he? How do you know about him, then?" asked Libby innocently.

"Oh, come on, Lib. Don't you ever follow the news?"

"Not often," said Libby. "Except the local stuff."

"Berini's famous, take my word for it. I can't remember if his name is Massimo, but I bet it's the same family."

"It sounds as though it's quite a common name, though," said Libby dubiously. "Are we doing another of our well-known leaps of faith — otherwise known as jumping to conclusions?"

"I'm sure not," said Fran, sounding quite excited. Libby was surprised.

"So where does old Pietro come into this?"

"Where does Terry come into this?" countered Fran. "If Massimo has brought the boat down here it must be for a reason."

"Terry's in hospital," reasoned Libby. "It can't be for him."

"Why not? They could get him out."

"He's got a police guard."

"Come to think of it," said Fran, ignoring Libby and retracing her steps towards the hard, "it was very risky to bring a boat registered in the family's name down here, wasn't it?"

"But they don't know about all the connections that have been made. They don't know Andrei has been identified, or that Rosa had told Jane the whole story. Why should they worry?"

"I want to know why it's here now," said Fran, coming to a halt above the *Ladana*. "There's been someone around apart from Terry for weeks, now, but they haven't needed the boat."

"Do you really think it's Terry?" said Libby. "I don't want to believe it."

"Neither do I," said Fran with a sigh. "But there's still someone else around."

"Yes, signora," said a voice behind them, "and he's right here."

340

Before either of them could scream or turn round a hand clamped over both of their mouths. Libby felt her hands being roughly pulled behind her and tied. Through a haze of fear she realised there must be two people, men, because the hand was still over her mouth. Then, to her horror, she was blindfolded.

"Now down the ladder, ladies," said a different, more heavily accented voice. "We will guide you."

She was unceremoniously turned round and felt a hand grab her ankle. Instinctively, she kicked out and was brought to her knees as she was dealt a ringing blow to the head. She heard scuffling, and then realised she was being dragged over the side of the hard, lifted and then almost flung into what she hoped was the *Ladana*. She heard a heavy thud and a yelp and realised Fran had joined her. For a while she lay there, listening to almost perfect silence. Her brain, for the last ten minutes a confused jumble of sensations rather than coherent thought, began to settle down.

Who knew where they were, first. Well, Ben knew she was in Nethergate. Guy knew they were going to The Swan. Mike knew they'd been *in* The Swan. But nobody knew about the *Ladana*. Her heart lurched. Except Ian.

She tried to move and finally succeeded in locating what she hoped was a part of Fran. A muffled squeak assured her it was.

"Fran!" she whispered.

"Yes?"

"Is anyone else on here with us?"

"I don't know — I can't see."

"Ian knows about the boat — do you think he'll investigate —"

"Ladies, ladies!" The heavily accented voice called down. "No conversation, or we might have to gag you, too."

"Bugger," whispered Libby. "But hey, Fran. It can't be Terry."

"No." Fran's answer was a mere breath.

The unmistakable sound of boots on metal rungs indicated the arrival of one of their captors.

"Now," said the more English of the two voices, "we're going to have to take you for a little ride. You need to be out of the way for a while, and we have no wish to kill two such nice ladies, so just keep quiet and you'll come to no harm."

Libby was so full of fear she couldn't speak. She heard, and felt, the engine starting and bit down hard on her lip.

Suddenly light flared across her blindfolded eyes and someone shouted. The boat lurched and crashed against the hard. Libby was flung sideways and ended up almost on top of Fran.

More shouting. Someone landed heavily on the deck and then a voice, a voice Libby recognised.

"They're here!" called Constable Maiden. And then, blessed relief, the blindfold was ripped off and through blurred eyes Libby saw him doing the same to Fran. She wriggled upright as he started on her hands and looked up.

And there, held firmly by two policemen, stood Mike Charteris.

CHAPTER
THIRTY-FIVE

"What I want to know," said Harry, pouring champagne into flutes, in what had become a traditional post-case celebration, although Ben preferred to call it post-chaos, "what I want to know is, was her name really Rosa?"

Jane, tucked into a corner of The Pink Geranium's big sofa with her Terry, nodded.

"Oh, yes. Rosa Berini. And Mike is her brother."

"And what exactly did he plan to do with you two?" asked Guy, who was holding on to Fran's arm as though he was afraid if he let go she would float up to the ceiling.

"As far as Ian can make out," said Libby, holding on to Ben in much the same manner, "they were going to take us somewhere and dump us while they ransacked Peel House. We were blindfolded so we couldn't see it was Mike. And he'd disguised his voice."

"Who was the other guy — I mean, bloke?" asked Terry, with an apologetic nod to Guy.

"Not Pietro," laughed Fran. "We really did run ahead of ourselves there. It was the chap who owned the flat in Lansdowne Square. He's a Berini cousin."

"Hang on," said Harry, "who's Pietro?"

Libby and Fran explained.

"And he was being paid by Mike — or Massimo, as I suppose we should call him," said Jane. "But only to employ Rosa to get close to me."

"And the reason behind this miscellany of misunderstandings?" asked Peter.

"Get him," said Libby, reaching across to poke his arm.

"The reason," said Fran, "was some documents allegedly concealed somewhere in Peel House by Jane's Aunt Jessica's lover, Simon Madderling. They revealed, as we have now found out from the Italian communists after the story was covered in Italy, that Giacomo Berini was a supporter of Mussolini and subsequently Hitler throughout the war and responsible for some of the nastier war crimes. All the time being seen to be holier-than-thou."

"Which his family have continued to be." Jane took up the story. "Any revelations would mean the Berinis would lose all power, and great grandfather Giacomo, now 92, would go on trial. They also have a healthy underground organisation aiding illegal immigrants from the non-European states."

"Lena and Andrei?" said Libby.

"Yes."

"So was Mike the vanishing Italian businessman?" asked Ben.

"Yes. He was investigating where Lena had worked, which was near Bruce's firm, so came up with a cover story which was easy with all his family's connections." Fran sighed. "And poor old Bruce was found unconscious in the car park by the police. He'd approached Mike — Massimo — and accused him of reneging on the deal with his company, and Mike realised his persona was at risk of being exposed. It's a wonder he didn't kill Bruce."

"That would have been another reason to get us out of the way," said Libby. "Once he'd been into Peel House and got away, it wouldn't have mattered if Bruce had reported to us. We still wouldn't have connected his Italian to Mike."

"But if he'd come round and reported to the police —" interrupted Ben.

"He was hit at least as hard as Terry was," said Fran, "and didn't come round in hospital for ages. Chrissie was there by then. Blaming me, of course."

"So Mike would have been long gone by that time," said Guy. "He was a real chancer, wasn't he?"

Fran nodded. "He had luck on his side a lot of the way."

"And he saw the ad I persuaded Jane to put in the paper," groaned Libby.

"And met Terry, who he realised was a real threat," said Fran. Terry tried to look modest.

"So was it Mike who attacked Terry?" asked Guy. "I don't see how."

"The first time, he hit Terry as he was coming in, took his keys to search his flat, then heard Mrs Finch taking her bin out. So he waited until she'd gone back in, dragged Terry on to the step, and pretended to discover him there," explained Libby. "Apparently."

"And the second time?" asked Harry.

"He had been to The Swan and the Carlton, as he said, but then left and realising we were both out, took the opportunity to search my flat. He turned out the lights and hit Terry when he went up the stairs, then rushed down past me," said Fran with a shudder, "then arranged himself neatly on the lower landing as though he'd been there a long time."

"But how did he fool the ambulance people if he hadn't really been knocked out?" asked Peter.

"He deliberately banged his head on the banisters," said Fran. "It didn't knock him out, but gave him a convincing bump."

"Blimey," said Harry. "There's dedication to the cause."

"He'd already killed, remember, or the family had at least," said Libby. "The body on the island which started it all."

"Hang on again," said Harry, topping up with champagne. "You've lost me re the body."

"Andrei," said Jane, Libby and Fran together.

"I know who he was, but why did they kill him and why did they put him on the island?"

"They killed him because he knew too much," said Fran.

"And they put him on the island as a warning to anyone in their organisation who didn't toe the line," said Jane. "Not to warn me."

"How would people from their organisation know what it meant?" asked Guy.

"Most of the migrant workers would recognise one of their own, even if they didn't know him personally,"

346

said Libby. "It was a general warning. And of course, none of the migrant workers would have volunteered any information, so they were safe."

"It was even their organisation that supplied the evil Budgen farmer," said Fran, "so all my strange floating visions linked up in the end."

"Except Terry," said Jane with a grin.

"He wasn't a vision," said Libby. "He was just bad adding up."

The others looked at her in perplexity. She sighed. "Putting two and two together?" she said.

"And making five. I see," said Harry. "More bubbles anyone?"

"And what about Rosa?" asked Libby later, when the last refried beans had been scraped off a plate.

"I don't know," said Jane. "I hope she's all right. She was a good person at heart."

"Not like the rest of her family," said Terry.

"And is there a document?" asked Peter. "Or was it all for nothing?"

"Aunt Jess said there wasn't. If there is, I doubt if we'll ever find it," said Jane.

"And I would far rather Libby and Fran didn't go looking for it," said Ben amid laughter.

"I've still got the bruises," said Libby, "so I won't be doing anything for a long, long time."

"We were lucky Ian turned up when he did," said Guy. "I hate to think what would have happened if he hadn't."

"Once I'd told him about the *Ladana* and he realised where it had come from and who it belonged to he thought he'd better take a look," said Fran. "It was lucky he didn't go on his own, though."

"So what are you going to be doing to keep out of mischief?" Harry asked her.

"I'm going to a creative writing class," said Fran. "I thought I might try to write a novel. Nothing much can happen to me there, can it?"

Also available in ISIS Large Print:

The Cruise Connection

Peter Kerr

Shipboard shenanigans for Detective Bob Burns

The droll Scots detective, Bob Burns, is once more aided by forensic scientist and ladyfriend, Dr Julie Bryson, and abetted by the ever keen Andy Green.

Working undercover on a cruise liner bound for the Canary Islands, Bob and his two sidekicks have plenty to cope with. The discovery of a severed finger in a passenger's quiche lorraine sparks an investigation that exposes greed, guile, deceit and double-dealing.

Does the finger belong to an alleged man-overboard victim? Was the man pushed, or did he commit suicide? Is it all just a cleverly engineered insurance scam?

ISBN 978-0-7531-8282-6 (hb)
ISBN 978-0-7531-8283-3 (pb)

Lonesome Road

Patricia Wentworth

There were times when Rachel Treherne fervently wished that her beloved father had left his fortune to somebody else, so overburdened did she feel with the administration of the estate. And never more so than now for, although she was surrounded by relatives who depended on her, whom she loved and who must surely love her, there was no doubt in her mind that somebody was trying to kill her. Threatening letters could be ignored, odd-tasting chocolates can be rejected but when snakes are left in her bed, Rachel is convinced that someone means her terrible harm. Her only chance of a future life lay with Miss Silver, and Miss Silver was well on the way to unmasking the murderer when they struck again.

ISBN 978-0-7531-8124-9 (hb)
ISBN 978-0-7531-8125-6 (pb)

Under Suspicion

The Mulgray Twins

DJ Smith is sent to Tenerife to infiltrate a money-laundering organisation run by Ambrose Vanheusen. DJ knows she is in deadly danger from such a ruthless criminal but luckily he has an Achilles heel: his obsession with his Persian cat, Samarkand Black Prince. DJ's passport into Vanheusen's empire comes in the form of Gorgonzola, a moth-eaten ginger Persian and sniffer cat extraordinaire, acting under the pedigree alias of Persepolis Desert Sandstorm.

With drug dealing, money laundering and murder to contend with, not to mention a cat with attitude, DJ has her hands full. So it's not surprising she doesn't realise that the greatest danger lies in Vanheusen's determination to steal her supposedly pedigree moggy. He's prepared to go to any lengths necessary to get his hands on a mate for his brute of a cat, and only a tooth and claw confrontation will determine who survives . . .

ISBN 978-0-7531-8216-1 (hb)
ISBN 978-0-7531-8217-8 (pb)

No Kiss for the Devil

Adrian Magson

A young woman's body is found dumped in the Essex countryside. Investigative reporter Riley Gavin recognises her as Helen Bellamy, a former girlfriend of her colleague, PI Frank Palmer. Ex-military policeman Palmer is accustomed to death, but this is different; this is the brutal murder of someone he was once close to. He knows only one way to deal with it: find the killers.

Meanwhile, Riley's next job is a profile of controversial businessman "Kim" Al-Bashir. She soon realises that there are sinister forces working against him, and if she doesn't tread carefully she could end up losing her assignment. And, like Helen, quite probably her life.

ISBN 978-0-7531-8190-4 (hb)
ISBN 978-0-7531-8191-1 (pb)